love me never

love me never

SARA WOLF

Entangled Publishing, LLC
2614 South Timberline Road Suite 109
Fort Collins, CO 80525
Visit our website at www.entangledpublishing.com

Entangled Teen is an imprint of Entangled Publishing, LLC

Edited by Stacy Abrams and Lydia Sharp
Cover design by Louisa Maggio
Interior design by Sabrina Plomitallo-González

Print ISBN: 978-1-63375-229-0
Ebook ISBN: 978-1-63375-230-6

Manufactured in the United States of America

First Edition April 2016

For my mother, D, and all the other girls who have faced the monsters. You are infinitely brave and strong, and I am infinitely with you.

chapter one

WHEN I WAS SIX, Dad told me something really true: everyone has a to-do list.

It took me another eleven years to actually get around to making one, but thanks to a certain asshole in my life, it's finished:

1. *Don't talk about love.*

2. *Don't think about love.*

3. *Thinking and talking about love leads to Love, which is the enemy. Do not consort with the enemy. Even if those hot-ass actors in the movies make it look cuddly and nice and tempting, don't fall for it. It's the biggest bad in the world, the worst villain ever created by hormone-pumped pubescent morons. It's the Joker, Lex Luthor, that one overweight guy who's always messing with the Scooby-Doo gang. It's the final boss in the massive joke of a video game you call your life.*

Everyone at Avery Brighton's party right now has their own to-do list, and most of them look identical to the following:

1. Get drunk.

2. Get more drunk.

3. Try not to vomit on anyone cute.

4. Try to score with the cute person you tried your best not to vomit on.

It's a foolproof list that's easy for even idiots to follow. It ensures you're drunk enough to think everyone is cute, so that you don't throw up on *anyone*, and so you try to score with *everyone*. It's basically a how-to for people who watch too much TV and think having fun is getting blind drunk and making out with someone they don't remember. It makes everyone here intolerable. Especially the boys. One of them slings his arm around my shoulders, red in the face and murmuring suggestively about going somewhere quieter.

He has no idea who I am. He has no idea what I've been through.

He's an idiot. But then again, most people are.

I wrinkle my lip and push him off before I hurry into the kitchen. People are too busy boozing up here to bother hitting on girls. Not that I get hit on a lot. Getting hit on is still a new thing, a weird thing, because boys don't generally hit on fat girls and that's what I used to be. The fat girl.

I pull my Florence and the Machine T-shirt lower to make sure it covers everything. Flaunting your stretch marks to the entire "cool" populace of East Summit High probably isn't the best way to make influential friends. Or friends, period. I'd settle for either. Hell, I'd settle for an enemy at this rate. Without an anchor, the sea of high school is the shittiest ride in the world.

"Isis!" A drunk girl sloshes up to me, black hair plastered to her face with sweat. "Hiiiii! How are . . . What . . . You're doing in here?"

"Uh, yes?" I try. She giggles.

"I'm Kayla. We met in history of the . . . planet."

"World history," I offer.

"Yeah!" She claps and points at me. "Wow. You are *really* smart."

"I'll be really wet if you don't stop that." I gently position her hand upright, her red cup of beer precariously dripping on the floor and my jeans.

"Oh, will you be wet?" She closes both her eyes really hard and smiles. When I don't react, she does it again.

"What are you doing?" I ask.

"Winking!"

"Where I come from, that's called drunk."

"Drunk?" She buzzes her lips in a laugh, spraying a bit of beer-spit over me. "Not little a even!"

"Look, you're really"—I pause as Kayla burps—"great, and thanks for talking to the weird new girl, but I think you need to lie down. Or possibly go back in time. Before the invention of liquor."

"You're so funny! Who invited you?"

"Avery."

"Ohhh, she's doing that thing again." Kayla laughs. "Don't drink the punch!"

"What thing?"

"She invites alllll the new kids to a party. If they stay the entire night without crying or wetting themselves, they're cool in our book."

Great. Seven hours of binge drinking crappy beer bought by someone's older brother is the proving ground for who's cool and who's not. I should've expected that from a boring, sterile little Ohio suburb like this one.

"What's in the punch?" I ask, looking over my shoulder at the giant plastic bowl filled with ruby liquid.

"Powdered lax . . . laxa . . . pooping powder!" Kayla concludes. A few boys circle around her like sharks, just waiting for the moment she passes the threshold from drunk to too-drunk-to-protest. I glower at them over her shoulder, pull her by the hand upstairs, and go to the second landing, where it's quiet and not full of horny vultures. We lean on the banister and watch the chaos below.

"So where are you from again?" Kayla asks. Now that she isn't swaying crazily, I can get a good look at her. Her dark hair and eyes make her one of the few nonwhite people in the school. Her skin's amber, the color of honeycomb. She's really pretty. Better than most of the girls here, anyway, and definitely way better than me.

"I'm from Florida," I say. "Good Falls. Tiny, boring place. Lots of mosquitoes and football jocks."

"Sounds a lot like here." She giggles, chugging the rest of

her beer. Someone downstairs opens a can of cocktail wieners and starts throwing them around. Girls shriek and duck and pick them out of their hair and boys chuck them at each other and try to get them down girls' shirts. A wiener flies up and gets stuck in the chandelier, and Kayla *ooohs*.

"Avery's mom isn't gonna like that," she says.

"Her parents are probably loaded snobs."

"How did you know? They're VEOs or something."

"CEOs."

"Yeah! I guess it's a really important job, but then I thought about it really hard and how can it be so important if it's only three letters?"

"You may be onto something. Something very drunk, but definitely something."

She beams at me, and then reaches over to touch a piece of my hair. "I like that color."

"Violet Madness," I say. "That's what the box called it."

"Oh, you dyed it yourself? Cool!"

It was part of my pact with myself: lose weight, dye my hair, get clothes that actually fit. Become a better person. Become the person a certain someone would wanna date. But I don't tell Kayla that, because that was the old me — the one who thought love wasn't stupid. The one who'd do anything for a boy, even lose eighty-five pounds dieting and sweating like a pig. The one who'd go to crappy little clubs to drink and smoke just to hang out with his friends. Not even him. His *friends*. I tried to get accepted by them, like it'd make him like me more.

But that's not me anymore. I'm not in Good Falls, Florida. I'm in Northplains, Ohio. No one knows the old me, so I won't drag her into the limelight just to embarrass the new me. I'm desperate for friends, not socially suicidal. There's a fine, pathetic line between the two and I'm toeing it like a ballet dancer at her first recital.

"Oh shit," Kayla hisses suddenly. "I didn't know *he'd* be here."

I look to where her eyes are riveted. It's unmistakable who she's talking about.

Amid the chaos of the wiener-throwing and drunk flail-dancing to Skrillex is a single island of still calm. He's gotta be six feet at least. His shoulders are broad, and everything about him is lean—his waist, his long legs, his ridiculously sharp cheekbones. His messy hair isn't quite blond but isn't quite brown, either, more like a tumble-weed color. Next to me, Kayla is ogling him with all she's got, and she isn't the only one. Girls froze when he walked in, and guys are throwing him stink eye. Whoever he is, I can already tell he's one of those people who are popular in all the wrong ways.

He walks farther into the party, keeping to himself. Normally you nod at people as you walk in or look for someone you know in the sea of the crowd. But not this guy. He just walks. He doesn't have to push or shove his way through— people part naturally. It's like he's got an invisible shield around him. He wears a permanent bored expression, like everything around him is completely uninteresting.

"That's Jack. Jack Hunter," Kayla whispers. "He never comes to parties like this. They're way beneath him."

"*Beneath him?* He's in high school, Kayla, not the royal goddamn court."

"He's got a nickname around here—Ice Prince. So he sort of *is* royalty."

I laugh. When Kayla's face remains serious, I stop.

"Wait, you're not kidding? You guys actually call him that?"

She flushes. "Well, yeah! Just like we call Carlos the Mexican quarterback Hot Tortilla and the creepy guy with too many knives who likes to hang around the library Creeper McJeepers. Jack is Ice Prince because that's what he is!"

I splutter another laugh, and this one must be too loud, because it makes Jack look up. Now that he's closer, I can see his face well. The bored expression does nothing for him. Kayla's whispering, "He's cute," to me, but that's not it at all. He's *not* baby-faced, boy-next-door cute in the way girls giggle about during sleepovers or between classes. He's handsome; the kind of lion-eyed, sharp-nosed, broad-lipped handsome you see in Italian suit ads. I can see why they call him Ice Prince. Aside from the thick fog of pretentiousness that follows him, his eyes are the color of a lake frozen through—a blue so light it looks almost translucent.

And they're looking right at me.

Kayla makes a noise disturbingly similar to a small monkey and hides behind my shoulder. "He's looking at us!" she hisses.

"Why are you hiding?"

Kayla mumbles something into my shirt.

I roll my eyes. "You like him."

"Not so loud!" She pinches my neck and pulls.

"Ow, *ow*! You can't have my vertebrae, I need those!"

"Then don't say dumb things like that so loud!"

"But you *do* like him!"

She twists, and I yelp. Our din is doing nothing to avert Jack's eyes—or anyone else's. I manage to pry her fingers off the part of my nervous system that keeps me breathing and duck into the bathroom to pee. In the semi-quiet only a bathroom surrounded by a raging party can offer, I realize Kayla's the first person who's bothered to talk to me since I've moved here. Everyone else stared, whispered, but never actually talked to me. I was beginning to think I was diseased, or awful, or possibly even dead. Either Kayla can talk to ghosts or she's just a nice person. Too nice.

I was like that, once upon a time.

The toilet's a mess, and I pat it in sympathy on my way out. Stay strong, buddy. One way or another, this will all be over soon. Either we'll all drop dead of alcohol poisoning, or your bowl will erode from the acidity of the gallons of vomit you've been subjected to. Do they give you retirement benefits? No? They should. We should protest. Picket. Toilet Union United.

When I'm done talking to the toilet in a completely sane manner, I walk out to the exact thing I didn't want to see— Kayla, downstairs again. The boys are leaving her alone, thank God. All except one. Or rather, it's one boy *she's* not leaving alone.

"I don't u-usually see you at these kinds of parties," Kayla stammers to none other than Jack Hunter himself.

"No. I don't particularly enjoy rolling in mud. Tonight's an exception." He looks around the room, his lip curling. "But you do, I'm guessing."

"W-What? No, I mean, I'm just Avery's friend. She makes me come. I don't even really like these parties—"

"Your speech is slurred and you're stumbling. You can barely control your own body. If you have to get this drunk to stand the parties your friends make you go to, you're an idiot who's made the wrong friends."

Kayla's expression stiffens, like she's been slapped, and then her eyes start watering. My blood boils. Who the hell does he think he is?

"That's n-not what I meant—" Kayla starts.

"And you seem exactly like the type of girl to stay with friends she hates. They probably hate you, too. It must be easy, hiding it behind all that booze and all those name brands."

Kayla's tears overflow onto her cheeks. Jack sighs.

"You're so spineless you collapse into tears the second anyone says the truth?"

My heart's thumping in my chest. My fists squeeze so tight I can't feel my fingers. His cruelty leaves a bitter taste in my mouth—it's a lot like someone I used to know.

Someone who ruined my life forever.

I shove aside the red-faced boy who tries to hit on me again and launch myself through the crowd. Kayla isn't my friend. No one here is. But she's been four seconds of nice to me—true nice, not Avery's sugary poison of inviting-me-to-this-weird-test-party nice. And four seconds is more than I ever thought I'd get. It's the most I've had in a long time. Jack's lip quirks up in a sneer. *Say it. Say one more thing, pretty boy. I dare you to.*

"You're pathetic," he says.

That's the first time I punch Jack Hunter's face.

And as my knuckles connect with his stupid high cheekbones and he staggers back with a furious blizzard brewing in his icy eyes, I somehow get the feeling it won't be the last.

"Apologize to Kayla," I demand, and the entire house goes quiet. It starts like a ripple, the people next to me and Kayla and Jack falling silent. And then it moves, jumping like a flea, like a disease, silent and ominous and spreading faster than a cat picture among aunts on Facebook. It's like the entire party has stopped, slowed down just to see what Jack will do. They want a show. They're a pack of ruthless little hyenas and I just bit the lion. Maybe Jack can sense that, because once he gets over his shock, he glances around carefully like he's plotting his next move, and then fixes me with a glare so frigid it could probably freeze lava.

"Judging by your expression"—I cross my arms and glower—"getting punched for being an ass is something new."

He dabs at his nose with his hand, a little blood trickling down to his mouth. He licks it leisurely off his thumb. Kayla's white-faced and stuck in place like a mannequin. The music blares hollowly and the bass thumps, the only thing daring to interfere with the tense quiet the entire room is waiting on.

Jack doesn't speak. So I do.

"Let me use really small words so you understand," I say with exaggerated slowness. "Apologize to Kayla for what you said before I make you bleed harder."

Someone in the crowd snickers. Whispers move into people's ears and out their mouths. I don't care what they think or whether or not I failed the stupid party test. I only care that he apologizes to Kayla. He hurt her in more ways than he knows.

"Why are you defending a girl you don't know?" Jack finally asks, his voice deep and with a sable deadly quality to it. "Correct me if I'm wrong, but aren't you new? That would explain the moronic ignorance. Do they have schools in Florida? Or do you learn from the crocodiles and the rednecks?"

Of course he knows where I'm from—word spreads fast in a town like this. A collective "ooooh" goes around the room. A flush creeps on my cheeks, but I don't let it faze me. I've gotten worse insults. This is nothing. I scoff.

"I can't stand by and watch while a stuck-up bastard steps on another girl's heart. It's not my style."

This second "ooooh" is a lot louder. I feel pride blossom in my chest. My hands and face are hot, and I'm shaking, but I won't show it. I won't let him win. I won't back down. I dealt with entitled mama's boys like him by the dozens in my old school in Florida. They're all the same; we'll trade insults until I humiliate him in front of these people so badly he can't fire back. That's the best way this could happen. Kayla would get her justice.

But that's not how it happens. He doesn't fire back. He leans in for the kill, over my shoulder, his lips so close I feel hot air glancing my earlobe.

"Because that happened to you, didn't it?"

My breath catches. I try to suppress it but I flinch, and when Jack sees that, he laughs. The sound is brittle and cool, like a frozen thing snapping in two. He *laughs*. Like it's nothing. I feel like I'm the one who's been punched. A second of tension passes between our eyes, and then he holds up a hand as if in farewell to the room and leaves through the door, the night lawn crowded with poorly parked cars swallowing him up.

The house starts talking again. People laugh and dance and drink again, making out against walls with renewed vigor. Heat and ice are sloshing through my veins all at once, back and forth. A heavy iron fist is squeezing my heart, and I can't breathe.

Kayla puts a hand on my shoulder. "Are you okay, Isis?"

How did he know? Could he really read me that well? Yeah, the same thing happened to me. A boy broke my heart— No, more than that. He broke my soul, my heart, and who I used to be. After three years, nine weeks, and five days, I should be able to hide it better. I thought I was good at hiding it. So how the hell could Jack tell?

Everyone's watching. I can't run out the door, since that's the way he went, or they'll assume things. I can't go upstairs to be alone, or they'll assume he won. Won what? I'm not sure yet, but the antagonism that arced between us felt like a fever, uncomfortably warm and refusing to be ignored. I want nothing more than to crawl into someplace quiet and nurse the scab he ripped off my gaping wound, but I can't. People might be going back to partying, but they're also watching me for confirmation of what exactly happened, and what I do next will determine that.

He attacked me on my most personal level.

He opened the one injury I never wanted to think about again, the one I came here to escape.

The one that destroyed me.

But I can't let anyone see that. I can't let it show. I'm someone else here. I'm not the weak, broken girl I used to be.

It's time to play my favorite game—pretend.

"He kissed me!" I announce loudly to Kayla. "It was disgusting! All tongue and no skill."

Kayla's eyes widen. My words echo back at me over the music in snippets of different people's voices. *Kiss. New girl. Jack Hunter. Ice Prince kissed New Girl.* While it spreads, I pull Kayla by the hand and take her into the kitchen. She's shaking. I put my hands on her shoulders and look her in the eyes.

"You— You and him—" she starts.

"Didn't do anything," I murmur. "I swear to you. I just said that to make him look bad."

Her eyes brighten momentarily, then dim, and somehow that makes me sadder than it makes me angry. She still likes him, even after he called her pathetic in front of a bunch of people. I feel so bad for her. I used to *be* her and that's why I feel so damn bad for her.

"I can't believe you actually punched him!" Kayla says. "You're crazy!"

"You're crazy for liking a guy like that." I sigh. "Didn't your mother ever tell you to stay away from feral dogs?"

"He's not a dog!" she protests. "He's never hit on me!"

"Because he's gay."

"He has mature college girlfriends! A new one, like, every week!"

"Because he's ordering them from Russia. Or Saturn. Whichever has more girls depressingly desperate for money."

Kayla wobbles, and I help her sit on the polished wood floor against the kitchen counter. There's a large cupboard. She feels it against her back and drunkenly opens it and crawls inside, closing the doors behind her. I become extremely patient and understanding for an entire ten seconds. I knock. A mutter reverberates from inside.

"Go away."

"C'mon. I'm not sorry. He deserved it, okay?"

"I've liked him since fourth grade!" Kayla mourns. "That was the first time I've ever talked to him! And you . . . you came in and ruined it! It's over! My life is over!"

"It was a life well spent." I nod.

"I'm not actually going to die!" She flings the cupboard doors open to wail at me.

"Oh, but you are! In about seventy years. But for now you are very much alive and very much wasted, so I think I'll drive you home."

"No! I can drive myself!" She gets out of the cupboard and promptly slips on some Cheetos. I catch her and pull her up, and together we make it through the front door.

"You can drive yourself off a cliff, yes."

"I might as well!" Kayla moans. "Jack hates me now!"

"Oh pishposh. I'm sure he'll remember you fondly as the four hundred and thirty-sixth girl he made cry."

Kayla bursts into tears, and I half drag, half pull her across the lawn and into my tiny VW Beetle. It's light green and rusted, with a broken headlight and soda cans littering the floor, but it does its job of letting everyone know I'm poor and that's really all I ask from a car.

"Isis!" a voice calls to me.

Kayla tries to bolt, but she's so drunk she just wobbles in place a bit and burps. I help her onto the seat and shut the door, turning to face the voice. Avery Brighton makes her way over to me, red curls bouncing and green eyes bright. She's a picturesque Irish doll with porcelain skin, slender proportions, and a perfect spate of freckles across her button nose. It's like God airbrushed the crap out of her, ran out of paint for everyone else, looked down at all the babies he was chucking to Earth, and went, *Ha-ha-ha whoops but check this one out it's a masterpiece.*

"Are you kidnapping Kayla?" Avery asks, smiling a china doll smile.

"*Theoretically*, I am totally not the sort of person to do that, but *also theoretically* if I knew how to kidnap people from looking it up on Google when I was really bored over Christmas break last year, then *theoretically* there'd be a lot more duct tape and chloroform involved. In theory."

"Yes, well, that's very interesting, but I'm going to ask you to give her back. I need her here. To do things for me."

"She sort of seems out of it? And also she's really bummed because of some things I don't know if you saw or not that happened?"

"I saw. It was interesting. Probably the most interesting thing that's happened all year besides Erika's suicide attempt," Avery muses. She looks me up and down, as if seeing me in a new light, and then points at me. "But that doesn't excuse Kayla from certain duties she needs to perform tonight."

"That's sort of weird? Like, it's a really vague and threatening thing to say about someone? Also I don't think you own her and she needs to lie down and chill so I'm taking her home?"

I inch around the car to the driver's side as Avery's face grows darker and more perfectly deadly vampire-esque.

"Why are you talking in questions?" she asks.

"Why are *you*? Talking in questions?" I crane my neck over the hood and maintain eye contact. She's like a bear. A really big, really rich bear. I can't look away or she'll charge and use my insides to line her Louis Vuitton purse.

"If you leave now, I'm not inviting you to another party again."

"Okay? That's kind of good because I don't think I want to associate with people who say suicide attempts are interesting? And who make pooping juice and pretend it's punch? That's almost as bad as playing Skrillex on loop?"

I quickly jump in, start the car, and pull out. Avery watches with a detached yet irritated twitch in her brow. I roll down the window as I pull up close to her.

"You're sort of popular so I guess I should thank you for inviting me? Also for threatening me? Like wow, that was a really bad party but a really good threatening? I give you two stars for effort? I'm babbling?" I pause. "Stay in school?"

"You go to my school, idiot."

She did it. She called me the I-word. The most popular girl in school just called me the I-word. I either have to kill myself, go back to Florida, or drive away really fast and not give a damn. I jam on the gas and swerve around a lion statue as I tear down her driveway, except I don't swerve fast enough and one of the lion's testicles goes flying in a fine haze of concrete. I leave behind a bunch of new enemies and a one-balled lion and I'm taking home a maybe-friend who thinks I ruined her crush and even if that sucks, it's still better than what I came in with, which was just three years, nine weeks, and five days of bad memories.

chapter two

I DROP OFF A considerably more sober Kayla at her modest house on a quiet cul-de-sac. She stares blearily at me, her makeup tear-smeared, and mutters softly, "Thanks."

"Man, I'm sorry." I sigh. "I really am, Kayla."

She shrugs. "It's whatever. I'll see you on Monday."

It's not whatever. People just say "whatever" when the situation is too hard to put into words, or they don't want to. If she still considers me a corporeal item worthy of being visually registered on Monday, I'll be happy as hell.

As I drive home, the dark road winding around cow pastures and cornfields, the imprint of Jack's icy blue eyes and his infuriating words echoes in my head. *Because that happened to you, didn't it?*

I grip the steering wheel hard. He has no idea what happened to me.

I don't go out with ugly girls.

A new voice echoes. Nameless, the guy I used to like. Love? Like. I don't know anymore. All I know is he hurt me.

I call him Nameless in my head; his real name still causes me physical pain. I breathe evenly, in and out, trying to dull the ache in my chest. I'm over it. I really am over it. After three years, nine weeks, and six days I am oodles over it.

I pull into the driveway of home and turn off my car. I sit in the darkness, pushing out all the bad memories and pulling in some new ones. I made a sort-of friend. Mom's happier here. I haven't seen Nameless in more than two months. That's good. Those are good new things to fill up the holes in the walls of my mind left behind by the decaying bad things. The good new things are flimsy, but they'll keep the cold wind out for now.

I flash myself a smile in the rearview mirror. Being anything but happy is dangerous around Mom lately. So I have to fake it hard, or at least fake it long enough to make it up to my room.

Our house is a two-story, with white doors and walls and blue trim. A rusted wind chime clinks faintly over the patio, and the garden is nothing more than a few patches of scraggly yellow grass. A broken barbecue slumps dejectedly in the corner by the leaking hose, and a dozen or so wilting maybe-red-maybe-poop-colored roses struggle to push up from the dying bush that separates our front yard from the street. It's ugly in the day, but at night, with light shining through the curtains, pretending it isn't a dump is a lot easier. It's the only decent place Mom could afford, but it's a far cry from the little Florida cottage I grew up in.

"I'm home!" I push the screen door open, chilly September air following me in. Our cat, Hellspawn aka Coco aka Get-out-of-the-fridge-you-idiot, minces delicately over to me and rubs on my ankles as I put my keys in the dish and take off my coat. Mom follows, her bathrobe pulled tightly around her and her face eager to hear every detail of the night. She's beautiful, in an aged-painting way, with gray streaks in her hair and soft smile lines. Her dark eyes are clear.

"Did you have fun? How many boys did you make out with?" she asks.

"Seventy. At least."

"How many shots did you take?"

"Fourteen. I let go of the wheel halfway home and Jesus drove me the rest of the way."

She laughs and strokes my head. "I'm glad you had fun."

We both know I don't drink (much) or kiss boys, so it's more of a morbid inside joke than anything. She shuffles into the kitchen where her newspaper and some tea wait. Hellspawn jumps on the chair opposite of where Mom sits and politely starts licking his balls.

"Did you take your meds?" I ask. Mom sighs, shooting me a reprimanding look.

"You don't have to worry after me. I'm a grown woman. I can take care of myself."

I look at the kitchen counter. It's stacked high with crusted pots and pans. The floor is filthy, and she hasn't opened the curtains all day, I can tell. But that isn't her fault.

Some days are better than others. It's the asshole who beat her black and blue who's really to blame. If Dad were here, he'd be able to do something more for her; make her smile, at least. Except he's not. He's moved on with his new family. I'm here, though. But all I can do is wash dishes and try not to make her worry. So I do that with everything I've got.

I roll up my hoodie sleeves and turn on the hot water, squeezing soap into a pan.

"I'll wash the windows tomorrow after school, okay? They're super dirty; whoever lived here last must've liked fog machines."

Mom smiles faintly, but it's not a real smile. "Thank you. I have work tomorrow, but I'll be back before dark."

Mom's an art restorer, the kind who takes old paintings and historic vases and fixes them up for museums. But after her breakup with Leo, she's been having a tough time finding—and keeping—a job. She works at the local tourist-trap train museum for now.

"I'll make dinner tomorrow, if you want," I offer.

"Let's treat ourselves. I'll get pizza."

"All right." I grin. She'll forget. It's not her fault, though; she'll just get absorbed in her work or the darkness of the past and forget to feed herself, and by proxy, me. But I'm used to it. I've learned to make back-up plans, always. I take chicken out of the freezer to defrost it when she's turned around.

"I'm a little tired," she says, sweeping over to kiss the top of my head. She smells like lavender and sadness—and that smells like ripped tissue paper and sun-dried salt.

"Okay. Sleep well." I squeeze her hand and she squeezes mine before slowly ascending the stairs. She moves so timidly still, like around every corner there's someone waiting to hurt her. Tonight should be an okay night, if she was honest about taking her meds.

She shouldn't have to take meds at all.

I wince and scrub the pots harder. I channel my rage and put enough elbow grease into cleaning the kitchen to lubricate a small car. The counters shine, the floors are smooth, and the sink is more spotless than a Disney Channel star's criminal record. I strip off my clothes and hop in the shower, rinsing away the last remnants of booze, cigarette smoke, and glitter from the party. My knuckles are red and raw, the top layer of skin jagged. Ah, well, a few injuries are to be expected when you punch an iceberg like Jack Hunter.

I come out smelling less like adolescent angst and more like almond shampoo not tested on animals. I bandage my knuckles and inspect the damage on my soul from tonight in the mirror. Mom's curly brown hair (though I've streaked it up with purple) and Dad's warm cinnamon eyes stare back at me. They look a little goldish-red in the middle. Dad used to say they were like little shards of ruby and topaz, but people with brown eyes search for the tiniest bit of color to make their hue unique. I proudly call them cinnamon, but the fancy-dressed DMV lady refused to put "cinnamon" on my license and so here I am, fighting for brown-eyed equality still today. They have not heard the last of me. I will rise from the ashes and tango with pink-nailed, hoop-earringed DMV oppression yet again.

It's still strange to see my thinner face in the mirror. I used to have fat cheeks with massive packets of pudge slapped on my chin and eyelids. My neck had rolls. Even my earlobes were fat. Dad used to send me to weight loss camp every summer, but that never worked because I'd hide in the incinerator to escape sports time—a risky but ultimately effective tactic. I preferred becoming bacon to embarrassing myself by showing off my bouncing rolls and wheezy lack of stamina. I took up an entire bus seat by myself. I have to remind myself constantly I don't take up that much room anymore.

If I were rich like my old best friend, Gina, I would've gotten lipo for my sixteenth birthday along with a BMW or something. You probably could've powered a BMW for a few months with oil made from the fat I lost, but alas. I wore layers of clothes and watched my calories carefully and ran every morning and every night, so there was just gradual muscle and no surgically removed bags of fat to convert to something useful. I remember hating every second of my diet and exercise, but now it's a foggy, painful memory, the opposite of the clear, sharp memory that kicked my butt into gear in the first place.

I don't go out with ugly girls.

Ugly.

I touch my face, my reflection moving with me in the damp mirror.

Ugly.

Ugly ugly ugly *ugly*. Purple streaks didn't make me prettier. Losing weight didn't make me prettier. My face is the same as ever. A little thinner, yeah, but still the same. My nose is flat and my chin is too wide. The usual bit of eyeliner I wear every day is half washed off, making me look pale and exhausted. Nameless's voice haunts me even as I dry my hair and pull on the boxer shorts and comfy T-shirt that serve as my pajamas.

My stretch marks —*ugly*.

My zits —*ugly*.

The way my thighs jiggle —*ugly*.

I'm an ugly girl. And I've come to terms with that. It's who I am. Right now I'm New Girl at East Summit High, but soon the glamour will fade and they'll give me another nickname, and it'll be Ugly Girl. That would be the most logical, accurate thing to call me. Nameless was cruel for saying it, but he was right. He pointed the truth out to me, and for that I'm sardonically grateful, the same way an artist is grateful someone pointed out his left hand is a little shakier, a little less masterful. It helped me know my weaknesses better, and therefore my strengths.

Love isn't one of my strengths. Dating definitely isn't one of them, either. I like to think being genuinely nice is one of my strengths, though, you know, minus punching guys who deserve it. So I'll be nice. I'll keep myself away from everybody else. No one wants ugly. Even if they did, it wouldn't be good for them. I'm loud and angry and sarcastic. No one wants that. Nameless taught me that, too. He taught me to spare everybody from myself. That's true kindness.

I sigh and flop into bed. Ms. Muffin, my faded but somehow still sinfully soft panda bear plushy, waits for me. I hug her and bury my face in her made-in-China chest.

"Ms. Muffin, I punched someone tonight. I might've fucked up."

Her beady black eyes seem to say, *Yes, I know, sweetie. It's what you do. But I don't love you any less for it.*

I manage to get four hours of sleep or so before the lights in my room snap on all at once. I sit up quickly, rubbing my eyes to clear them. It's still dark outside. Mom stands in the doorway, shaking like a leaf beneath her robe. I throw off my blankets and dash over to her.

"Again?" I ask. She nods, eyes glassy and locked onto some faraway point. I put my arm around her shoulder and lead her back into her bedroom.

"I'm sorry," she whispers as she crawls into bed. I pull the covers over her and smile.

"It's fine. I'll go get the air mattress and sleep in here with you."

When I come back from the attic with the mattress, she's gone.

"Mom? Mom!"

The window is open. I launch myself toward it and peer over the edge. Please, no. Please, don't let her be—

"I'm here."

Her voice is tiny and distant-sounding. I follow it to the

space beneath her bed, where she's lying, her knees pulled up to her chest.

"Mom, what are you—"

"It's safer here," she says. "Can you come under?"

"You'd be more comfortable on the bed—"

"No!" she shrieks, pressing her hands over her ears. "No, no, I can't! You can't make me!"

"Okay, okay," I soothe her and press myself flat. I inch over the dusty carpet, the box spring pressing into my ribs, and grab her hand. "It's okay. I'm here. I'll stay under here with you."

Her panic fades, and she slowly nods off, clutching my fingers with her own trembling, ice-cold ones. Sometimes she'll whimper in her sleep words I can't understand or don't want to, and all I can think about is how I would've probably murdered the guy if I'd been there. I should've been there. I should've been with her instead of at Aunt Beth's. I should've protected her, should've seen the signs when I visited for Christmas, should've—

"I'm sorry," she whispers in her sleep, childlike and small. I wrap my arms around her, pull her into my chest, and drift uneasily into sleep with the smell of lavender and sadness in my nose.

๏　๐　°°

School on a Monday after a party is really awkward. A lot of people know something embarrassing happened but no one can remember what exactly. Somebody used too much teeth while kissing somebody's girlfriend and maybe someone forgot to tell someone they'd broken up and maybe someone put a Mentos in their ex-boyfriend's rum and Coke. Or maybe some guy and girl hooked up, and his dick was too small. Somebody's dick is always too small.

"That's what I'll do!" I exclaim halfway through a heinously practical tuna sandwich. "I'll spread a rumor that his dick is small. That's the only thing guys care about—their dicks. I'll hit him where it hurts most, metaphorically and also non-metaphorically."

Kayla raises an eyebrow and nibbles her baby carrots. "Do you really hate him that much?"

When I pulled into the parking lot today she was waiting for me, all tentative and smiley. And now she's eating lunch with me! It's a miracle worthy of the book of Revelation. It's the very first entry in my book of Fuckups-With-a-Semi-Happy-Ending, anyway. She's as tender as a rabbit and loyal as a dog and very, very into a certain icy pig, but that can be corrected. Hopefully without firearms.

"Isis!" A totally random girl I've never seen before runs up to me. "Is it true? Did you and Jack make out at Avery's party and then you punched him?"

"Uh, there was no me and Jack, *Jack* macked on *me*," I correct. "And drooled everywhere. It wasn't a kiss, it was a disaster. It was so bad, I *had* to punch him. It was so bad my hand formed an unconscious fist and my biceps twitched forward in a defense mechanism against his suckitude. All girls everywhere need to beware of his dismal skills. Pass it along."

The girl nods eagerly and darts off to a circle of her friends. Kayla folds her arms and harrumphs at me.

"What?" I try to look innocent.

"Why are you spreading that rumor, anyway?"

"If I tell everyone he sucks at kissing, beautiful and kind girls like yourself won't fall for his tricks and date him. The power of gossip will smite evil in its lair, where swords cannot reach!"

She shakes her head. "You're so weird."

"I'm also super excited to freeze his expression in amber and make a necklace out of it when he realizes what everyone's saying about him. Revenge is sweet."

"What did he say to you at the party that's made you hate him so much?"

I clear my throat, not all that eager to wade through my nasty past with a potential-maybe-almost friend.

"Just, you know. He insulted you. Then he insulted me, which is totally not cool because there's really nothing about me to insult, objectively. If I were less than perfect I would probably be bothered by insults. But I'm not. He still did a vaguely negative thing, though, and according to the law, doing vaguely negative things is sometimes bad. So I have to pay him back. An eye for an eye and all that."

She tilts her head, a confused carrot hanging out of her mouth. I clarify.

"Shakespeare said that. The dude traded eyeballs a lot, apparently."

Avery comes in then, flanked by two other girls I can never remember the names of, but who try and fail to look as waifish and savagely stylish as Avery. Kayla bolts up instantly, grabbing her lunch and stammering.

"S-Sorry. I have to go."

"Uh, yeah? Sure?"

She jogs over to Avery, hemorrhaging baby carrots across the floor as she goes. The janitor in the corner makes a face that's only slightly different from his usual I-would-become-a-serial-killer-so-quickly-if-given-the-chance face. Kayla apparently doesn't want Avery knowing she's hanging out with me, which is fine, because Avery dislikes me and Kayla was friends with Avery way before me. So it's logical for her to pick Avery over me, and I say that with the least amount of bitterness I've ever held for a person in my life. It makes honest-to-God perfect sense. I briefly entertain the thought that what Jack said the other night might be true—Kayla really hates what her friends do, yet forces herself to go along with it.

I shake my head and laugh into my sandwich, spraying tuna in an elegant pattern across the table. No. Somebody that pretentious and self-absorbed has no idea how to relate to other people. Jack has no idea what Kayla, or anyone, is going through. And that includes me.

I get up and throw my lunch trash away, then head to my next class early. No sense in eating alone in the cafeteria and looking like a friendless moron any more than I already do.

The September day is crisp and chilly, but the sun is warm. East Summit High looks like any other school—white buildings, glass-walled lobbies. There's a giant quad area made of grass and pine trees and water fountains and benches, and all the buildings are situated around that. There's a flag in front of the office and a stadium in the back where we apparently lose more than we win. It's Middle America at its finest, and blandest. At least at my old school we had cool banyan trees and the occasional raccoon invasion to spice things up. But here it's just been nothing—nothing but old memories and trudging through a series of classes and homework assignments alone. Until this weekend, of course. Now I'm riding high on a twisted sort of false popularity with no real lasting power. It's slightly awesome.

I'm halfway to Mrs. Gregory's class when I see him.

Jack Hunter's talking with Principal Evans, a balding man in a suit that always smells like a mixture of mothballs and old fish. Next to tall, effortless Jack, Evans looks like a little bumbling gnome. Jack's nose looks fine from here, which pisses me off. I wanted a scab, or at least a mark of some kind. They can't see me since I'm behind a tree, but I can hear both of them perfectly.

"You shouldn't let that keep you here, Jack. I know it's been hard for you, but it's not a good enough excuse to ruin your future over," Mr. Evans says. "Do you know how many calls from Princeton and Yale I have to field a day? They want you, Jack. You could go to any Ivy League for free! Don't ruin that for yourself."

Jack's eyes remain cold, but for a second I think I see a flash of hot anger run through them. He tames it quickly, his voice even and purposefully pleasant, the kind of pleasant you reserve for grown-ups you want to get off your back.

"I'm aware of this. Thank you for your input."

"But you're not, Jack! That's just the problem—you're not. She'll get better with or without you here."

Jack spots me over Evans's shoulder. He smiles at Evans, nothing about the grin sincere, and pats him on the arm.

"I should go. My friend's waiting for me."

To my shock, Jack walks over to me, Evans watching from behind him. Jack keeps the creepy not-smile in place.

"Hey. Sorry I couldn't meet you for lunch," he says.

"Uh, what?"

Jack leans in, his fingers glancing across my hair. I can smell his cologne on him—nothing strong, but it's a soft sweet scent beneath the smell of his sweater. Blue eyes bore into me. His voice gets so low and gravelly he sounds like a beast instead of the cheery person he was a second ago.

"Pretend you're my friend."

"Give me one logically sound reason why I'd even think about it," I hiss back.

"Will Cavanaugh. That was his name, wasn't it?"

A bolt of pain ricochets through my chest at his name. Nameless. How the hell did Jack find out?

"Look at that horrible flinching movement. You have a physical reaction to his name. You must be in terrible pain. Pretend to be my friend or I'll say it again. Louder."

"You wouldn't—"

"Wil—"

"I couldn't find you in the cafeteria!" I say loud enough for Evans to hear, but he can't see my face. I glare fire into Jack's eyes as he makes his voice light again.

"Come on. I'll buy you pizza. My treat." He slings his arm around my shoulder and leads me away. Every nerve in my body goes on point. A boy's touching me and I gave him absolutely no permission. I'm ready to punch him out like a WWE special, but for the sake of not hearing Nameless's name again, I'll do anything. His ribs are pressing into mine and our steps are in a creepy sort of sync. Jack doesn't look back once, and neither do I, and once we're completely around G-Building, Jack lets go and I pull away like I've been stabbed with a red-hot poker.

"What the hell was that for?" I snarl.

"I should be the offended one," Jack says coolly. "You're spreading rumors about me. Punching me wasn't enough, you bloodthirsty harpy?"

"I enjoy constructing eventual social downfalls," I say. "And harpy's really the best you can come up with? That's cute."

"I hope you realize how accurate it is."

"Oh, I do. But you might want to get something a little more original. It doesn't sting at all. I've heard that a thousand times before, trust me."

"I won't. Trust you, that is. But I will disappoint you—my social standing is fine. I've spent years building it, and a few seconds of slander from a jaded little new girl won't scratch the surface."

"*I'm* jaded?" I scoff. "What does that make you? Diamonded?"

"Let's not argue semantics—"

"Let's."

"No. Unlike you, I have a life to attend to. I can't afford to waste my time arguing the finer points of what makes you an idiot."

He tries to duck around me, but I block him with my body.

"You still haven't apologized to Kayla."

He scoffs. "This is far beyond just her now. Stop using your protective instincts as an excuse to harass me. Do it normally, like all the other starstruck girls in this school."

"I'm surprised you manage to get your head off your pillow in the mornings with an ego like that. Not everything with a vagina likes you, dipshit."

"Then why spread a rumor about how I kiss? Whether you acknowledge it or not, it's a very specific rumor. You must've used it as cover at the party. Thought of it on the fly? It was the first thing that popped into your mind, right? There's a very smart man named Freud I think you should read up on."

"There's this awesome sandwich you should try called my knuckles, but, whatddya know? You already did."

"So that's a no, then, to my request about not spreading any more rumors." His eyes are deathly cold, but for some reason that only makes me smile brighter.

"Oh, I'm going to spread the rumor even more now. Thanks for letting me know it was bugging you."

I wink at him and walk off. He doesn't show much emotion, but I caught the tiniest glimmer of annoyance flit across his face before I turned. I won this round.

The bell to end lunch rings and people start streaming out of the cafeteria, and I plot heinously. I'll keep harassing him like this until he apologizes to Kayla, at least. I won't let another asshole strut around lording himself over other people. Never again.

Someone grabs my wrist, hard. I whirl around to yell at him, or possibly fight him off, when a blur roughly pulls me in, hard hipbones pressing into my stomach and height dwarfing me in shadow. I barely register the flash of blue eyes before he tilts my face up and kisses me, a tongue tasting the corner of my mouth and a lip tracing the curve of my cupid's bow. The kiss spreads buzzing heat from my tongue, to my throat, to my lungs, to my heart, all the way down to my stomach and even below that. Everything is on fire. I can't breathe—the kiss has me frozen, locked in place, completely immobile. This is my first. This is my first kiss and I'm going weak in the knees; I'm making some kind of stupid little moan. How moronic am I for reacting in such a cliché way? How stupid am I for letting this person—

And it's then I realize the blue eyes belong to Jack.

And it's then I realize Jack Hunter stole my first kiss in front of the entire school. People are whistling, hooting. The smell of Jack's cologne wafts up, and the taste of his mouth is pepper and mint on my tongue as he leans in to whisper.

"If it's a war you want, Isis Blake, it's a war you'll get."

Forty entire seconds after Jack Hunter kisses me and walks off, I'm too stunned to move. Just like that. Just like that, my first kiss went to East Summit's Ice-douche Prince. Not to someone I really loved. Hell, not even to someone I liked. It was sacrificed helplessly, like a little ritual priestess on the altar of callous assholery.

And all of East Summit High saw. He couldn't have picked a more perfect time for the entire lunch crowd to see, and like an idiot I stumbled into the perfect place—the only hall connecting the cafeteria to the main entrance. I set myself up, and he pounced on it like a jaguar.

As my shock wears off, two things hit me:

1. He's good. Very, very good. Not at kissing. No, definitely not. I was just in shock, that's all. That's why I couldn't breathe. No, what I meant is he's good at the game. I started it at the party by initiating the rumor, but he just fired back his first shot, and it was a perfect ten. I couldn't have done it better myself. I'm dealing with a mastermind. Possibly a criminal one. It depends on how many cups of baby's blood he drinks a day.

2. He took my first kiss. Now that everyone's seen me go weak in the knees from a kiss (weak knees run in my family, we all have to get canes, it's nothing special), they'll never believe the rumor that he kisses bad. That he kissed me bad. Now I'm a liar. He proved me a liar in front of everyone

in ten seconds flat. My title's expanded from New Girl to New Girl Who Lied and Said Jack Hunter Kisses Bad. He took my first kiss and ruined my reputation, but most importantly, he took my first kiss when I thought no one would ever take it. No one had up until now. I'd gone seventeen years without a guy once trying to kiss me. Ugly girls don't get kissed—that's a fact. Nameless never even tried to kiss me. I'd buried my hopes of ever getting kissed deep beneath the nine-billion-foot grave that contains my respect for men.

My feet start taking me to Mrs. Gregory's class again. I hear my name on people's lips, and I feel them staring. I need to be plotting my next move against Jack. I need to make him apologize to Kayla no matter what. I need to somehow turn this around and salvage my reputation. But all that just melds into a cacophony of faint buzzing in my head, with three huge words echoing over it.

I got kissed.

I got *kissed.*

I shake my head so violently to clear it one of my ladybug earrings nearly flies off. I cup the small creature and pet the enamel of it soothingly. Hush now, Mr. Ladybug. Don't go anywhere. I still love you. You're the only one for me. That kiss didn't mean anything at all; it was just Jackoff's way of making me look like a liar.

Once Mr. Ladybug is soothed and I'm in my seat comfortably zoning out while Mrs. Gregory yammers about matrix equation shit, I expertly piece together what just happened, edited to my taste of course. I white out the entire kiss. That goes first—I don't need to remember that ever again. Men are scum and Jack Hunter is the worst scum of all. If anyone asks, I lost my first kiss to Johnny Depp and/or Tom Hiddleston. Possibly at the same time. Note to self: verify that with your Realistic Likelihood Calculator™ before committing to it.

As for the other parts, I know I saw Mr. Evans and Jack talking. Apparently some stuck-up colleges want Jack to attend. Maybe he has good grades or something? I wouldn't put it past him to be smart. I'd seen that much with the way he took advantage of the perfect timing in the hall. And he uses big weird words, so he's probably a huge nerd. To be fair, I do, too, but that's because I'm mildly fabulous. Jack has no such excuse. Evans and Jack also talked about a "she," as in, *She'll get better with or without you here*. Who's "she"? And is she somehow preventing Jack from going off to college?

It's a huge mystery I obviously don't have time for. I ferret the information away in my brain in case I need some really heavy-duty ammunition against Jack in the days to come, but I leave it at that. I need to take this guy's ego down a peg, not get all weirdly concerned over his future. Unless said future involves me strangling him. Then that's fine and I should probably concern myself with that in order to make absolutely sure it gets locked down on the permanent dimensional timeline.

And how the hell did he find out Nameless's name, anyway? It's not like I'm in the newspapers back in Florida. That's really private, sensitive, and particular information.

And if Jack somehow found out Nameless's name, is he capable of finding out what happened between us?

I quickly scribble down a battle plan on the back of my hand with ballpoint pen:

1. *Assess the threat.*
2. *Pinpoint weaknesses.*
3. *Exploit said weaknesses.*
4. *Win.*

"Isis?" Mrs. Gregory snaps. "Are you paying attention to the problem on the board?"

"Seventy-two," I say, and get out of my chair to sit beneath my desk.

"Excuse me?"

"The answer," I call from underneath the wood. "Seventy-two."

She looks startled, but quickly takes in the board and scribbles on a loose sheaf she thinks I can't see. The whole class is staring at me with bated breath, wondering what the hell is going on. Mrs. Gregory finally looks up.

"Correct. But why are you sitting—"

The emergency bell rings then, shrill and in short bursts. Mrs. Gregory tells everyone to get under their desks and remain calm. Her bug-eyed face is anything but calm. The lockdown lasts for four or so tense minutes in which I pick the black polish off my nails while everyone debates whether it's a shooting or a drug raid. Mrs. Gregory crawls over to me and frowns.

"Isis, how did you know there was going to be a lockdown? Are you"—she lowers her voice and leans in—"*involved* with shady characters? It's okay to talk to me, you know. I can convince the police you didn't mean any harm. There are programs for students like you—"

"I saw the kid who likes knives too much run across the quad in his underwear with a plastic one."

She looks understandably shocked. Principal Evans gets on the PA and announces it's safe. On my way to the parking lot, I pass the open principal's door, where Knife Kid sits in a chair, surrounded by three cops arguing what to do with him. I flash him a thumbs-up, and he makes scissors with two fingers and drags them across his throat in a jovial greeting, but it doesn't faze me. I'm still in a daze.

I got kissed.

The one thing I never thought would happen to me, happened.

chapter three

I QUICKLY FIND OUT two things about East Summit High:

> 1. *Avery might be the most popular, but Kayla is widely regarded as the prettiest.*
> 2. *Every boy in school has had at least five wet dreams about her.*

This means that Kayla didn't have to earn her popularity by groveling to Avery like everybody else. She simply showed up, grew a pair of fabulous knockers and had a face to die for, and Avery recruited her into her friend group solely based on how pretty she is, and how spineless. And I say that with the utmost respect. Kayla is, comparatively, spineless. But she isn't stupid. This means that Kayla might actually like being popular, or she might actually like Avery. I'm willing to bet it's the first more than the second, because who honestly likes contract slavery other than two-hundred-year-old racists and the raunchy BDSM crowd? No one.

Kayla invites me over to consume cookies and interpret the giant stack of world history homework she can't quite seem to grasp, which is understandable—grasping the true glory of Genghis Khan is a little difficult to do when he's not there himself, shooting fletched arrows into your ass.

"Hello, spawn!" I coo at Kayla's baby brother as he waddles into her room. He burps at me.

"It looks like you guys speak the same language," Kayla quips.

"Where was that sass when Jack was making you cry at Avery's party?"

"Uh, hello? He's my crush? I'm not going to sass him."

"Flash 'em the sass before you flash 'em the ass."

"What kind of saying is that?" She laughs.

"Grandma-saying. She's the head of the motorcycle gang at her nursing home."

I amuse myself for a few minutes by showing her brother how to blow spit bubbles. Kayla's still a little beat up over the fact that Jack kissed me, for real this time, and I've spent the past hour assuring her it was nothing, but she still won't believe me.

"Everybody's saying you looked shocked. Like, a good shocked. And what the hell is that?" She points at my hand. I hold up the leather wallet.

"Oh this? I just, uh, picked it up."

"It looks like something from a cheap cowboy movie."

Her brother squeals and pulls my hair. I blacklist him.

"Hey, don't call my wallet cheap. Do you have a leather wallet? No. Even if you did, yours would be uncool, whereas mine was both free and satisfying, by which I mean I stole it from my nemesis's butt pocket while he was macking on me."

"You stole Jack Hunter's wallet?" Kayla's eyes bug out. I wave it in front of her with a smirk.

"What, you think I'd go down without a fight? Wanna see what's inside?"

Her curiosity wars visibly with her crush, but curiosity kills all types of cats, including people. She scoots next to me. I peel it open and expect some sort of unholy glow to emit from within like in cartoons, but all that comes out is a piece of lint and the smell of pine. Inside is Jack's ID—him glaring at the camera intensely.

"He's so hot," Kayla says through a sigh. "He even takes good ID photos."

"That's a sure sign of being an alien. Or plastic surgery. Possibly both."

"Look at the age!"

I peer at the age stamped on the ID and frown. March 20, 1990. There's no way he's that old.

"That's not his birthday," Kayla insists. "It's January 9, 1998."

I give her a long, meaningful look and she flushes. Fake ID—fine. We all gotta buy booze and get into clubs somehow. It's pretty standard. I riffle through the rest of the wallet . . . five bucks cash, some change, a library card because he's a nerd, some receipts for chicken and milk and measuring tape. Pretty basic high school kid stuff, but surprisingly tame coming from the wallet of a guy who talks like an Einstein

clone and looks like an underwear ad. I was expecting loads
of condoms and maybe a line of molly.

Kayla's brother screams in my ear for candy. I tell him
the plants in the yard need watering and he immediately
trundles toward the kitchen spewing spit bubbles.

"Look!" Kayla grabs something from the wallet. It's a
stack of business cards. Or, at least I think they're business
cards. But they don't actually have any business addresses on
them, so they can't be business cards. They're a deep black
with a single red stripe on the bottom, with the same name
and same phone number in dangerously svelte red text:

JADEN 555-354-3310

"Jaden must've really liked Jack to give him this many
cards," Kayla muses. She's so dense sometimes.

"They're his, Kayla. He's passing them out. That's why he
has so many."

Her mouth makes a little O. "But . . . but his name isn't
Jaden."

"It's a pseudonym."

"Why would he need one?"

"It's probably for a job."

She nods. I bite my lip and torture my brain into thinking
more clearly. I take a single business card and put the rest
back, handing the wallet to her.

"Here. You can do the honor of returning that—he's
probably stressing that it's gone. This is your chance to tip

the scales in your favor. Even if the scales are made of misogynism and the bones of small infants."

She takes it, beaming. "Thanks!"

"Is Avery still mad at you for leaving the party?" I ask.

"Oh, no. I mean, Avery never really gets *mad* mad, you know? She sort of just, doesn't talk to you. Or look at you. Or acknowledge you exist."

"Ah, yes. Perfectly reasonable."

"At the party, I was supposed to, um, talk to Wren. You know, student council president guy."

"Your student council prez goes to boozers? Consider me impressed."

"He's cool like that, but at the same time he's also intimidating. Like, really intimidating. He's going to MIT and he doesn't look anywhere at you except your eyes. No lips, no boobs, not even your eyelashes. Just. Your. Eyes."

She stares at me as if demonstrating, wide-eyed and unrelenting, and I shudder.

"All right, all right. I get the picture. Mega creep."

"Yeah, but like, a socially accepted mega creep. It's weird. He's friends with everybody. And I mean *everybody*. He watched an entire season of *Naruto* just so he could talk to the anime club kids."

I whistle. "He's certainly impressive. Hell-bent. Also possibly from actual hell."

"Anyway, Avery wanted me to, um, talk to him."

"Just talk?"

Kayla nods a little too hard for my liking. "She wants

more funds for the French club. She's president of that. She's trying to set up a trip to France for them or something."

"So you *talking* to him would get you funds? Are you that good at talking?"

"Just, you know. I'm nice. I can get things from people."

"You're pretty."

"But I'm also nice! And I'm smart! Okay, maybe not in world history, but who even cares about stupid plagues anyway? We have vaccines now! I'm really good at home ec and Mrs. Gregory said I have a natural talent for calculus, okay? I'm a lot of things besides pretty, so don't just say that like everyone else!"

Her chest is heaving, and her face is a little red. I put my hands up in surrender.

"Okay. I'm sorry. You're right. You're a lot of things besides pretty. I just meant . . . I just meant—"

"You just meant what? I know I'm pretty, okay? I know that! That's all anyone talks about! But I'm not pretty enough, I guess, because you're the one Jack Hunter kissed and not me!"

She shouts the last sentence. It hangs in the air like icicles, cold and jagged.

"I didn't— I'm sorry—"

"I don't wanna talk about it anymore," she murmurs. "I have to watch Gerald, so if you could just leave, that'd be great."

I feel all the air punch out of me at once. "Oh. R-Right. Sure."

I grab my backpack and books, shuffling them away. Kayla gets up and goes into the kitchen, wiping dirt off her brother's face and scolding him for trying to eat daisies. I want to say bye, or apologize again, but there's a thick curtain of awkward closing on the stage that is our tenuous friendship. I want to say a lot of things to her. I want to thank her for being the first person to really invite me over to her house, to talk to me, to eat lunch with me. But those words get stuck in my throat, the gratitude I have for her dammed up by shame.

As I leave and start my car, I mentally kick myself. Of course she gets told she's pretty. She gets it all the time. Pretty girls like her are sick of hearing it. I was insensitive to even say it—but how could someone like me understand what pretty girls experience?

Ugly girl.

Jack kissing me—was it really such a huge deal for her? Maybe I underestimated her feelings for him. She must really like him if she's that upset. Hell, if I still believed in love and had someone I liked and he kissed my sort-of-friend, I'd be mad at that friend, too.

She has every right to hate me.

But then again, a lot of people do. I'm not exactly a saint.

Mom texts, asking me to buy sponges and some blueberries on the way home. I'm feeling terrible about what I said, so terrible I grab a bar of chocolate. Or three. When I get home I sneak into Mom's bathroom and count her pills. She's down two. That's good. That means she took them. I can breathe easier, and maybe get a solid night's sleep.

"There's a package for you from your father," Mom says. She's up and baking muffins, hence the blueberries. It's a good sign. No, scratch that; it's the best sign I've seen in a while. She used to bake all the time when I was a kid.

"Thanks." I smile. Forced smile. Always a little forced. It won't be a real smile until she's really better.

But I don't remember what better looks like anymore.

The package is wrapped in brown paper and on my bed. The box inside is labeled "Chanel." Dad married a rich programmer from New York; they've got three-year-old twin girls and a boy on the way. I've never met them, but just knowing I have stepsiblings wigs me out. I see them on Facebook through the pictures Dad posts, but it's like they aren't real. It's like they're Photoshopped Loch Ness monsters and the University of Whatever is going to prove the hoax by showing me the beam of light in the background is wavy or something.

They're real.

Sometimes I wish they weren't.

And that's horrible, so I stop wishing that. Or at least I try to.

Inside the box is a beautiful chiffon top. It's light and fluffy, with dozens of frills, but a little big. Dad's new wife wheedled my size out of me two summers ago when I visited. She's nice enough, but it's things like this that remind me she just wants me to like her. She thinks gifts of expensive name brands are all it takes to woo a high school girl. She doesn't know me at all—she doesn't even know I'm eighty-five pounds lighter now.

But she's half right. A top like this would woo any girl. Any girl who isn't ugly. Maybe if I put this on, I can be prettier, and understand a smidgen of what Kayla's problems are, what she feels. Maybe I can understand her better.

I pull my shirt off and slip it over my head. It's so cool and airy, and the ruffles bounce with my every step. I can see my angry red stretch marks on my stomach through the gauzy fabric, but they don't bug me as much for some reason. I smile at myself in the mirror; I look different.

Maybe Nameless was wrong. Maybe I am pretty.

The door to my room opens just then, and I'm frozen in the headlights that are Mom's eyes. She looks me up and down, and immediately shakes her head.

"Oh, honey, that doesn't suit you at all."

The air punches out of me again, but this time in a deeper way. A more final way. Mom opens the door wider, totally oblivious to how deep the wound is.

"The muffins are ready. Come down and have some."

"Awesome. One sec. Just, uh, let me change out of this stupid thing."

When she's gone, I can't look at myself in the mirror without flinching. The ruffles seem to droop idiotically. The color is an eyesore, especially on me. It's not my thing. Being pretty is not my thing and I was stupid for testing the logical facts and practical boundaries. There are rules. And the number one rule is don't try to be someone you're not. Trying to be someone prettier is stupid, a waste of energy.

I stuff the shirt in the box and chuck it in the closet.

chapter four

FOR APPROXIMATELY TWO WEEKS, I debate the validity of ruining Jack Hunter's life-slash-reputation-slash-all future prospects with women. Or men. Just love in general, really. Guys like him shouldn't get to be happy. He ruins a girl's happiness at least once per hour. On Wednesday, someone left him a love letter tucked between the wipers of his black sedan. He tore it off without a second glance and ripped it in two. A distant wail could be heard as a well-dressed, beautiful blond girl from drama club had her heart shattered and smeared all over the pavement. She'd been waiting for his reaction, and now she had to watch the pieces of her carefully crafted letter-feelings whisk across the parking lot.

I chased the pieces around, grabbing as many as I could, and comforted her for three hours in a stairwell while she cried on me. I pieced the letter back together. It was full of Shakespearian references and a particularly well-thought-out passage in which she drew comparisons between Jack and Romeo. I informed her she was right—Romeo's manic

mental illness and pigheaded refusal to acknowledge another person's feelings are mirrored exactly in Jack. She
thanked me for that keen assessment by calling me a bitch.

Drama Club Wailer was just the first. In two weeks of
stealthily following Jack around campus, I've counted four love
confessions, each more creative than the last. The girl who runs
the morning announcements says Jack's won a prize from the
announcement committee, and to come to the PA room after
school to get it. She does this every. Single. Day. And yet every
day Jack never goes near the PA room; he doesn't even walk
in the same hall. He takes a route that leads him around it and
makes him almost late for fourth period. I sneak a peek at the
PA room after school for a few days. Sure enough, Announcement Girl waits in that room for thirty minutes before finally
locking up and going home with a defeated look on her face.

A girl in art club is working on a *marble statue* of him
(it's definitely him, everyone can see that) complete with
resplendent Greek posture and a perfectly replicated face.
She's left the crotch area blank and goes red if anyone asks
her about it, but according to Kayla she's diligently chipped
away at it since freshmen year, and she's now a senior. Another girl writes poetry and leaves it in his locker.

Through all this, Jack is impervious. It's like he's numb to
whatever a girl does to get his attention. On top of that, no
one dares to call his name out loud in the hall. He doesn't
have any guy friends; he keeps to himself at lunch, and
during recess he's in the library. He's always alone, and it's
definitely by choice. But why? That nags at me more than

anything—pretty people are never alone. That's what I've learned, in my scant seventeen years on this green earth. Why is he defying the one law I thought I had pinned down?

At first I stayed far away from Jack to quell the rumors, and to maybe-hopefully get Kayla to forget the fact that he kissed me. But there are so many rumors now; it's just one irritating slurry. "They're going out" is the usual; the most out-there one is that he's my pimp and I'm addicted to lean. My favorite is the one where I'm his long-lost half sister and we're doing the incest and doing it hard. None of them is helping my relationship with Kayla, of course, but today she sat at my table and we ate together. In total silence. Which isn't exactly a step in the right direction, but it's a step nonetheless. She only started sitting with me after she returned Jack's wallet to him, which I watched. It went much smoother than their first encounter— she handed it over and he actually nodded at her! A positive signal! I didn't see his lips form the words "I'm sorry," though, so technically he hasn't swallowed his pride and technically I am not regrettably still at war with him.

Kayla's smile lasted for hours after the exchange. And that only fuels my need to see Jack apologize. It's incredible how much control he has over her emotions, and how little he cares. Any guy in school would kill to make her smile like that. Jack's indifference toward her only makes me hate him more. No one should pour their entire heart onto another person without even an acknowledgment.

And so, armed with only a single business card and my indomitable charm, I go hunting.

My prey is easy to find. He moves like clockwork — always the same boring places at the same boring times. I open the door to the library. Frigid air mixed with the pulpy smell of old books greets me. The librarian eyes my purple streaks but doesn't say anything. She's seen worse. I meander through the aisles, looking up and down for him. Finally, I find him in the romance section. His sandy hair grazes his eyes as he leafs through a book with ... a beefy guy on the cover? I feel my eyebrows shoot up.

"You could do the fair maidens of the school a favor and inform them you're gay," I say.

"Didn't you read the sign?" he asks coolly without looking up. "No harpies in the library."

"If I was any fantasy animal I'd be a majestic unicorn, thank you, but I'll forgive your transgressions. It takes keen eyesight to differentiate a harpy from a unicorn. Also, common sense."

He looks up, blue eyes growing irritated. "I don't have the patience for you right now."

"Listen to yourself! *I don't have the patience for you,*" I mock in a deep voice. "You sound like my freaking mom! Like a parent! Like a really old, decrepit man. You're what, seventeen? Start acting like it."

"They're spreading rumors about us. It'd be best for you to keep your distance."

"Aha! I've already thought of that! But let's be realistic. This is high school. No amount of space between us is gonna stop the rumors from breeding like rabbits."

"Your Freudian choice of metaphor is getting ridiculous now. If you want me, just come out and say it. Get it over with so I can shoot you down."

"You'd like that, wouldn't you? Nope. Not happening. You aren't my type, first off—"

"I'm everyone's type," he says tiredly.

"And second off, have you even *seen* that marble statue? It's incredible. You should at least give her a chance, okay? Someone with that much talent has to be cool."

He snaps the book closed and picks up another one. "No."

"You have to agree it's an incredible piece of art, creepy stalkerish qualities attached to it or no."

"You're the only stalker I see here." He sighs.

"And what about drama club girl—"

"Who?"

"Windshield love note girl."

"Ah." His face sours.

"But she's so cute! And short! And she has huge boobs! And she's got tenacity! But mostly *huge* boobs. That's a thing with guys last time I checked. Boooobs!" I make a cupping motion around my significantly flatter chest. "And if she has tenacity, she'll be able to put up with your arrogant bullshit longer! It's a perfect match!"

He snorts. "You don't know anything about me, let alone enough to match me with some pathetic girls."

"Stop saying they're pathetic! They're nice, okay? You just haven't given them a chance—"

He moves so fast I barely have time to blink and he's

looming over me, arms on either side of me and that same deadly cool look in his eyes I saw when he was talking to Evans. A strange pressure threatens to collapse my lungs, but I stay strong. For Kayla. For the sake of the war. I'm strong and I can't let him see anything otherwise.

"All they do is grovel," he snarls. "I am a thing to them, not a person. They worship me because they don't know me."

"Yeah, but you keep it that way. Everybody thinks you're intimidating and hard to approach, just how you like it. You don't make any effort to be nice or make friends. It's easier to be worshipped by people than it is to be friends with them."

"What the hell do you know?"

"I don't know anything—except that you're here, in the library, reading corny-ass romance books." I gesture around me. He holds my gaze, like he's looking for something inside me, some weakness to exploit. He is the spitting image of a lion circling its prey. But I'm no wildebeest to be eaten.

I'm a tiger.

He must see that, because he backs off. He returns the book and takes out a few others, piling them on his arm.

"These aren't for me."

"I've heard that before."

"I have a friend who enjoys them," he says, voice now softer. "But she can't get out a lot. So I take them to her."

"Oh. Well. That's nice of you. Also kind of weird, since you seem to intensely dislike all women."

"I don't dislike them. I'm tired of them. There's a difference."

"*Tired* of them? You're seventeen! Why do I have to keep reminding you of that? There are soooo many women you haven't even met yet! Don't act like you're tired of the puss-puss; no guy is ever tired of the puss-puss."

He shoots me a withering look, but for a split second I swear I hear him half laugh, half scoff quietly under his breath.

"You're bizarre. And a moron. But I suppose it could be worse. You could be normal."

"I could be normal," I agree. "It could be even *worse*—I could like you."

"True. I don't like you, either. In fact, I despise you."

"Can we maybe not talk about your gross little feelings for me?"

"Trust me, they're anything but little. And gross is an understatement; they cause instantaneous vomiting."

"Oh, good! That makes two of us. I threw up four times on my way to the library to ask you about this."

I flash the black-and-red card between my fingers. Jack's expression doesn't change from one of utter boredom. I flash it again in front of his face, waving it back and forth a few times for good measure.

"Aren't you the least bit concerned I have one of these?"

"I knew you had it. I counted the cards when your friend returned the wallet you stole."

"How did you know I was the one who took it?"

"How else would Kayla get it?" He sneers. "She's not the type to steal. You are."

"I'd be insulted if I wasn't rolling in five cubic tons of hot-ass self-confidence."

"I have twenty-two cards, and there were twenty-one when she gave it back."

"Are you OCD or something? You keep count of how many business cards you have in your wallet?"

"Can you just get on with threatening me?"

I treat him to a brief glare. "I haven't called the number on this card. Yet."

"But you've written it down somewhere else."

"Of course," I breeze on. "And if you have an ounce of brain in that thick head of yours, you'll apologize to Kayla before I call it and leak to the campus cop whatever sordid drugs you deal as a side job."

He scoffs. "Drugs. That's what you think it is? You think I'm that predictable? I'm almost offended."

"The people in juvie will certainly be offended by your holier-than-thou attitude. Offended enough to beat you up on the daily."

"You poor girl." He laughs, pinching the bridge of his nose like he has a headache. "You poor, naive little girl. You talk a big game, about how much smarter you are and how you're different from them. But at the end of the day, you're just as oblivious as all the other girls."

"Don't patronize me!" I snarl. "I know you're doing some-thing illegal to make money. If you don't apologize to Kayla—"

"You'll what? Out me? Go ahead. Call that number." He leans in. "I dare you to."

"Back the hell off," I hiss up at his face. He narrows his icy-flint eyes but doesn't lean away.

"Do it." He holds out his phone.

It's a trap. I'm walking into the biggest trap in the world. Jack looks at me with a keen, almost hungry interest. He wants me to find out what this card means. By the time I do, I might've sprung his trap closed. But I want to know, too. The part of me that wants to know is louder than the part of me that's a prudent, tactical battle master. If I call this number, I'll get a huge amount of blackmail material. In theory. What's the worst that could happen? It's not like he's rigged a bomb to the number or anything. It could be nothing at all, a huge dud, but I won't know until I try.

I dial slowly and raise it to my ear. There's a ring. And another ring. Jack isn't moving. He's barely blinking. I'm barely breathing, anticipation heavy on my chest.

"Hello, Madison speaking," a pleasant woman's voice chirps. "How may I help you?"

"Uh, hi, I'm—"

"Looking for a rose," Jack says softly. He's so close I can smell him—pepper and honey? His hair falls in his eyes and I'm pretty sure I'm in the middle of a photo shoot, but I can't tear my gaze from his to confirm that.

"Looking for a rose," I finally croak.

There's a brief pause. "One moment while I bring out the books. May I ask your name?"

I look to Jack again, but he just shakes his head.

"Isi— Isabelle."

"All right Isabelle, and who are you calling after?"

"Um ... "

"The name on the card you were given?"

"Oh. Jaden."

If this is a drug request line or something, it's the weirdest one ever. There's a tapping noise as the woman types on a keyboard. Jack's eyes are scanning over my shoulder, watching people walk by, but I can tell he's still fully tuned in to the conversation I'm having.

"And is this your first time with the Rose Club, Isabelle?"

"Y-Yes? Yes." Club? What kind of club—

"All right, thank you so much for choosing to book with us, Isabelle. Jaden's one of our most popular escorts, so I'm afraid there's a bit of a wait. The soonest opening I have is on December fourth, at twelve thirty p.m., in Columbus. In addition, I'm obligated to mention to any and all customers his fees are considerably higher than those of our other escorts—"

I scrabble for the button to cancel the call and end up fumbling the phone onto the floor. It slides beneath a shelf and disappears. Jack hefts off the shelf and picks the phone up in one fell swoop.

"I set my phone to record that call," he says. "I now have you and the operator's conversation on tape. I will edit it to only implicate you. If you tell anyone what you know about that card, I will sue you for character defamation. Is that clear?"

I swallow so hard I swear I hear my throat crack. Jack

Hunter an escort? A real-life escort? At seventeen? It's not possible—

"I said, *is that clear*?" He hardens his voice. I don't dignify him with a nod. I'm gone before he has the chance to form another imperious sentence. It was a trap. And I fell for it.

◉ ◉ °◉

I watch Isis go, her footsteps petulant. This isn't the first time I've seen her angry. But it's definitely the first time I've seen her off her game. She's thrown, imbalanced by my reveal. If this isn't enough to get her off my case for good, I don't know what is. I gambled on the truth, scaring her enough to keep her away from me, but I'll only know if it worked for sure in the next few days.

I want it to work.

I want her to stop following me, harassing me. She's clearly misguided, or just bored—either way, I remind her of someone who hurt her in the past. Even an idiot can see that much. How can a girl be this infuriating and stubborn? Most of them give up after I tell them off, or at least quietly go about their business and leave me be. But she has no sense of boundaries, no tact. She's raw and forward and never holds herself back. She throws herself headfirst into any problem she comes across. It's utterly baffling. It's driving me *crazy*.

"Another girl you've scared off, eh, Jack?"

I look up. The librarian has an armful of books, and she puts each back carefully on the shelf next to me. She and I haven't always gotten along, but she lets me stay in the library whenever I want, and for that I'm grateful.

"It's none of your business, Ms. Schafer."

She laughs. "Oh, I know. But keep going like this, and you'll end up like me—all alone."

"Maybe that's what I want."

Ms. Schafer sighs and puts a book back on the highest shelf. "That's very romantic and tragic and all, but I'll let you in on a secret—nobody actually wants that, kiddo. Only poets and psychopaths want to be left alone forever, and after three years I know you're not either of those."

"Thank you for your words of wisdom, but forgive me if I don't take the bittersweet ramblings of a high school librarian to heart."

I start to walk away, but she speaks after me, sounding exasperated.

"You don't have to keep punishing yourself, kiddo."

I keep walking. She doesn't know anything.

The air outside is warm and smells fresh, but my insides are rotting. They've been rotting since that night, five years ago.

But I deserve to rot.

This is my punishment.

Somewhere deep down, I am relieved. I'm relieved someone knows what I really do now, even if it is an insensitive girl like Isis. I've kept the secret for so many months, I forgot it was festering. But now it feels freer—no. *I* feel freer. I've chained myself to this side job to help Sophia. Or at least, that's what I keep telling myself. Of course I'm helping her. At the same time, it's bothersome. It's tiring. And sometimes, it feels like I'm being used.

But this is my punishment for the evil I've done.

And I will accept it.

○ ○ ° ○

I am getting my *shit* kicked in.

I say that admiringly about Jack Hunter, even if I hate his guts. He's pulling out all the stops, hitting hard and heavy and never relenting. I would be wounded, my pride shattered and completely defeated if I were anyone but me. Thankfully, I'm Isis Blake, and word on the block is she's a pretty rad girl who is never defeated. Nameless couldn't do it. I sure as hell won't let some random pretty boy do it. The only one who's worthy of defeating me is me!

Feeling mildly more pumped, I blast my radio louder at a stoplight. My brain's working overtime. I make a list in my head.

1. Jack knows a girl. He brings said girl romance novels. She can't get out a lot. Maybe she has overprotective parents or something? Is she the same girl I heard Evans trying to convince him to leave behind? More investigation is necessary. The girl could be the key factor in turning the tide — Jack seems to care about her, mildly more than he cares about himself, anyway. I need to find out who she is.

2. Jack is an escort. It's like something out of a stupid drama on TV, but I heard the lady on the other line. If she

was a hoax, she was a very good one. Something in my gut tells me she wasn't—Jack's good at this mind game stuff, but not *that* good. He couldn't have set up an entire fake telephone line and hired a fake lady to convince me he's an escort, and even if he did, what would he gain from it? Why would convincing me he's an escort prove helpful to him? It wouldn't. So that means it has to be true.

2A. The word "escort" has a buncha definitions, but "a man who is a companion of a woman, especially on a social occasion" is the one that fits here. People hire Jack—no, Jaden. Women escorts more or less are hired for sex. Is that true with the men, too? Is Jack—for all intents and purposes—having sex for money?

2B. If it's true he's an escort, then I can't use that info, since he has the recording to use against *me*. It kills me that I can't say anything—revealing he has a part-time job as an escort would be the ultimate retaliation for him stealing my first kiss. But I don't wanna get dragged down with him. I don't wanna get sued—even if it is a bluff, Mom doesn't need the extra stress of the legal system right now. And we definitely don't need another chip in our finances. So I'll just have to find other ways to make him regret ever touching me, or insulting Kayla, or being the Massive Douche Bag of the Century™.

I've never fought someone this confusing.

My enemies in my old high school were straightforward assholes, the kind who shouted "bitch" and "dyke" and sometimes spread rumors about sleeping with certain (pretty) girls. But that was all they did. That was the limit. They were easy to see through (insecure, compensating), and easy to shut down with a well-placed comment about their inferiority complexes or urge to fit in.

But Jack? Jack is steel and black ice. He's deadly serious, sharp as a katana, and as disorienting as a mountain blizzard in December. I have no idea what his deal is. All I know is he isn't what he seems; a boy who takes a girl the romance novels she likes to read because she can't get out much can't be a monster. That's the act of a kind person.

But then again, I learned the hard way that even kind boys can turn out to be monsters.

Since Jack is good, and I've never quite faced this good of an enemy before, I need answers, information, and tactics. And I need them fast. So I'm going to the one person who might know something about Jack.

Wren volunteers on Saturdays at the local food bank. I know this because every time Mrs. Gregory sees his face on the morning announcements she feels the need to list each one of his accomplishments, starting with how often he volunteers and where. I park and get out, mincing through the crowd of single moms with screaming kids and the half homeless. A guy looks me up and down and whistles "Ay mami" but he smells like booze and pee and that makes sense—only people with severely impaired judgment would think I'm pretty enough to whistle at. Wren's at the front of the line but behind the tables, stocking cans of corn and tuna. He talks with the other volunteers and coordinates them with a brisk, clear efficiency. He has dark midnight hair perfectly slicked back. His glasses make him look way older than he is. He isn't handsome like Jack, but he's terribly cute in that bumbling, wide-eyed boy-next-door way. I sidle up beside him.

"Your mom should've just named you Chicken."

Wren looks up, hazel eyes confused. "Excuse me?"

"You know, it's a more common word than Wren. Plus people wouldn't be bugging you about how to spell it all the time. If you're gonna name your kid after a bird, at least have the courtesy to make it a bird people can spell."

"It has four letters," he says.

"Those little paper fortune-teller hand doohickeys have four things, too, but do you even know how complicated that shit can get?"

"I'm sorry." Wren squints at me. "Do I know you? Oh, wait. I do know you. The new girl. Isis Blake."

"The one and only!" I smile.

"July 1, 1998. Blood type O positive. You previously lived in Good Falls, Florida, with your aunt. You're allergic to strawberries."

I'm shocked, but I keep my smile. "How do you know so—"

"I've read your school record. I volunteer in the office." He stacks another can on top of the small pyramid of tuna.

"Ah. Right. That makes less creepy sense!"

"Is there something I can do for you?" He grins, locking eyes with mine, and it's then I'm subjected to his fabled stare. He doesn't move his gaze in the slightest, boring a hole deep into my head. I glance away, but when I look back he's still staring with that same pleasant smile on his face. I clear my throat.

"As you may or may not know, I'm engaged in casual war with Jack Hunter."

"Yes, it's hard to go anywhere without hearing about the newest tantrum you two collectively pull."

"And a little bird—not a chicken—told me that you know everyone. Like, *everyone*."

"I make it a point to speak with everyone on campus. I enjoy being on amiable terms with many people."

"So that's a yes?"

"Yes. I know everyone. And if I don't know them, such as in your case, I hope to soon."

His smile brightens, but it only creeps me out more.

"Right," I say slowly. "So anyway, I'm betting you're the only guy who knows Jack."

Wren laughs. "'Know' Jack? Sure. I know him. As much as anyone can. He's like a wolf—he comes and goes and doesn't really give you any explanation about anything. But sometimes, just sometimes, he'll visit you in the dead of the night. If you're looking for information about him, I'm afraid I can't help you. I'm a little busy."

Wren pulls out a can of tomato sauce and inspects it like it's a precious gem. He hands it to a lady working with him.

"It's dented. Send it to the back pile."

"But it feels fine!" the woman protests.

"No, right here." Wren guides her fingers to the side of the can. "See? A nick. Tin doesn't stand up well to denting. You could poison someone like that."

The lady has to be postcollege, but she flushes a darker red than any schoolgirl. Wren turns back to me, and I make a low whistle.

"That's a hell of a metaphor, prez. Personally, I'd liken Jack more to a limbless, ooze-leaking amoeba, but wolf works, too."

"My name is Wren," he says sternly.

"Do you like burritos, prez? There's a burrito place around the corner. Saw it on my way here. They look huge! I can't eat one all by myself. But I'm hungry as hell and it's nearly lunchtime, so . . . " I jerk my thumb behind me. "I'm gonna go get one. I guess I'll see you around."

The burrito truck is situated in the middle of a ring of picnic tables, colorful umbrellas shading the parking lot and tired construction workers from across the street lining up to get a bite of cheesy, beany glory. I order a chicken and green salsa one. I cut it neatly in half and place one half across the table, and dig into my own. And I wait. It's the perfect lure. Wren might hide his exhaustion well, but I know he doesn't eat enough. He's the kind of student who's so busy buzzing around doing extracurriculars he constantly forgets to eat.

A shadow falls over my table, and Wren slides into the seat across from me. He pulls the burrito half to him, pleasant smile faint.

"You don't mind, do you?"

"Nope." I dribble lettuce eloquently on my shirt. He wolfs the burrito down with impressive speed. When he's done, and wiping his mouth with a napkin, I clap.

"Very good, prez. There's hope for you yet."

"I didn't have breakfast," he admits sheepishly.

"I know."

"You . . . knew?"

I nod toward his hands. "Your nails. See how they're all translucent, and ribbed with those little raised spots? Mine used to get like that when I was dieting. Not enough iron. Hell, not enough anything, period. I can get you another burrito, if you want."

"No, no I'm fine," he says a little too quickly, and does the creepy eyelock thing with me. "You're very observant, aren't you?"

I shrug. "How else would I maintain such a fabulous awareness of human existence at all times?"

"You *are* like him." Wren laughs and stands. He starts walking back to the food bank tent, and I trash my napkins and quickly follow.

"Like who?"

"Jack. You two have the same eye for detail. The same eye for delving into what people are all about."

I roll my eyes, but Wren merely shakes his head.

"He already came to see me. About you. That just further proves you two think alike—except you might be the slower one."

I shoot him a withering look, but he just smiles.

"I didn't say much about you. If you want to know about him, I can only tell you a few things. There's a lot I don't know."

"Who's the girl?" I immediately ask.

"What girl?"

"The girl he takes books to."

"Oh. You must mean Sophia."

"Sophia," I repeat quietly. "Is she his sister?"

"No. She's a friend. Maybe more than a friend. She's the one thing he guards very closely. I know she's ill; she's in the hospital almost always."

"Sick Sophia. Got it." I catch a falling can and hand it to the blush lady. "Anything else?"

"He lives with his mom in Coral Heights."

"That's that fancy gated suburb with the huge houses, isn't it?"

"Yeah, a lot closer to Columbus."

"Where's his dad?"

"Died in a plane crash, I believe. It was a long time ago, but I read articles about it. He was a pilot for a major airline. The insulation melted over the wing. It came right off." Wren inhales. "He landed the plane and managed to keep the cabin area safe. Two hundred people escaped. But he and his copilot were crushed under the impact. Jack's mother got a substantial amount of money from the company after a lawsuit against them."

I squeeze my eyes shut. My heart sinks. I pull it back up by the ventricles. *Now is no time to be feeling sorry for the enemy, heart! Get it together! Extremely together! Get it to-gether so well you fuse!*

"So . . . what did you tell him about *me*?"

"I told him about Will Cavanaugh."

I flinch so hard I jolt into the table behind me. A pyramid of soup cans wobbles and comes crashing down. I bite back a swear and hurriedly help them clean up my mess. When the pyramid is back on the table in a mass of tin and cheery labels screaming "SODIUM FREE," Wren sighs.

"My cousin is kind of a cruel little shit. I can understand why his name affects you like that."

"He's—" I swallow what feels like the entire contents of a staple box. "He's your—"

"Cousin," Wren confirms. "I don't know if you've been told, but it's a very small world."

"Microscopic." I laugh nervously, but no part of me feels happy. Nameless is closer than I thought. No—it's not him. Calm down. It's just a relation of his. He's not here, and he won't ever be. Hopefully. I mentally make a note to search for the closest cliff to dive off of just in case.

"I don't know the full story between you and my cousin, but he's said you and he were involved at some point."

"Yeah. Involved. That's hilarious."

"Are you okay? You look green."

"I'm— I'm fine." I put a hand on my stomach to steady it and send it a memo.

Can you wait until we're alone to recalibrate the burrito? Thanks and love, The Management Upstairs.

My stomach replies with a rebellious gurgle. Wren checks off something on a clipboard, eyes burrowing into me all the while.

"Anything else I can help you with?"

"Yeah, how legal is underage prostitution?"

He blinks. "Excuse me?"

"Like, it's not death sentence illegal, but it's not booze-legal either. So it's somewhere in between those two, right?"

"Presumably, yeah."

"Okay. Cool. Thanks again, prez!"

He flinches at the nickname as I wave and walk off, my mind brewing with a fantastic, ultracool, surefire plan.

Jack Hunter might be a little more human in my eyes now—he might have a sick girlfriend and a dead father—but he's still a dick. We're still at war. And he's still gonna apologize to Kayla, if it's the last thing I do.

chapter five

DOING A BIT OF Google research on the Rose Club clues me in on two things:

1. *There is no Rose Club. At least, not out in the open. People on sketchy Ohio sex forums refer to something called the "Club," but they don't ever detail the name. I guess it makes sense; things like this are pretty illegal. And if the Club is hiring minors, it's even grosser and illegaler. Or maybe Jack lied about his age—his fake ID certainly looked convincing enough.*

2. *Clubs with good-looking men for escort hire are usually gigolo clubs, run by a smart, older gigolo from overseas, where the practice is widely common in Europe. It's not unheard of for rich, wealthy daughters to hire equally beautiful guys for proms, weddings, family functions, and the weekend usual of wild-ass rave nights. The Duchess of Orlan-Reis (eighteen and gorgeous)*

was busted last month in Los Angeles for a DUI with fifteen pounds of Versace couture and two Portuguese gigolos in the car. Bill Gates's daughter has been going out with a rumored gigolo for a year and a half. Rich girls like pretty guys. And Jack is a lot of hugely negative things, but he is, I hate to admit, a pretty guy. But it's hard to believe a gigolo club would be here, in Ohio. I mean, there are some pretty rich people in Columbus, so it makes sense, but only a pie slice of sense versus an entire pie of sense. And why would Jack sign up to be in one to begin with? Last time I checked, sex for hire isn't exactly one of those jobs you like. Or do you?

I shake my head and open a can of tuna. Let's not think about sex. Ugly people have sex, sure, but me, particularly? It's not in my future. I've made it through most of high school without having it, and I'll probably make it a couple more years. Even if I do have it, it won't be with someone who actually likes me for who I am, and whoever I have it with will have to like stretch marks and zits, and last time I checked a significant portion of the population thinks all three are gross as hell. I'll get it over with someday. It'll be, like, a fling. A bar thing. What do grown-ups do to get laid again? Dating sites, I guess. It's a pretty bleak future, but it's not like I can expect anything else—I'm sparing people from me, and that includes relationships.

"Honey." Mom comes in. "Your father wants to know what schools you're applying to."

I smack my hand against my head but there's a can opener in it. As I rub away the bruises, I sigh.

"I've told him a million times: Redfield, Oregon U, Idaho U, and that one Mormon college in Seattle with the creepy brochures."

"Why are you applying if it looks creepy?"

"Because creepy is awesome? They're like a cult. I'm all about that shit."

Mom shoots me the disapproving-mom-subtle-lip-frown.

"I'm all about that *poop*," I correct delicately. She laughs, and it's a good sign. Two good signs in one month. I quash my optimism for stark realism—it won't last. I hope it does, but it won't. That won't stop me from enjoying it while I can, though. I assemble the tuna melts and slip the sandwiches in the oven to, well, melt. The doorbell rings, and I answer. Avery stands there, flaming hair lit from behind by the half-setting sun and a little scowl on her face.

"Awesome, thanks so much for coming!"

"I'm not staying," Avery drawls. "Just give me the money so I can leave."

"Uh, right! How much do I owe you?"

"Twenty bucks."

"Okay, one sec, lemme go get my wallet."

I take the stairs two at a time to my bedroom and rummage frantically in my wallet. I pull out two tens and hurtle downstairs. Avery passes me a brown paper bag, squished small, and I give her the money.

"Thanks for this." I smile. "Means, uh, a lot."

"Stay in school," she mocks what I told her that night at the party.

"Haha." I laugh awkwardly. "They aren't for me. They're for my high-anxiety . . . aunt's . . . boyfriend's . . . daughter . . . who is my cousin."

"Sure." Avery snorts. "Whatever."

There's a moment of quiet in which I think she'll turn and walk away, our business done, but she stays.

"Can I give you a piece of advice?" She narrows her eyes at me.

"Sure."

"Stay away from Jack's past."

I raise an eyebrow. "Any particular reason? And how did you know—"

"Wren and I talk. You asked Wren about Jack. And I'm telling you to stay out of Jack's past. People don't do well when they meddle in there."

"Like, they're struck by a terrible illness? Did he steal a crystal skull from a tomb? I told him that wasn't the brightest idea—"

"He's dangerous." She cuts me off. "Okay? He's fucking dangerous when you try to get close to him, and if you keep it up, he's going to turn that danger on you and I won't be able to stop him this time."

"Oh, is that a friend, Isis?"

I immediately stash the paper bag down my shirt. It bulges awkwardly and I pray she doesn't notice I've suddenly gone up an entire lumpy cup.

"Uh, yeah. Mom, this is Avery. Avery, this is Patricia Blake, my mom."

Avery takes one look at my bathrobed, watery-eyed, slightly fragile-looking mother and sneers.

"I gotta go."

She's gone in her green Saab before Mom has the chance to rope her into the living room. Smart girl. Also all kinds of hells rude, but smart.

"That girl . . . she looked familiar," Mom starts.

"Yeah? You've seen her before?"

"I have. I just can't for the life of me remember where."

○ ○ ° ○

I manage to slip the paper bag past security at school by almost rear-ending the janitor's truck as he pulls in to the parking lot Monday morning. He gets out, face a beet-red pimple ready to pop, and as he's lecturing me on safe driving and checking my fender to make sure not a speck of his red paint is on it, I slip the bag into the bed of the truck, under the tarp. At morning recess, I go behind the maintenance shed by the art room, where the janitor parks and dumps out the bed of his truck. A pile of rakes, brooms, bleach, sponges, and hammers crowd the ground, and the paper bag looks perfectly at home. I quickly pull the bag out from under a window-washing pole and scamper off.

Lots of people in the movies break in to lockers with elaborate ear-to-the-lock techniques, and when that fails, there's always the good old bolt cutters. But what the movies don't tell you is it's tons easier to just go through the door. Federal school district funding ensures the metal is the lowest quality nickel-tin hybrid, and all high school lockers are essentially made with a two-bolt drop system, which means if you take a hairpin and a pair of tweezers and wedge the center bolt to the left, you can crack the door open enough to slip something inside—for instance, two dime bags of weed that definitely are Jack Hunter's because they are in his locker now. I go to the bathroom and call the school office, anonymously tipping them that locker 522 has the smell of weed coming from it.

Campus security is all puffed up after catching that "criminal" the other day. Knife Guy's suspended for a week, and everyone sniggers openly about the fact that it took three security officers to catch one naked guy, but that doesn't matter to the officers. In their minds, it was a triumph of Adult Good over the General Evil of Teenagers, and that's enough ego puffing to have them walking around like balloons with mustaches and bald spots. In ten minutes they're at locker 522, the janitor cutting the lock and the officers riffling through Jack's things. I watch from around the corner of the hall as they take out his books, his pencils, dumping them on the floor unceremoniously. When they find the dime bags, they sniff the inside of them and assure one another it's weed. I cackle softly on my way back to class.

Jack Hunter: two. Isis Blake: one. It's a big difference, but I'll make it up quick.

Right about now some people somewhere would probably like to sit me down and give me a stern talking-to about how bad and evil and dangerous planting drugs in a dude's locker is. I would politely notify them: 1. Jack is rich and white and underage and a model student—let's get real, the police won't press charges all *that* hard. And 2. Jack is beyond cruel to everyone around him. It's a wake-up call. Jack Hunter has skated through life thinking he can get away with being cruel. Thinking he's smarter than everyone else. Fortunately, neither of those things is true.

And I'm the perfect girl to inform him of this.

This was long overdue. Like, borrowed-the-fourth-Harry-Potter-book-from-the-library-for-seventeen-months-when-I-was-a-kid overdue.

The rumor spreads like fire on an oil spill. Jack Hunter is suspended for two days pending minor drug charges with the local police, while they confirm at a lab that it's weed. Life is sweet. I bite into my sandwich and hardly notice it's the third day in a row I'm eating tuna. My taste buds can only perceive sweet, sweet victory.

"What are you doing?" Kayla asks, staring down at me with a tray of chili in her hands.

"Savoring my win," I say.

"That *was* you, wasn't it!" Kayla slams her tray down and hisses. "You were the one who planted weed in Jack's locker!"

"Uh, no? He's the stoner, not me. I wouldn't even know where to buy weed."

"Avery said she sold you two dime bags."

"Oh. Well, in that case, yes. I do know where to buy weed."

She makes a disgusted noise, but her face is the opposite of disgusting. It's beautiful. It's like watching a purebred show cat hack up a hairball.

"In my defense—" I throw up my hands. "Everybody knows the popular people have weed, okay? It's like a universal law, up there with 'the apple falls on Newton's nerdy head' and 'the sky is a distinct bluish color.'"

"I can't believe you." Kayla sighs. "I thought you were cool, and now look at you, planting drugs on some guy you don't like?"

"Uh, it's a little more than 'don't like.'"

"Newsflash—the rest of us do like him, okay? So can you just lay off?"

"He still hasn't apologized for making you cry, Kayla."

"He makes me cry all the fucking time, okay? I've kind of cried on the daily into my pillow about him for six years now!"

"Even more reason to kick his ass!"

"This isn't second grade, Isis," Kayla snaps. "Biting and kicking isn't ladylike, and it's not gonna get you anywhere with any guys, either."

"Maybe I don't wanna fucking get with any guys!" My voice is so loud it's drawing attention. "Maybe all guys are scumbags. Maybe I'm the only one who apparently can think clearly anymore and see an asshole for who he really is!"

"He's not an asshole—"

"I'm not going to listen to your excuses, Kayla! I know them all. I said them all once, too, for a guy, okay?"

"I have a hard time believing that," she says nastily.

"Yeah? Believe this!"

I yank my sleeve up, and Kayla does three things in quick succession—she sees the dark thing there, understands it, and recoils, flinching from it. From me.

I pull my sleeve back down and grab my backpack. I leave the sandwich there. I leave the short triumph over Jack I had there. I leave my secret there, with her.

The rest of the day is a blurry soup of anger and half-held-back tears. When I get home, the house is dark. All the windows are closed and the curtains drawn, like usual. The house is sleeping, or that's what it feels like. I call out for Mom. She didn't have work or a psychologist's appointment today, and her car is still in the garage. She should be home. I take the stairs two at a time and freeze when I see into her open room.

Everything is trashed. The lamp is broken, amber glass shattered across the carpet. Her documents and work canvases are scattered like the scales of a paper snake. She's ripped some of them to shreds, her bed littered with scraps. Her makeup is dripping off her dresser in ugly, flesh-colored liquid rivers. The mirror in her bathroom is broken, her pill bottle open and the pills clogging the sink. Water overflows from the tub onto the floor, a pool just beginning to form. My heart turns cold, my fingers going numb.

"Mom?" I shout. "Mom!"

I check under the bed, her closet, tearing clothes and chairs aside as I look for her. She's not in the living room, or my room, or the kitchen. I dial her cell phone but it rings upstairs, under her pillow. My mind crowds with images of her beaten, kidnapped, that man holding her by the arm and yanking her back to Nevada, back to where she was miserable.

I dial Dad frantically. But it only rings twice before I hear the faint sobbing. Mom. I leap after it, following the sound into the garage. She's curled up in the backseat of the car. It isn't running, thank God. I yank the door open and touch her face, her shoulders, inspect her for wounds or cuts.

"Mom, what the hell happened? Are you okay?"

"He came," Mom gasps into my hair, clinging to me like a baby monkey clings to a large one. "He found me."

The police take fifteen minutes to get here. They comb the house, interrogate Mom to the point of tears and back again, and all I can do is hold her and snap at them when they get too nosy or invasive. When the sweep of the house is done, one of them pulls me aside.

"Look, Miss Blake, you said your mom has a history of mental illness—"

"She has PTSD," I correct angrily. "From a recent abusive boyfriend. Not an entire history of fucking mental illness."

"I understand—"

"Do you?" I laugh, half hysterical.

"Look, I'm sorry. PTSD can be hell. Shit, some of our guys have it, too. Some of our guys have to be *let go* for it. Fact of the matter is, there's no male-size footprints in the house, and the locks weren't forced open. Nothing was stolen. There's no sign of a two-person struggle in her room, either."

"She said she heard him walking downstairs."

"It could very well have been a flashback. You said she's on medication, right?"

"And seeing a psychologist every week."

"Well, I'm sorry, kid, but if she's doing those things already, there's not a lot we can do for her."

"She's not crazy! Stop treating her like she is!"

"I'm not. I'm just stating facts. We can keep a cop outside your house for seventy-two hours, if it makes you feel better, but that's about it."

"Yeah. That'd be good."

He pats my shoulder. "Keep your chin up. She'll get better."

I watch his retreating back and murmur, "That's what they all say."

○　●　°○

After Mom's scare, I sleep in her room on the air mattress every night. I do my homework in there with her as she reads or naps. We eat meals upstairs, since she can't bring herself to go downstairs for more than a few minutes at a time. My own room starts to look weird and foreign when I walk in, like I'm a stranger in it. The cop outside helps. When she gets jumpy in the middle of the night, I point out her window to the cop car sitting under the streetlight, and she relaxes and manages to get some sleep.

But I don't. I stay awake, listening for the sounds of the heavy footsteps. Waiting. Praying. Praying that the bastard comes in and gives me an excuse to slit his throat. He got away easy. Beating a woman nightly when he got too drunk or she did something he didn't like is unforgivable. Beating a woman period is unforgivable. And the beatings are the only things I know about. There's more darkness lurking beneath Mom's surface, but she doesn't want me to worry, so she never told me the whole story. And that gives me more agony than the guilt. Whoever said not knowing is better than knowing was grievously full of shit.

I wait and I pray and I thank any god who's listening. Nameless might've fucked me over, but he didn't mess me up as much as that guy did to Mom. My thing is nothing compared to hers. It doesn't even deserve to be called a thing in light of what happened to Mom. To what happens to women everywhere, every day.

I call the office at school and Mom tells them I'm sick when I'm not. She calls her work and uses all her sick days. I search the house high and low for any sign of Leo. But the guy hunts deer during the summer—he knows how to cover his tracks so he can't be found. Mom used to tell me how much she hated the fact that he only hunted does and their fawns. It's illegal, but he'd do it anyway like the sick bastard he is. I remember thinking, when I heard Mom say that, that he wasn't a good guy. That a hidden darkness lurked below in the worst way. I remember wanting to tell her to leave him, but she was too happy at the time. Happier than I'd seen her since Dad left us. So I kept my mouth shut. And I regret it every day.

Anyway, I can't find anything that's evidence he was here. Was Mom really hearing things? She's had flashbacks, but none of them left her this terrified and drained. My gut won't give it up—if he was here, I'll find him.

The house has since been cleaned thoroughly by Mom. But the yard hasn't been touched. I get on my hands and knees and scour every inch of grass and rosebush for a footprint. Something, anything the police overlooked. After an hour, I sit back on my heels, my hands covered in dirt. I wipe sweat off my face and growl.

"Ugh! Whose idea was it to make humans leak salty water?"

God, understandably, has better things to do than answer me. And that's when I see it, half buried in the dirt below the roses.

A cigarette butt.

Mom and I don't smoke. I pick it up carefully. It could've been left by one of the cops when they smoked on break, or maybe even just a lazy kid who couldn't be bothered with a trash can. I sniff it tentatively and instantly recoil.

I'd know that smell anywhere. Gudang Garam, a clove cigarette, the same brand I used to see in Leo's back pocket. I only ever visited twice—both times for Christmas. But I keenly remember him stepping out during the day to smoke. The clove smell would waft in through the windows. Leo was in the army. He was stationed in Indonesia, he'd told me with an oily smirk. That's where he picked up Gudang Garam.

A cold sweat breaks out all over my body. What's the likelihood someone else in the neighborhood smokes Gudang, and decided to drop a butt in our yard around the same time Mom "saw" Leo? I could be paranoid. I could be *really* paranoid. Or I could be right. Something is wrong; my every nerve screams that at me. But I can't tell Mom. Not when she's so fragile. Confirming her fears would push her into a deeper darkness. And if I'm wrong, if it was just a coincidence, I'd be freaking her out for nothing. She needs to get better first, or at least more stable.

She falls asleep at random times—in the middle of the day, or just before dinner. I take those times to slip out and do errands, breathe fresh air—air free from the stagnant heaviness inside our house. I make sure the windows are open, but the breezes never whisk away the sadness like I want them to.

On my way back from the grocery store, I pass the South Rise Bridge. It's the highest bridge in the city, looming over the highway below. Most cars avoid it to take the much faster highway, but I like the drive. And today, I'm not the only one.

A familiar green Saab is parked on the side of the bridge, a girl with flaming red hair standing near the bridge edge, elbows on the railing. A chain-link mesh erected above the railing ensures nobody jumps off, but the girl definitely looks like she wants to.

I park far away and walk slowly toward her to make sure my eyes are working right. It's Avery. Her pale skin is sick-pale today, made even more obvious by her bright green dress. Her ballet flats sit just to the side of her, her bare feet white against the dark sidewalk. Her eyes are riveted on the horizon, where the line of city buildings bursts into flame with the sunset.

I don't say anything, but once I'm close enough, she does.

"It looks like the apocalypse." Her voice is hoarse. I follow her eyes to the illusion of fiery death.

"The sky bleeds sometimes," I say. "Just like we do."

She snorts, tracing a circle in the dirt of the railing with one manicured finger. I can see the dark circles under her eyes now, the ones she usually covers with makeup at school. We stand there, watching the sun die.

"Get out of here," she says finally.

"Nah." I shove my hands in my pockets. She looks at me sideways, green eyes like an angry leopard, but they look too tired to sustain any anger for long. I'm right. The fire in them wilts, and she looks back at the sky.

"Don't get jealous." Her voice breaks the distant static of the cars on the highway. "It eats you alive. Makes you do bad things."

The words are too dark for her. I might not like her and she might not like me, but no one deserves to sound this sad. So I keep it light.

"You should start an advice column."

"Shut up," she says, but nothing about it is acidic. It just *is*, plain and there and heavy on my chest. Her chest. I don't know what to say. I'm afraid if I talk too loud, too fast, make any sudden movement, this surreal moment will break like a spider's thread in the wind. Avery clenches her fists on the railing, then looks at me with dead eyes—the kind of eyes you see on a fish in a polluted lake, swollen with corruption and disease.

But somewhere in them is a glimmer of purity. I can see it in the way her right eye is tearing up ever so slightly.

"I'm not good. I'll never be good again."

She sounds like I did, when it first happened. I spent months telling myself the same thing after it happened.

"I know it feels like that right now," I say slowly. "But time helps. Makes all the sharp edges soft."

"And what am I supposed to do in the meantime? Let the sharp edges cut me?"

I look out at the sunset, quiet. I think about Leo. About all the evil he's done. Finally, it comes to me.

"If you did something bad, then maybe you deserve to be cut."

Her face goes slack, then darkens.

"But not forever," I say. "No one deserves to be cut forever. At least, that's what I think. I could be wrong, though. I usually am."

Avery picks up her shoes and slips them back on, and without a word she walks to her car and drives away, leaving me to the blood in the sky and the blood on her hands. Whatever she did, it tortures her. It doesn't forgive her for being a controlling, nasty asshole. But it makes more sense now. When you think you're evil, you punish yourself for it most of all. With that logic, whatever she did had to be heinous.

And she did it because she got jealous . . . But of who?

        ◐ ○ °◦

By Friday, Mom's improved enough that she can go back to work. Or so she says. I don't believe her, but I try to. If I believe, maybe that'll make it real.

Fridays at school are always good days, but today it's just shitcake on a shitpie sandwich. Every part of me feels like I'm rotting from the inside out. I've gotten barely any sleep and I can't focus on the work I have to catch up on. All I can think about is Mom—if she's all right at work, if she's coping okay, if she'll remember to eat the lunch I made her. All thoughts of the war with Jack Hunter fly out the window. I've got no tactics, no urge to show him up. No nothing. I'm drained, and tired. And done.

I watch him from my place under a tree during lunch break. Of course he's back at school—two days later and the police labs determined the weed in his locker was fake. Like I planned it. I took out the real stuff and substituted crushed whole oregano stems—visually enough to fool campus security. But the smell would never fool them. So I used the plastic baggies the real stuff came in, and filled it with my fake oregano weed. The real weed is currently a pile of fine ash fertilizing a very nice patch of dying roses in Mom's garden. The goal was to scare him, after all. Show him I can get to him. It's the fear of what's in the dark that scares us, not the dark itself. Thanks, ancient Chinese philosophers. You guys are the best. And the deadest. But mostly the best.

Jack's currently going into the front office, but so is an older woman in a wheelchair. Half the football team likes to hang around the disabled ramp leading up to the office, and today's no exception. They shove at one another, put one another in headlocks. They barely notice the woman struggling to get through their crowd. And then, to my utter surprise, Jack makes them notice. He stops heading up the stairs and doubles around to walk up the ramp instead. The football team immediately sobers as he gets closer, moving out of his way with a wary skittishness. Jack eyes them, then looks down to the woman in the wheelchair and says a few low words to her.

His face is soft.

I blink once, twice, trying to clear my eyes to make sure I'm not hallucinating. His expression is . . . *kind.* A smile even plays at his lips. The woman smiles back and he takes the handlebars of her chair, pushes her gently the rest of the way to the office, opening the door for her. The football team kicks back into riotous life, flipping the bird and sneering in Jack's general direction—but only after he's gone. One of them mutters, "Freak." The girls hanging around the team, however, have a completely different opinion; they're sighing dreamily among themselves and squealing about how cute Jack was.

Something twists around in my stomach. Guilt. Either Jack has a split personality or he's not as bad as I think he is. He's definitely not as bad as Nameless. Nameless would never help an old lady like that.

Even if Jack isn't as bad, he's still just as confusing. Why is he an escort? It doesn't make sense. Beyond his looks, there's no reason he'd be good at it. He's a jerk. Unless his weird dual-personality is in effect while he's working, too. Maybe I'm overestimating him. Maybe he's just a horny teenage boy who likes sex with women who know what they're doing after thirty or so years of being alive. He's so confusing I don't know what to believe anymore.

As I'm stewing in a delightful mix of guilt and utter confusion, Kayla nervously approaches me. She clears her throat.

"Hi," she starts.

"Hey."

"What are you doing?"

"Trying to get some sleep."

"Oh. Didn't sleep well?"

"For a couple of nights," I agree. "It's just, you know. Insomnia crap. Typical wacky teenage circadian rhythms."

"You were absent."

"Yeah. I was sick."

"Oh." She bites her lip and looks at her shoes before she blurts, "I'm really sorry. For what I said earlier this week. About you, and things. I'm sorry. I didn't know."

"S'cool. I've been pretty mean to you too, lately."

"Nu-uh!"

"I've been insensitive. About Jack, and how you like him. I'm sorry."

There's a long quiet. She reaches out her hand.

"Let's start over? I'm Kayla Thermopolis."

I shake her hand. "Isis. Isis Blake."

"You're really good at that history of the planet thing."

"World history." I smile as she repeats our first exchange at Avery's party. Speak of the horned red guy with a trident—Avery walks by at that moment. Kayla clearly sees her, but unlike most times, she doesn't scurry away to Avery's side. She stays in front of me and keeps talking.

"I'm . . . I'm having a party tonight. My parents are out of town, so. It's just a little get-together. It'd be really awesome if you could be there. There'll be pretzels. And a piñata. You could even punch someone! But only if you really have to. Like, really really *really* have to. Like, if your life depends on it." She thinks on that for a moment. "Actually, can you just not punch anyone at all?"

"I'll try." I laugh.

"Okay! It starts at eight, so be there."

I glance at Avery, who's glaring swords at me. Claymores. *Axes*.

"Is Avery coming?" I ask. Kayla shrugs.

"No. She said she had something to do."

"Are you sure you're okay with her seeing me and you talking?"

"I'm— I don't know. She doesn't like it, but I owe you an apology, so. She's really awesome and stuff, but I'm not gonna let her stop me from being polite."

"Right. Cool. I'll see you tonight, then."

Kayla rushes back to Avery's side, and Avery rips into her with snapped, quick words.

After school, I rummage through my closet for something badass to wear, and settle on a black shirt with a red flannel over it, and a black skirt with tights. I used to not be into clothes. It's hard to be into clothes when the only thing people see about you is the fat, not the fashion. After losing all that weight I couldn't help but cultivate a newfound joy in dressing the body I'd worked so hard for.

"Are you going out tonight?" Mom peeks into my room and catches me applying eyeliner. I grin sheepishly.

"Uh, yeah. Kayla invited me at the last minute."

"And who's this Kayla?"

"The first person at school to call me something other than 'New Girl.'"

Mom makes a little applauding motion. "I like her already."

"Are you…" I trail off. "Are you gonna be okay alone here?"

I still don't know if it was her having a flashback, or if Leo really tracked us down. Either way, my stomach boils nervously when I think about what could happen if I leave her alone too long.

"I'll be fine," Mom assures me. "Don't worry about me. When are you coming home?"

"I . . . I don't know. Before midnight, definitely."

"Good."

"The cop will still be out there tonight, so you don't have to worry."

She sweeps over and kisses the top of my head. "I know. Hurry now. You don't want to be late."

"But I do! It makes me seem important and busy!"

She laughs. I pull my hair into a side braid and grab my purse. Gum? Check. Cash? Check. Tampons? Check. You never know when someone will start her period or when I'll punch somebody and make his nose bleed. At least with tampons I can be considerate to my enemies.

Speaking of enemies, I have no idea if Jack will be there or not, and frankly I don't care. I'm still not feeling the whole war thing, and I'm just barely in the mood to party to begin with. I throw together an easy beef casserole and stick it in the oven for Mom before I go, and she waves as I pull out of the driveway. Halfway to Kayla's house, Kayla texts me to pick up red plastic cups. I make a haphazard U-turn and gun it to the nearest supermarket for the timeless keg party staple. I'm still feeling like crap, so I grab a jar of frosting to snack on. After losing eighty-five pounds, putting on two or three because of my still-shitty comfort eating habits is small-time crime.

"Speaking of crime," I whisper as I look into the rearview mirror. Two someones stroll along the sidewalk across from the supermarket, coming out of a fancy Italian restaurant.

The guy's messy-but-way-too-perfectly-messy-if-you-get-my-drift hair and towering height give him away—Jack Hunter. But he's smiling. A warm, sincere smile decorates his angled cheekbones and makes him look more human than ever. A young woman in a to-die-for fur coat clutches his arm. I know the people of Northplains are mostly rich, but this woman looks Columbus-class rich. She belongs in the capital, in Seattle, L.A., not here—her hair perfectly red and her lips soft and pouty. She can't be more than four years older than me. Probably some rich guy's daughter.

It hits me just then; Jack's working. That would explain the smile. He's getting paid to smile. I fight the urge to leap out of the car and follow them, and I resist for a record point four seconds before I pull my hood up and bolt out of the car and follow them. It's a romantic walk, I have to admit. The streetlamps are wrought iron in an old Victorian style, and the warm glow they produce drives off the chilly October night. Little tourist-trap shops filled with stained glass animals and soulless watercolors of the lake crowd the avenue. I duck behind potted plants and café signs whenever Jack or the lady's head swivels too far. I'm so nervous and excited I uncap the frosting and dip my finger in it, eating it as I follow them. It's like watching a movie with popcorn except a hundred times funnier, because it's watching ice-pole-up-his-butt Jack try to be nice. Also, it's intensely disturbing. Seeing him smile is as unnatural and weird as remembering your parents had to have sex in order to make you.

"I didn't know your dad was an idiot," Jack says. His voice is . . . teasing. Light. Nothing about it is boredly flat, like it usually is. The lady punches his arm playfully.

"Don't make fun of him. He's the one paying you, technically."

"Ah, but I'd do this for nothing. That's how beautifully distracting you are, Alice."

I shovel more frosting in my mouth before I rip a hole in the space-time continuum with my explosive laughter. The lady finds it much more sincere and giggles, leaning her beautiful head on his shoulder as they walk.

"Do you want to go back to the hotel?" she asks, quieter. "I bought new rope that needs breaking in."

I yelp as I bite my own frosting-covered finger. Alice looks behind her first. Her expression gets flustered and confused. Jack turns around, and his face goes from a faintly smiling mask to deadly angry not-mask in less than point two seconds. I swallow and raise a sticky hand in abrupt greeting.

"Uh, hello! Don't mind me! I'm just walking behind you. Not following you."

"You're really close," Alice says warily.

"I'm just . . . watching so I can manage things!"

"Manage?" Alice raises a brow. Jack's ice-blue eyes are colder than a snap frozen mountain river in December.

"Yup! I manage stuff. I'm a . . . manager! I'm his manager." I point at Jack and wink and put on a corny-old-timey voice. "You're going to Hollywood, kid!"

"I paid the fee, if that's what you're here about," Alice starts. Jack looks to her, smile flashing on for a moment.

"Let me talk to her. Give me one second."

"Okay." Alice giggles.

Jack kisses her passionately, so passionately I almost feel embarrassed for watching. When they part, she's breathless, and Jack strides over to me with a brewing sneer. He grabs my elbow and pulls me in the other direction.

"Is that how you kissed me?" I ask, nearly tripping as he pulls me along. "Golly gee, it looks kind of mildly fucking embarrassing! No wonder people at school have been talking about it for weeks now. Golly gee!"

"Stop saying golly gee."

"Tallyho, chaps!"

"Stop saying things!" He snarls, letting go of me only when we're around the corner and a tea shop separates us from Alice's view.

"Things!" I shout.

"How did you find me? If you hacked into the Club's computer to look up my appointments—"

"Whoa, I think you overestimate me, shitlord. Last time I checked, all I did was be in the wrong place at the right time. I saw you and had to—"

"Stalk me."

"—delicately approach you. In a sideways manner. From behind. Without being seen at all. For ten minutes."

"Why are you even out? I thought you were sick."

I briefly ask myself when he'd been paying attention to

my presence closely enough to realize I'd been absent, but then stop. Figuring this guy out is as impossible as writing a note in invisible ink for a blind person.

"I was. See, it's this thing called an immune system . . ."

He holds up his hand and rubs his eyes. "Okay, stop. Shut all systems down and just. Stop. Talking."

"Why?"

"It's annoying."

"That's never stopped me before!"

"Why did you follow me?"

"I was . . . curious?"

"Not good enough."

"You want me to be honest?"

"Preferably yes, so you don't waste any more of my time."

"We *are* at war. Wars don't exactly demand honesty. How did you enjoy my little gift, by the way?"

"Wonderfully, thank you." His voice drips acid sarcasm. "It would've been quite the scare, if it had any resolve to it."

"What's that supposed to mean?"

"It means you're softer than you pretend you are, Isis Blake. All bark and no bite. If you really hated me like you claim, you would have planted real weed and gotten me suspended. But you didn't, so you don't."

"Don't what?"

"Hate me." Jack smirks, but something about it is playful. The golden streetlights dye his razor cheekbones and set his blue eyes on fire. "Don't tell me you're falling for me like all the others. That would be such a disappointment."

I freeze, my heart squeezing strangely and every nasty comeback I had in my head flying right out of my ears. My mouth opens, but I close it quickly. Jack sees my hesitance, and something in his smirk changes—it goes from playful to slack, then serious, and then confused. He knits his brows. The Ice Prince is clearly bewildered by my inability to fire back at his comment. I always have a comeback. But not this time. *Why?* Why not this time? My irritation starts as a buzz in my head and snaps me out of it.

"And I'd just hate to disappoint." I bitterly smile back. "How's work going, by the way, *Jaden*?"

"I've booked seven new clients and earned a thousand extra this week."

"Impressive. Is that how much they pay for the dick, or for the hilariously cheesy compliments? Or are those extra? If so, count me in! I want to hear you serenade me with them while I choke on my own bile." I point at him with a frosting-covered finger. "I saw you help that older lady."

Jack quirks a brow. "Alice?"

"No, idiot. The woman earlier today. The one in the wheelchair, going to the office."

"Ah," he drawls. "You caught me."

"What interests me more than the fact that you were possessed by a completely different personality for a split second and helped a disabled woman is the fact that the football team let you. What did you do to them to make them so scared of you?"

He rolls his eyes. "They're not exactly hard to scare.

They're like a herd of horses—one of them bolts, the rest of them follow."

"What did you do to them?" I press.

"They picked on me freshman year," he snipes. "I got tired of it. I fought back. They haven't bothered me since." He looks down at the jar of frosting I clutch in my hands. "Are you eating that out of the can?"

"Are you the king of stupid questions?" I fire back. "Of course I am! Frosting is the ambrosia of the gods. God, if you're into that religious thing. Are you religious? Somehow I get the feeling the only church you'd join is the church of self-worship. Your body is your temple. Work it, boy."

"What are you saying?" he snarls. "You're blabbering!"

"At least I'm not whoring!"

He rolls his eyes. "It's not that simple."

"Uh, really? Because it sounded as simple as a bunch of new rope and a hotel room, and frankly that recipe means you're either going to get some kinky sex on or you're going to mutually hang yourselves."

He sighs. "She likes being tied up, okay? I don't. I don't like any of this. I'm getting paid. So you need to just piss off and go to whatever immature party you were heading to in the first place."

"How'd you know I'm going to a party?"

"The receipt for red plastic cups sticking out of your jacket. Your eyeliner. Girls don't make eyeliner wings that big unless they plan on drinking."

"Touché. You're smarter than I gave you credit for."

"And you're far more annoying than I first suspected. If I had known you'd stalk me like all the others, I never would've kissed you, even as payback."

"Seriously, you kiss everyone like that, though! It was nothing special."

"Exactly. It was nothing special. So back off and leave me alone."

He whirls around and strides away, and I wave madly at his back, jumping up and down.

"Bye, loser! Try not to suck! Or I guess you have to since you're getting paid for it, huh?"

He flips me the bird over his shoulder but it only makes me laugh and fist pump in self-congratulations. This is the first time I've really seen him perturbed. Everything before now was just a bunch of cold sarcasm and stony glares. I got under his skin this time. I, Isis Blake, got under his permafrost skin. I skip the entire way to the car and blast a triumphant Katy Perry song on my way to the party. I don't even particularly like Katy Perry. But for this second my victory is so sweet even mindless pop sounds like the battle trumpets of Roman gladiators, and I'm shouting along to it anyway.

chapter six

KAYLA'S FRONT LAWN IS crowded with cars. I wedge my Beetle into a parking space between a tree and a BMW, and rush into the warmly lit house.

"I come bearing gifts!" I shout above the already thumping music. There must be a hundred people here, if not more. *A little get-together*, Kayla said. Pft. I could power a small jet plane on the body heat crammed into this room.

I dump the cups in the kitchen, where bottles of Jack and Bacardi crowd the counters. I guard my frosting jealously, nibbling on it as I meander through the party looking for Kayla. The usual writhing group of dancers congregates around the speakers, and the equally writhing make-outs are happening on every chair and couch. Someone throws a roll of purple streamers around, someone has on a plastic horsehead mask that creeps me out, and someone else is wiping puke off the bookshelf with a TV remote. I don't recognize half the people in here; some of them must be from Midvale High. Kayla's in the garden, a gorgeous gathering of ivy trellises and a gently burbling fountain. She's breath-taking—her blue tube top and white skirt make her look like a tanned tennis goddess. She's talking to some of Avery's crowd, but when she sees me she trots over, smiling.

"Hey! You made it!"

"Yeah, cups are in the kitchen."

"Awesome. Thank you so much. You look really great."

"You, too. Gonna be on high alert tonight, fight off those creepers with a baseball bat if I have to."

"Oh, chill out." She laughs. "Go get something to drink!"

When I come back with a rum and Coke, Kayla's gone. I look around for her and find her dancing with some guy. He isn't grinding on her or staring at her tits 99 percent of the time, so he's fine with me. For now. When he happens to catch my eye I point two fingers at my eyes and then at him in an *I'm-watching-you-fuckstick* warning, and he must get it because he smiles nervously back and nods. Good boy.

"Threatening the male populace as usual?" a familiar voice says. I turn to see Wren in a casual polo shirt and jeans. He's clutching a drink, grinning in that sunny way and staring at me in that creepy hell-bent way.

"Yup. What's up with you, homes? Why are you here? Oh, that's right—you're the super cool prez. You don't tattle on boozers."

"If I did tattle I wouldn't be friends with quite so many people now, would I?"

"Ah, I see. You're hungry for that popularity game."

He laughs and shakes his head. "It's not so much

popularity as it's . . . What's the word? Amiable? I just like being liked."

"Huh. Is that rooted in a deep-seated need for approval fostered by your alcoholic mother and workaholic father? That'd explain why you volunteer so much—trying to do good because no one does good for you."

He looks like I zapped him. I wave my hand and laugh.

"I was kidding. I get crazy conclusion-y when I get buzzed."

"How did you—" He stops himself. "I guess I should stop asking that at this point. You and he never cease to amaze me."

He. He means Jack. I point at his cup to get him off the subject.

"Whaddya drinking?"

"Grape juice."

I laugh. "Seriously?"

"Seriously. I'm the designated driver for quite a few people tonight."

"Ahh, prez." I slap his back and he slops juice on the floor. "Always so straight-edge. You gotta learn to live a little!"

"I do! I live constantly!"

"Yeah, but it's all living for other people and shit. No time to yourself. You're gonna start resenting everybody pretty soon if you keep doing stuff for them and not you."

Wren looks away. I smile.

"Look, sorry. I'm poking my nose where it definitely doesn't belong. Like in an armpit." I stop. "Gross."

Wren sheepishly looks back at me and laughs, and I laugh with him. There's a silence the music fills, and before it can get too uncomfortable, I change the subject.

"The football team sure doesn't like Jack, huh?"

"You could say that." Wren nods. "They liked him even less freshman year."

"And then what happened?"

"And then Jack snapped. Before Christmas break, they tried to give him a swirly in the bathroom, and, well ... Let's just say Brett's nose wasn't broken in three places from playing football. And Jeremy won't stay in the same room as Jack for more than a minute for a good reason."

"So he beat them up."

"All four of them," Wren confirms.

"Jesus," I hiss.

"He's done worse," Wren says. His eyes are distant, like he's deep in a memory I can't see. The words ring ominously, and I'm both curious and concerned. But the alcohol is hitting me quickly. I can only grab on to thoughts for a half second before they slip away. The song changes to something I like for once, and I scream a little and shove my cup at Wren.

"Hold this! I gotta go dance!"

"You dance?"

"Uh, yeah, I am well-versed in the butt-tango, thank you."

Wren looks between the dance floor and me, his eyes darting back and forth.

"You wanna dance with me?" I shout.

"What?" His face drains pale in a split second.

"C'mon! It'll be fun!"

"I don't dance."

"Yeah, I don't poop."

"What? That sounds a little unhealthy."

"C'mon, prez!" I grab his hand and pull him toward the "dance floor," which is just ten-by-ten of carpet in the corner pushed free of couches. I do my stupidest dances—making myself look like an idiot so Wren won't feel so uptight about dancing "right." People who don't dance worry about making fools of themselves, but when you make a fool of yourself as often as I do, dancing is kind of easy. Sort of. I still keep thinking people will point and laugh at the way my fat jiggles, but the urge to push those nasty thoughts out of my head has me dancing harder. Wren laughs when I kneel on the floor and try to do a breakdance head-spin. I end up taking down two people before Kayla kicks me in a friendly manner to get me to stop. Wren bobs a little to the beat, looking nervous as hell. I dance around him, mostly, and when a slower song comes on, I put his arms around my waist and show him how to slow dance. Except he already knows.

"You lied! You do know how to dance."

"Ballroom classes," he says. "My mom made me take them when I was little."

He doesn't have cologne on like Jack, but his natural smell is pleasant compared to all of the sweaty boys who are dripping Axe from every pore. It's then I notice someone sitting on the couch on the other side of the house, staring at me. The icy blue of his eyes is very familiar. What is he doing here? Did Kayla invite him? And why does his gaze linger where Wren's arms are around my waist?

Finally, I get bored of being stared at, and rush back to where our drinks are. Wren follows, downing his grape juice in one thirsty gulp. I do the same, the stale Coke burning as it goes down.

"I'm wayyyyy too hot," I say. "Physically my booty is hot, but I'm also hot temperature-wise, so I'm going outside."

Wren laughs. "All right. Thanks for the dance."

"No, thank *you*, prez."

"Wren! There you are!"

I watch Kayla run over to him, beaming. Wren almost drops his cup and his glasses slide off his face. Kayla bends to pick them up for him and he stammers an apology. I take my exit and let them fumble through the awkward.

I swallow cool air and try to catch my breath. I haven't danced in, well, forever. I hadn't been invited to parties after what happened with Nameless in Florida. His influence spread far and wide, so I was kind of barred from any and all get-togethers. Not that they invited me, the fat girl, to begin with. But still. I'd danced before but this was the first night in a long time, and it felt good. I sweated off some of my worry over Mom in those few minutes. And to think, I danced with Nameless's cousin. The devil's kin! I laugh and slap the bench I'm sitting on.

"Hitting inanimate objects now? Your violence knows no

bounds," a bored voice says. I don't even have to turn around to know who it belongs to.

"Jackoff!" I slap the bench harder. "Weren't you being paid to bed a girl tonight? Where is she? Did you bring her?"

"She canceled. Her father had a stroke."

"Poor guy. Probably will have another stroke when he finds out the money he sends her for college goes to blow and hookers."

"I'm not a hooker."

"You're an escort."

"They're separate things."

"But you get paid to bed girls."

"Women are different. Most of them aren't sex-obsessed like men are. I get paid to take women out to dinner, too." He sniffs. "Or go to weddings and high school reunions as their arm candy. Or I pretend to be their boyfriend to make their exes jealous, or I cover for their lesbianism in front of their more traditional family. Sex is only sometimes a part of it."

I quash the weird wave of relief I feel at his words. I couldn't care less if he bangs the entire population of suburbia, but now that I know he doesn't, a bunch of anxious weight I didn't even know I was carrying lifts from my chest.

"Excuses, excuses!" I crow. "Come! Come sit by me. It's a nice bench. Nice and lovely on the butt."

"You're drunk," he counters, and runs his hand through his bangs. They flop back in his eyes like he's in a soft drink commercial.

"Yeah, and you're ugly, but do I complain about it? No! Because I don't complain about things that I can't change. That's called intelligence. How'd you find the party, anyway?"

"I remember Kayla squeaking to me about it earlier today. Then I saw you with the red cups and put two and two together."

"Wow. So smart. Such intelligence."

"You reek of rum." He sits by me and sniffs the air.

"It's a good thing I'm not a sexy-ass pirate, otherwise I'd repeat the same line to you over and over about the rum being gone and make a movie out of it."

"You like Johnny Depp, then."

"Like him? The man is my dreamboat on my dream car in my dream house in my actual dreams!"

Jack's lips crumple into a half sneer, half incredulous scoff. "Riiight."

"Ah, what do you know about sexy?" I sputter and wave him off. "You know nuthin."

"I know some things, I like to think."

"Yeah? Don't tell me—sappy compliments are your idea of sexy. You just lay 'em on thick and hope some girl—I'm sorry, *your client*—is stupid enough to buy them."

"Most of my clients are fairly stupid. And shallow. It's sort of inevitable when you work for a club that hires you for your looks."

He sounds tired; that exhausted, world-weary edge is in his voice. I lean against his back. His spine is rigid, his shoulder blades a comforting sort of hardness on my own.

"D-Did you at least get to use the rope?" I hiccup.

"Not at all."

"Dang. Must've been some nice rope, since she was rich. Like, golden and shit, with gold threads, and, like, sapphires in the knots."

Maybe I'm so drunk I hallucinate, but I swear I feel him laugh, the rumbling vibrating through his back and the sound clear. But it's quickly swallowed up by the music before I can concentrate through the drunken stupor and determine if it was an actual laugh or just another angry scoff. The garden is quieter, people making out behind bushes. I point at the slightly yellow fountain.

"Somebody peed."

"I'd bet money it was you."

"I wish! How awesome would it be to pee in that thing! Us girls don't have the luxury of a portable piss-tube, okay? We can only pee on things we can squat on. A fountain is not one of said things."

"With your pigheaded stubbornness, I'm sure you'd find a way."

"Absolutely. I'm gonna try it right now."

I stand a little too fast, wobbling on my feet. Jack grabs my wrist, pulling me back to the safety of the bench, but when I collapse backward on it, I sit slightly on his knee. I squeal and reposition quickly.

"Phew! That was almost a disaster. Dis-ASS-ter. Get it? I'm so good."

"You're so drunk," he insists.

"You ain't seen nuthin' yet."

The fountain burbles, and somewhere a cricket starts up his high-pitched engine legs.

"I wanted to thank you." I squint hard at Jack's face.

"For putting you in your place, you little hellion?"

"I don't even know what hellion means. Where do you get all these words? You're like that one nerdy dude they put on *Jeopardy!* all the time. Minus the neckbeard. And the English degree."

"It's like, a crazy person. An insane sort of . . . tornado type of person. Someone who just tears through people like paper in his or her madness."

"Oh. Yup. Cool that they made an entire word just to describe me."

"It's Shakespearian."

"He had a vision. Of me. A million years in the future. And that caused him to make up that word. Little-known fact."

The world is spinning. I've definitely had too much to drink. Somewhere someone breaks something made of glass and yells, "Oh shit." I see Kayla rush upstairs through the windows with a broom and dustpan.

"As I was saying before I was so rudely interrupted," I start again. "I wanted to thank you."

"For what, exactly? I thought you hate me."

"Oh, I do! But I still owe you a thanks. You . . . It's hard to explain, but I never thought, um. I never *thought*. It's, when you're someone like me, you don't think it'll ever happen to you. I just sort of gave up on it, you know? I was happy with never getting one, because people like me don't get them, or deserve them, really. We're not the sort of people those things happen to."

"What on earth are you talking about?" He narrows his eyes.

"I just!" I shout, then whisper. "I just wanted to say. Um. Thank you. For. Um. Kissing me."

He arches a brow. "That was a joke kiss. You were annoying me with the rumors; I had to put a stop to them somehow. It wasn't serious."

"Oh, I know! I think we, uh, previously discussed that, actually. No, I mean, I know. It was, ha-ha, definitely a joke! Just. Thank you anyway."

Jack goes very still, and then looks at me like he's seeing me in a new light all of a sudden.

"Do you mean— You've never— That was your first kiss?"

"Ha-ha. I mean, it'll be my last, too, since, you know, people like me don't get kissed, except when it's a joke of course. Ha-ha. But it was, uh, an experience. And. And I'm happy it happened to me, since I never thought someone would ever want to do something like that with me. So. Um. Yeah. Thank you. I mean it."

"You've never—"

"No! But that's not really weird for someone like me; I mean, look at me!" I gesture to my clothes and face. "I'm not, uh, you know, Kayla. I'm not even close. And plus I have too many huge dumb issues. I'm never gonna trust anybody to do those things with. But still. It was nice. And cool. And a joke, duh, but things can still be nice even if they're jokes, I think. Ha-ha."

Jack's blue eyes are shocked, or maybe I'm just awfully drunk.

"But you're so—" he starts.

"Loud? Annoying? Bitter? Yeah, I know. Guys have called me that before."

"I was going to say," Jack adds sharply, "confident. Charismatic. And cheerful. You're like . . . It just seems like a lot of guys would've gravitated to . . . I don't know."

"There you go again with the really gross flattery. I'm not a client, okay? So you don't have to flatter me when you don't mean it."

"I do mean it. I don't say things I don't mean."

"Except when you're working."

"But I'm not working now. There is no girl I'm being paid to woo here, so what I'm saying is honest and true."

"Well, apparently you haven't quite flipped the correct switches from work back to your normal life, so. It's okay. The compliments are nice, even if you don't mean them."

"I mean them, all right? Stop questioning my sincerity."

"Stop saying lies." I sigh. "I'm none of those nice things you just said. But it's okay. I can pretend."

He rubs his forehead. "God, you're infuriating."

"Ooh, that's another good adjective to add to my list!"

"If I had known—" He runs a hand through his tawny

hair, but it flops back down to shade his eyes. "If I had known, I wouldn't have done it. A first kiss . . . that's something a girl should cherish. It's something you should share with someone you really love. You shouldn't lose it in a petty high school battle of wills to someone you hate."

"Yeah, well. Never gonna love someone again, so. It's okay. I'm glad I lost it, at least! It's sort of nice to have gotten it over with."

"You're so sure of that, aren't you?"

"Sure of what?" I blink.

"That you're never going to love anyone again. You said it with such . . . conviction. Like it's set in stone."

"Oh! But it is!" I smile.

"So you won't, in any one of the endless millions and trillions of possibilities that are your future selves, ever fall in love with someone again?"

"Yup! That's right. It's been three years, fourteen weeks, and zero days since I fell in love. And I'm never going to do it ever again. I learned my lesson."

I get up and stretch to break the awkward quiet between us.

"I'm gonna get some more booze. You want any?" I ask.

"I don't drink."

"Oh ho! Is that so? You and Wren, both terrible Goody Two-shoes! Whodathunk it."

"We used to be friends, in middle school," Jack says softly. "He and I."

"And then what happened?"

Jack looks up at me, icy eyes glowing with an unholy fire in the faint light from the house. The shadows hug his cheekbones, making him look savagely handsome and savagely terrifying all at the same time.

"I did something very bad."

His tone sends shivers down my spine, but I keep my face light and unaffected.

"Oh. Like, uh, put snow down his pants? Kissed his girlfriend? Or does it have something to do with Sophia?"

Jack laughs. He really laughs this time, the sound clear like when he was with Alice. But nothing about it is pleasant or amused. It's bitter, old, full of guilt. Jack gets up and leaves; my curiosity roars through me and darts my hand out to grab his shirt to pull him back and make him explain. I trip on the lip of the fountain, and all at once there's a horrible jolting down my spine, a heavy weight falling next to me, and water in my nose, my ears, my mouth. The cold shock whisks my booze-haze away and leaves me sputtering and struggling to get out of the fountain. Jack is likewise wet from his pants down, and glowering at me, his jeans clinging to his thighs and showing me much more than I ever wanted to see. The entire party inside is mashed up against the windows, looking at us and laughing, and the garden crowd is practically rolling with laughter.

"How do you fall in there? It's like two feet wide."

"Fucking idiots!"

"Carl peed in there, too!"

Jack and I drip in solidarity.

"You did that on purpose," Jack mutters, and I swear I see his eyebrow twitch with controlled rage.

"N-No! I tripped and— Oh God, there's something green on your crotch. Not that I was looking there. It just happened to be very green! Right there!"

He picks a wad of algae off his crotch and throws it onto the face of a laughing guy nearby. It makes a wet splat, and Jack is gone before I have the chance to apologize properly. Not that I was going to at all, since I'm at war with him and what am I thinking, *apologizing*? And thanking him for kissing me? What the hell am I on other than ethanol-based depressants? I have to work this accident for all it's worth! I hold up my hands and pump my fist, shouting.

"Take that, Jackass Hunter!"

The party laughs, some people shake their heads. I go back inside, squishing over to a shocked Kayla.

"Sorry about your floor. I love you. Have I mentioned that lately? I really love you and please don't be mad I shoved your crush into a fountain, please, it was an accident but I'm making it look like it wasn't because that's how smooth I am."

There's an anxious span of quiet in which I reconsider all my life choices up until this moment. She wrinkles her nose and smiles.

"You smell like pee."

I exhale in relief, inhale, and immediately regret it.

"I smell *hells* like pee."

chapter seven

JACK HUNTER'S LEVEL OF menace is steadily increasing.

For a while back at the party I thought our pretty-damn-secluded moment of secluded-feelings-sharing was going to diffuse the tension between us, but alas. It appears, by the pictures plastered all over the walls and lockers of East Summit High, that I was wrong.

The pictures are of me. Fat. Coming out of my old high school building in Good Falls, Florida. My butt crack is showing, and I'm practically swimming in the old baggy shirt I used to wear. And my round face is turned over my shoulder, looking straight at the camera.

People look at the pictures, then point at me and laugh.

I immediately weigh the pros and cons of throwing a tantrum.

Kayla sidles up to me, a nervous look on her face. She walks with me to class. People really are huge meanies. Just really big fat meanies. This has to be Jack's doing, since we are at war and all, but this is the cruelest thing he's done yet. I've been pretty cruel, too, but I didn't dig around in his past or anything. Okay. Maybe I did. A little. I talked to Wren and he told me about Sophia and I mentioned Sophia at the party. So I guess this is Jack's way of telling me to butt out. I ticked him off. Super ticked. A very large tick that drank a lot of blood and got stuck in an armpit for so long it became a Godzilla-tick. That's how ticked off he is. As if I care! He's brought out the big guns, the guns of me being fat, and I still look fabulous even fat but how dare he reach his shitty little fingers into my past and air it out for everyone to see, and if I ever lay eyes on him again I'll tear his esophagus up out of his mouth and use it as a ceremonial headdress—

"Isis." Kayla pats me on the back. "You're thinking out loud again."

"I am upset." I sniff. "With certain persons in the immediate vicinity."

"Not me," Kayla clarifies.

"Never you."

"To be fair, it's a very pretty butt crack," Kayla offers.

"Thank you. What's Jack's first period?"

"Trigonometry with Mr. Bernard."

I storm over to J-Building. The bell still hasn't rung. I've got five minutes to give him hell. I casually kick Mr. Bernard's door open. Jack's in the back. I stride over to the whiteboard, pick up the eraser, and chuck it at his head. It dings off with considerable force. Jack looks stunned.

"You're a horrible little boy, Jackoff Hunter McShit-tington!" I shout. "You're mean and cruel and probably like boiled broccoli and I bet you have potted cactuses—"

"Cacti," Mr. Bernard offers timidly.

"—cacti, and you smell horrible and you're the stupidest asshole I've ever had the displeasure of meeting and if you could just go jump off a building and die alone I would be very grateful!"

I slam the door behind me and lean against it, breathing deep. With all the angst out, I can smile again, think straight again. I skip to class.

Kayla quirks a brow. "Are you okay?"

"I'm currently devising terribly fiendish torture scenarios in which Jack doesn't get out alive with his penis intact."

"Oh."

"He is getting crossed off the decent human list," I assure her. "With red ink! And a million exclamation points!"

"Do you think he really did it? He taped up all those pictures by himself? Where did he even get them?"

"There's only one person who has access to my past like that," I murmur.

As I make my way to Wren's typical hideout at recess, I realize I haven't cried. Not a single tear. And why should I? I'm not proud of who I used to be, but it's not who I am anymore. I'm different. I have four streaks of purple in my hair, and I haven't fallen in love in three years, fourteen weeks, and three days. I'm doing well. I'm doing so much better than that girl in the pictures was. I hold my hand out and run down a line of lockers, tearing off the pictures as I go. I slam the wad into the trash triumphantly. My fat butt decorates the floor, ripped and shredded and made dirty by the thousands of footprints that've walked on it. Some people have scribbled "FAT" and "HUGE BITCH" over it. The janitor is sweeping pictures up by the dozens, his usual death glare turning a little soft when he sees me.

"No pity!" I point and demand. Pity is for people who need it. And I don't need it. Not anymore.

The janitor smiles crookedly before turning back to his sweeping.

"No pity," he agrees.

The student council room is clean and tiny and smells like pencils and stale doughnut holes. Wren is instructing a freshman guy with glasses and two freshmen girls with mousy hair on the merits of not running in the halls and getting good grades or some drivel. I come up behind him and slam my hands on the desk.

"Yes, hello, good evening everyone. It is I, Butt Crack Girl. Please evacuate the immediate vicinity before I show you my new and updated butt crack."

"Isis, what the hell?" Wren starts. The freshmen shoot him nervous looks, and he motions for them to go. When they've closed the door, I sit on Wren's desk and cross my legs over each other like a dainty lady.

"You gave my picture to Jack, didn't you?"

"I don't know what you're talking about."

"You talked to Nameless, and he gave you my picture."

"No! I swear to you, Isis, I haven't talked to Will—"

I flinch, and he clears his throat.

"—uh, Nameless, for weeks now. We're not all that close."

"How else would Jack get that picture?"

"Look, I'm not saying I know who did it, but didn't you notice there was no comment from the faculty? Principal Evans didn't get on the PA system to comment on the pictures at all. He usually reprimands defacing school property like crazy. But this time? Nothing."

"Are you saying Evans did this?"

"I'm not saying anything." He lowers his voice. "I'm just saying it's odd, is all, and that if you talk to Evans, you might get some more information."

He stares at me with his round, unblinking hazel eyes. I finally relent. There's no way someone as cute as he is could have done something as evil as supply my enemy with prime blackmail photos, even if they were friends once.

"All right. I'll talk to Evans. But—" I point in his face. "I'm not done with you. Not by a long shot. Jack told me at Kayla's party he did something bad. And you got scared. And I'm gonna find out what it was."

Wren's face goes so pale for a second I think he's had a heart attack. His lips get thin and he glowers. It's all the proof I need that what Jack said was true. He really *did* do something bad. Something that's making Wren tremble under his polo shirt and horn-rimmed glasses. But I can't pry it out of him now; I have a principal to confront. I stride out and leave Wren behind.

Mr. Evans's secretary is a pretty, dark-haired woman with a spotty birthmark over her forehead that makes her look half Dalmatian and half awesome.

"Can I see Principal Evans, ma'am? It's urgent."

"Sure, sweetie." She smiles. "He's free. I'll buzz you in right now."

I take a deep breath right before the door and compose myself. I can't kick this door down. I have to be sociable, I have to get the truth from him, and that means pretending I'm nice and pretending I'm easy to fool. So I smile my brightest smile ever and push through the door.

Evans is at his desk, typing away at the computer. Glass figurines of penguins litter his bookshelves, and an ostentatious, tacky gold bust of his own head sits on his desk next to his name tag: Principal Goodworth M. Evans. I swallow a snort. Goodworth. What kind of name is that?

Mr. Evans looks up, his bald patch more noticeable than ever. He grins.

"Ah, Isis. I figured you'd come in to see me today. Please, sit."

He figured, huh? That's not promising. I sit in the plushy chair across from him.

"My picture is everywhere," I start.

"I know. I saw. I'm terribly sorry—kids these days are just so cruel. I had Marcus clean them up as soon as I saw them."

"He's still working on that."

"I know. Poor man."

Nothing about Evans's voice sounds sincere; it's all

half-sweet, meaninglessly airy words. He doesn't care at all. He just keeps typing at the computer, with no time for me. Either that or he doesn't want to confront me. He can't look me in the eye, and it's not a good sign. Guilt does that to people.

"I wanted to ask you about Jack," I say. Evans chuckles.

"No, I won't give you his home address, his schedule, his phone number, or his social security number."

"What?"

"That's what the other girls ask for."

"I'm not other girls."

"So I can see." He smiles, typing on the computer even more rapidly. "You were expelled from your last high school because of— What did the police call it? Intent to harm? According to your permanent record here, you fought everyone you could get your hands on, anyone who looked at you a strange way. What made you so touchy, I wonder?"

"Oh, I don't know, maybe years of vicious bullying for being fat."

"But that teasing inspired you, didn't it? That's why you lost so much weight. So really, you should be thankful for it, and to the people who antagonized you."

I laugh incredulously. "Are you fucking kidding me?"

"Language, Isis," he says smoothly. "We wouldn't want another mark on your permanent record now, would we? It's already so scuffed up."

I underestimated this guy. He plays the game well. Of course he does. He's had years of adulthood—where everyone smiles when they hate someone and bottles up their emotions—to practice. He's a master of passive-aggressive-bullshit-tae kwon do. And I'm a master of the more aggressive style. We're basically dancing around each other in two incompatible styles, so neither of us is getting anywhere. I change my stance.

"I heard Jack's supersmart." I add a simpering tone to my voice. "That must be because this school is so good at teaching, huh?"

Mr. Evans looks up, his chest puffing. "Of course. Our faculty is top-notch, you'll learn that soon enough. Jack is the brightest student I've seen in years. He got a perfect score on his SATs."

I smirk on the inside, but smile on the outside. "So that means he'll probably go to a really good college, right?"

"Oh, the best. He just started applying to Yale today, as a matter of fact."

Today? That's an odd coincidence. When I overheard Jack and Evans just a few weeks ago, Jack seemed to hate the idea of applying to an Ivy League. So what changed? I narrow my eyes but keep smiling.

"Wowwww. Yale is an Ivy League school, right? That's pretty impressive."

"He'll apply to Princeton, too, or so he said. It would be a huge waste if someone like him stayed here."

"Right. Definitely. Is he the first person from this school to go to an Ivy League?"

Evans's eyes glint. "Well, not the first. There have been

three people before him. But he'll be the first in about twenty years, yes."

"That must make you so proud."

"Indeed. Extremely proud. More than that, it'll get us the funding—"

He freezes, and I blink.

"Funding?"

Mr. Evans clears his throat and drums his fingers on the desktop impatiently. "Regardless, Jack's choice of college is very important to many people."

I mull it over while giving him a limp, fake smile. So it's not just about Jack. Evans isn't just pushing it for Jack's sake. It's because if Jack goes to an Ivy, this school gets some kind of extra funding. Now everything makes perfect sense. People have done worse things than slander a teenage girl for money. I guess I should consider myself lucky he *only* slandered me.

"Everybody's gonna think it's because of your management!" I say finally.

"Oh." He laughs in a fake-modest way. "I wouldn't say that."

And that's when it hits me.

"You have access to everybody's permanent record, huh, Mr. Evans?"

Ever eager to show off his power, he preens, smoothing hair ineffectually over his bald spot. "Hm? Oh, yes. Yes I do."

"So you have everyone's past schools on record, too."

"Certainly."

"Including mine."

"Yes, that's how I know you were expelled."

"And you know where I went to high school before this. So you'd know how to get my yearbook, which has pictures of me."

Evans freezes, his fingers hovering over the keyboard. Gotcha, motherfucker.

"Let me guess," I say slowly. "Jack called you. Probably on Sunday. He asked you to find old pictures of the old me and post them up where people could see them. And in exchange, he would apply to the Ivy League schools you've been harassing him about."

He scoffs. "That's nonsense."

"Is it? Because that picture of me was taken by my old school's yearbook club, and they put it in the section titled 'Student Failsauces! XD.'"

"What's an XD?"

"A sideways laughing face of horrendous proportions. Don't change the subject."

"Isis, look, I really wish I could catch whoever did this horrible thing to you. But the fact of the matter is our camera system is in the process of being recalibrated. And Marcus said he saw no signs of a break-in—"

"Because no one broke in. You just unlocked the gate and doors with your master key. A student would've had to have broken a window or a vent grating or something to get inside."

His eyes flash dangerously, and instantly.

"I've had enough of this," Evans snaps. "Get out of my office, right now."

"What if I tell campus security? Huh? What's gonna happen then? Oh, wait, they're on your payroll. Maybe I'll just go to the police with this."

"You have no evidence. Get out!"

I sarcastically salute him, slamming the door so hard behind me I hear one of his stupid glass penguin statuettes fall and shatter. He grumbles and yells at his secretary for a broom, and I walk away with a smirk. His outrage confirms everything. I won, and we both know it. Principal Goodworth M. Evans is small fry, and never posed a real challenge at all.

I'm almost disappointed, but then I remember Jack.

I still have Jack.

I still have a lovely, satisfying challenge waiting for me.

◦ ◦ ◦

Someday, the world has to acknowledge my raw sex appeal.

Today is that day.

On Wednesday, I wear the skimpiest, most jaw-dropping outfit I can manage while still being inside dress code—a short denim skirt and a bright red shirt with slits cut in the side and a wide neck to show off my collarbone and shoulders. I wear red flats, put my hair up in a high ponytail, and wear five times more makeup than usual. I look, for all intents and purposes, hot as hell. Well, I always look hot. Now my hot just can't be ignored.

Jack was trying to insult my looks with those pictures. And he did. He insulted them so well, people will have no choice but to notice the difference. The before picture was plastered all over the school, and the after picture is breathing and walking around in a bright red shirt. If he expected me to cower, to wear dull colors and shrink away from the attention, he was very, very wrong. I might not be Kayla or Avery pretty, but I'm better than the girl in the picture, and that's all the school needs to see.

I park toward the front and make a big show of getting out—piling my books slowly into my backpack and locking my car with exaggerated key pressing. I wave at some people I recognize—Avery, who all but sneers at me as I pass. Kayla runs over, but Avery grabs her arm and yanks her back. I flash Kayla a "see you later" smile. It's better she doesn't come over and ask what's up, anyway. I've got places to go and people to shock. They're staring, whispering, but there's no laughing, and there's sure as hell no smirks. Boys whistle and a girl asks where I got my skirt. Half of me is terrified from all the attention—my hands shaking and my throat dry. But the other half of me knows this is what I need to do. Not just for the war, not just to prove Jack wrong. I have to do this for myself. For the girl in the picture. If there's anything I've learned this year, it's that I have to stand up for myself, or no one else will.

I make my way to Jack's first period when the bell rings.

"Hi, Mrs. Gregory!" I smile at her in the hall. She does a double take, like most people are doing.

"I-Isis? Oh my God, you look so . . ."

"Different? Awesome?"

"Tasteless," she sniffs.

"Not all of us have the luxury of a college English degree, Mrs. Gregory. Some of us have to hustle on the streets."

She goes white down to her toes. If only she knew her favorite Jack Hunter was really a high-paid gigolo. She'd flip. And probably hire him for a night two seconds later. I shudder.

I walk into trig. Mr. Bernard eyes me like I'm a rabid dog, but I smile really hard and try to look innocent. It works for all of two seconds before Mr. Bernard glances at the door behind me.

"You dented it, Isis."

"Sorry, Mr. Bernard. There are always unfortunate casualties of war. I'm just here for a second."

"Well, all right then. But only make it a second."

I have to kill time until Jack walks in. I see Knife Kid. He's in Trig with Jack? That's impressive. I sit at the desk beside him. He nods at me, but his frown remains.

"You look different," he says, voice croaking. It's the first time I've heard him talk.

"Thanks! You too! New haircut? I bet you did it yourself."

"A butterfly A-9 buck knife would cut hair pretty good, now that you mention it. Or I could use the classic rib eye backhand."

"Sounds about right." I nod, even if I have no clue what the hell he's talking about.

"Who are you waiting for?" Knife Kid asks.

"That obvious, huh?"

"Jack, then. Screaming at him wasn't enough?"

"He was the one who put the pictures of me all over school. Hell no, screaming isn't enough."

Knife Kid nods. "I saw the pictures. I had fun slashing them with my protractor. Nobody should be made fun of like that, I think."

I don't know whether to smile at how sweet he sounds or become extremely concerned at how creepy he sounds. I settle for a little of both just as Jack comes in. He walks right by and settles in his desk behind me. I turn and watch him take off his backpack.

"Hi." I wave.

It takes him a moment to recognize me. Or a million. He focuses his gaze on me, then looks boredly to the window. He puts his chin in his hand, studies a pigeon in a tree with utmost intensity, and then all at once his eyes go wide. He swivels his head slowly back to me.

"You," he murmurs.

"Me!" I chirp.

"What the hell are you doing in that?" he asks, eyes sweeping down to my chest, my legs, and up again.

"Damage control." I smile. "Do you like it?"

"I've seen pigs dressed better."

"Oh, I don't doubt that, considering you see one in the mirror every morning."

"I wasn't the one who put up the pictures, if that's what this idiocy is about."

"I know you didn't do it. Evans did."

Jack goes stock-still for all of three seconds before he snarls. "I asked him to give me a photo of you when you were younger, not plaster them all over the school."

"But he did it anyway. He knows we've been fighting; the whole school does. He probably wanted to impress you so you'd think about applying to more of those Ivys, huh? Pity. He gets funding if you do, you know. And also he really wants to brag about you to all his little educator friends. No offense, Mr. Bernard."

Mr. Bernard shrugs, trying and failing to hide the fact he's sneaking glances at my chest. Everyone is disgusting forever.

"Really." I turn back to Jack. "You should've known better than to go to Evans. I don't care if it's not what you told him to do—those pictures still happened. And you made it happen. So I can't forgive you. Ever."

Wren walks in just then, a stack of papers in his hands. He plops them on the desk and starts talking to Mr. Bernard about robotics club funding. And then he sees me. Wren's face is five times more expressive than Jack's. His mouth pops open and hangs there like an ajar door, and he clears his throat and adjusts his glasses quickly.

"I-Isis. Good morning."

"Hey, prez!" I get out of the desk and hug him. He makes a strangled-cat noise and adjusts his glasses so hard they fly off his face. I pick them up off the floor.

"You okay?"

"I-I'm fine. Um. You look— You look, uh, you look . . ."

"Nice?" I offer.

"Really . . . really nice." Wren exhales. "Nice doesn't actually cover it."

For some reason, the compliment coming from Wren means a lot more to me than the dozens of stares and wolf whistles.

"Are you just going to stand there and gawk, Wren?" Jack sneers. "Or are you going to get on with your presidential business? I'm sure more club advisers have papers that need delivering."

Wren turns red and glances sheepishly at Jack.

"Right. I should go. Bye, Isis."

"See ya!" I wave.

"And you, Mr. Bernard," Jack continues savagely. "Last time I checked they don't pay you to ogle teenage girls. They pay you to teach. So start teaching."

Mr. Bernard jumps in his chair, clears his throat, and hurriedly goes to the whiteboard and starts writing equations. Knife Kid laughs. I salute Jack as I bow out the door.

"Have a great day, Jackoff."

"Try not to get molested," he snaps.

"Oh my stars!" I fan my face. "Could it be? Could East Summit High's Ice Prince be expressing concern for me?"

"Get out," Jack says.

"That's the only command of yours I'll obey." I wink and flounce through the door. It's obvious I've won this battle. By lunchtime everyone is talking about how slutty I look instead of how fat my butt crack used to be. It's not much of an improvement, but it's the best I'll get. The whispers are the sound of me winning the war against Jack Hunter.

Boom, bitch.

⊙   ⊙   ° ⊙

The bell rings, and a flustered Mr. Bernard begins teaching. I glare out the window, directing all my anger at a particularly droopy tree branch instead of a person. I'm fairly certain if I aimed my fury at people right now, they'd wet themselves. I can't concentrate on a single thing Bernard is saying, and not only because I think he's a lecherous failure unworthy of respect, but because my mind is distracted. Buzzing. And I'm never distracted when I don't want to be. I'm very good at staying focused during class; it's why I learn as much as I do. But I can barely afford to think about learning. All I can hear is my own blood rushing in my ears.

Isis's wink replays in my mind, over and over again. Confidence radiated from her. Her usual outfits were too baggy for me to ever notice how tall she is, or how slender and smooth the space between her neck and collarbone is. In a ponytail she looked completely different—no, in that outfit she looked completely different. She wasn't the Isis I'd learned well; she was someone else entirely.

Someone beautiful.

And, judging by the starstruck look in every male's eyes in this classroom, I wasn't the only one who noticed that.

I snort and stab my pencil into my paper with excess

force. I knew she liked drawing attention to herself, but not this much. Not this . . . *flamboyantly*. She obviously did it to counter the photos that petty idiot Evans pasted all over the school. He went too far, and Isis did what she could to distract people from it. A part of me feels sorry for her. Another part boils at what Evans did. This is our fight, Isis's and mine, but he just had to stick his nose into it to try to get at me.

And it worked.

Class is over after far too long. In the halls, people pick up the torn remains of Isis's pictures and laugh at them, smirk and snigger. I see Avery leaning against a locker, showing the ragged picture to her gang and laughing shrilly at it.

"It's incredible. I knew she was a bitch, but I had no idea she used to be a whale. Do you think she's covered in stretch marks, or what? How much of her is flab?" Avery chuckles. Her back is to me, so she doesn't see me coming, but her posse does. They shrink back, but before Avery can whirl around and see who it is, I grab the picture out of her hands. She turns, her eyes wide, watching as I shred it to pieces.

"That's enough nasty gossip out of you," I say.

"Mind your own business, Jack," Avery snipes. It's bravado. I can see her shoulders shaking under the faux-fur collar of her jacket. She's still afraid of me.

"It's adorable," I drawl, "that you think this isn't my business."

"Why are you defending her? When did you start giving a shit about the new girl?"

I lean in and murmur in her ear before she can pull away. "When did you stop giving a shit about Sophia?"

Avery freezes, her breathing going shallow. I lean back and address her posse.

"Do me a favor, would you? Stop gossiping about Isis. Avery doesn't want you to do it anymore. Isn't that right?" I quirk a brow to her, and she nods tersely. "See?"

Her friends shift nervously, unable to meet my eyes.

I smirk as I walk away. "Try to be on your best behavior, ladies."

The entire school is laughing at Isis's old picture, like it's a monolithic joke offered for their amusement, a sacrifice on a silver platter. All they can see is a joke in that picture. But I see a girl—miserable and heartbroken, terrified and lonely. All I can see in the picture is a girl slowly convincing herself, day by day, that no one will ever love her, convincing herself that it's impossible for her to be loved.

I touch my fingers to my lips. I kissed that girl, as a throw-away tactic to get her to stop bothering me. I treated her first kiss like a disposable tool, a cavalier scheme. To me it was meaningless, but to her, to a girl who'd given up on ever being kissed . . .

"Oh man, is this what she used to look like?" I pass a few boys gathered around her picture at the water fountain. Their conversation is too loud to ignore.

"No way, it's gotta be Photoshopped. You saw how hot she looks today. There's no way this is the same person."

"I'd tap the shit outta that ho." A redheaded boy smacks

the air in front of his crotch lasciviously. I don't have time to stop myself—he's pinned against the water fountain in less than two seconds.

"Repeat that," I growl.

"W-What?" the redhead stutters. "C'mon man, let me go!"

"Repeat what you just said," I insist.

"Hey," one of his friends barks. "Get off of him!"

"Hold up," another friend hisses. "That's Jack Hunter. You *wanna* get beat hard? Just chill for a second."

I redirect my glare to the redhead. "If I hear you spewing your perverted bullshit about that girl again, well. Ask the football team why they avoid me, would you? It might enlighten you."

I throw him toward the trash can, and he stumbles, his hand digging deep in the trash in an effort to right himself. His friends throw me nasty looks, but I leave before they can work up the courage to retaliate.

chapter eight

I PICK MOM UP after her shrink session downtown. I wait in the car outside the brick building and watch the late-afternoon sun dance its golden fingers across the sidewalk and through the trees. Northplains might be quiet and chock-full of a whole lot of nothing, but it's incredibly pretty in the fall. Orange and red leaves litter the ground, dreamy clouds of steam and smoke pour out of the chimneys, and the sky is a cold, bright blue, like a chilled porcelain dish. I pull my scarf up over my nose. It's way chillier than Florida, but if I freeze to death, at least I'll die far, far away from where Nameless can see.

I bump my head against the headrest thoughtfully. Nameless. He hasn't crossed my mind in a while. He's always been there, like a massive poop stain in my brain, but with the war against Jack and Mom's problems, I haven't thought about him for weeks.

That's a lie, of course. I always think about him when I see a mirror, or the thing on my wrist. There's no escaping him.

He's the reason I look the way I do now, and I'm reminded of that every day. I am who I am because of him, and part of me hates that. Part of me hates everything I am because of him. Maybe someday I'll get rid of him. I hope so, at least. But hope is hard to hold without cutting yourself on it, so I try not to hold on too tight.

Mom's taking longer than normal, so I grab my coffee and head inside the building. Neat offices line the hall, and a lobby with fake plants and faker girls on the magazine covers greets me. The receptionist is a woman with gray hair and eyes and a sad sort of smile. She's helping someone at the counter with flaming red hair.

Hair that can't be mistaken for anyone else but Avery Brighton.

"Hey, Avery!" I wave.

The girl freezes, shoulders seizing up as she slowly, so slowly, turns around. It's Avery all right, bright green eyes glaring at me and her nose twitching. She says something to the receptionist and walks over to me.

"What the hell are you doing here?" she asks. Completely nonthreateningly.

"Uh, my mom goes here. For things. What about you? Why are you here? Oh, uh, shit, is that insensitive to ask?"

"Slightly," Avery drawls.

"You're here for someone else, too, huh? Duh. Avery Brighton doesn't go to a shrink."

"Of course," Avery says quickly. "I'm here to pick up my . . . cousin."

"Ms. Brighton?" the receptionist calls. "Here's your prescription. Would you like to schedule another appointment for next week?"

Avery winces, composes herself, and turns to the receptionist and takes the prescription. She marches back to me with a super-angry face.

"Don't you dare say anything."

"Uh, I won't. It's cool."

"It's not cool." Avery's voice pitches up. "Don't you get it? It's the fucking opposite of cool, what I'm doing here, so just keep your mouth shut."

"Look, it's fine, I'm not out for your blood."

"You would be if you knew about Kayla—"

I frown. "What? What about her?"

Avery's face relaxes visibly. "Never mind."

"Wait a second, I might not be after you, but I care about Kayla. What the hell did you mean by 'if I knew about Kayla'?"

Avery flips her fiery hair. "Remember how I said I'm never inviting you to a thing of mine ever again?"

"Vividly."

"Well, I'm inviting you now. And I hope you'll return the favor and not talk about what you saw here."

"Suuuree," I say slowly. Avery narrows her eyes.

"The Grand 9 bowling alley, in downtown Columbus. Saturday at noon. Be there."

"But what about Kayla?"

Avery scoffs. "It'll be clear when you come to the alley. So just come."

"Yes? Okay? I guess?"

She pushes past me and is gone before I can ask more questions.

"Isis!" Mom comes up behind me, hugging me and turning me to face her. "I'm sorry I'm late, honey, the session went long."

Her eyes are a little red, and she's clutching a wad of tissues. It must've been a hard session. Hard, and sad.

"It's fine." I smile. "Let's go. I've got some pizza dough rising in the oven."

"Homemade pizza!" She laughs and looks to the receptionist, wrapping an arm around me and pulling me into a hug. "I've got the best daughter in the world, I swear."

When we get home, I roll the dough out and put sauce on it and decorate with mushrooms, olives, and a few onion slices. I sprinkle it with garlic salt and mozzarella, and put it in the oven. The smell soon permeates the house in a cloud of cheesy, saucy scent. Mom is upstairs taking a nap when the phone rings.

"Hello?"

"Isis! How're you doing, sweetie?"

"Hi, Dad. Wow, I'm sorry I haven't called? It's been crazy over here."

"Your mother told me. Apparently you've made friends and have been going to parties. I'd be proud if I wasn't so insanely worried."

"I'm fine, Dad." I laugh. "It's really okay. I'm smart and careful."

"No boys yet?"

"Never boys."

"Good. Keep that off your plate for a while, you don't need the distraction when you're so close to graduating and going to college."

Jack's dangerously handsome face instantly pops into my mind, and I smirk.

"Don't worry. No distractions here."

◉   ◦   °◦

There are only two things people will ask you in your senior year of high school: what colleges you're applying to and whether or not you have a boyfriend. Everything else seems completely irrelevant. No one will ask after your mental state (deteriorating rapidly with all my homework and essays), what you do to have fun (stare at my bedroom ceiling and pick the nail polish off my nails), or whether or not you actually want to go to college (no, I don't, I'm tired of school, but I'll go because everyone is making me and flipping burgers at McDonald's for seven bucks an hour sounds revolting). So far I've applied to a couple, and the only one I really want is Redfield University. It's close to Mom, so I can take care of her if she has another breakdown or if she just needs me, period. I can't go too far, obviously, not with her nightmares and flashbacks. She'd forget to eat without me here to cook for her, I'm sure. And I'm not gonna let her waste away.

What I really wanna do is take what I earned from my

summers of part-time-jobbing and go to Europe, eat the food, see the people, bike around the countryside. It'd be incredible. And incredibly terrifying to be on my own like that. But I'd manage. Struggling through young adulthood is half the fun, or so I've been told.

Except we all know that's bullshit. It isn't fun at all.

It's painful, and now I just wanna go somewhere no one knows me, start the next chapter of my life fresh. But I can't. I have Mom. And I love her more than I love my freedom. I have to protect her and help her get better.

So I'll do the college thing Dad and Mom expect of me. I'll get a degree in Poopology or something. I'll be the daughter they want me to be until I figure out the person I want to be.

The Grand 9 bowling alley in downtown Columbus is awesome, a massive neon sign greeting me with the number nine and a dancing electronic bear of some kind draped over it. It's cheap and looks like it'll be greasy as hell, and I'm already loving it. I park and go in, and I'm instantly greeted by that particular bowling-alley smell—wax and sweaty shoes and soggy French fries. An overweight man jerks his thumb to the last lane and hands me a pair of size-seven shoes.

"Oh. Thank you? How did you know my size?"

"Pretty Boy told me." The man grunts. Pretty Boy? I walk over to the last lane, the counter riddled with soda cups, a pitcher of root beer, and empty nacho containers. Wren is bowling, arcing a perfect split. Kayla smiles and high-fives him as he comes off the lane. Avery is grumpily sipping her root beer, and to my surprise and general disgust, Jack

Hunter is sitting at the lane, looking even more insufferably cool, if that's at all humanly possible.

"I see everyone's here!" I cheerily bounce into a seat next to him and unlace my shoes. I glance over, as if seeing him for the first time. "All right, which one of you's been dabbling in demon summoning and hasn't told me about it?"

Avery rolls her eyes and takes out a flask of, presumably, alcohol, and dumps it into her soda.

"Nice to see you in something other than prostitute clothes," Jack says.

"You'd know all about prostitute clothes, wouldn't you?" I smile, and choose a bright pink ball before sitting down again. "Who—"

"I'm here because I was invited," he interrupts. "And I guessed your shoe size."

"Accurate guess."

"Your measurements are 38-28-36, and you're five five. It's not hard to guess a shoe size based on that."

"And you know my measurements!" I clap my hands excitedly. "However did you guess those? Wait, let me think— you were staring at me!"

"I have a gift," he says drily. "For observation."

"And for being extremely creepy."

"Your outfit the other day was the first time you wore tight enough clothes for me to estimate correctly."

"I would love to slap you right now, but I'm currently wielding a nine-pound ball and I'm afraid that would be called murder."

He half laughs, half scoffs, and gets up to pour himself a soda.

I turn to Avery. "So? Who's winning?"

"Can't you read numbers?" Avery sighs and motions to the board. Jack is ahead of everyone by a good fifty points and they're only in the fifth round, his card decorated with straight strikes.

"Look at all those Xs! It's like a strip club sign! You'd almost think they had some kind of hidden meaning," I muse aloud. Very loudly.

"The meaning that I'm winning?" Jack raises a brow.

"Or that you're a stripper at a gay bar," I announce.

"I've only stripped once, and it was for a woman, thank you very much," Jack hisses.

"Yeah? Do tell." Avery suddenly looks mildly interested.

Jack sneers. "As if I'd tell you, you disgusting weasel. You'd use it for blackmail, undoubtedly."

"You know me too well," Avery says, quieter than I've ever heard her. Something about Jack's presence is keeping her humble in a way I'm completely shocked by. Avery isn't quiet ever, just like Satan isn't a decent guy ever. Jack stands to bowl his turn. Kayla bounces over to me.

"Aw, Kayla, look at you! Eager as a puppy and pretty as a picture. Not of a puppy. Because pictures of puppies sometimes look kind of slimy and you are not slimy and oh my God Wren are you wearing contacts?"

Wren coughs and adjusts his shirt collar, eyes busy boring a nervous hole into the back of Jack's head.

"Y-Yes? I just came from volunteering at the Salvation Army, so I didn't have time to take them out. It's good to see you. We thought you weren't coming."

"Oh, I always come. Especially where I'm not wanted!"

Kayla frowns. "That's not true. Um. Avery, um, you wanted her here, right?"

Behind Kayla's back, I make a crazy cuckoo spiral around my head with my finger.

Avery narrows her eyes, then smiles like a fox with its tail caught in a chicken coop door. "Yeah. Sure. Whatever. Did you get the French club proposal, Wren?"

"Yes, I did. I've already looked it over. It's nice you took me out to bowling and all, but I'm afraid I just can't pass it. That much money for only the French club is pretty ludicrous."

"Ludicrous? C'mon, sweetie," Avery coos, running her finger up his chest. "You know I'll put it to good use."

Wren gulps. "Ah, still. No. I'm sorry, but I can't sign off on it. You could start four new clubs with that much funding."

"But they aren't being started!" Avery snarls. "The money's just sitting there. Why not give it to me? Kayla, back me up here."

Kayla shoots her a nervous look, but she can't meet Wren's eyes. "It's just a little money, right? Avery really needs it, Wren."

Wren's face flushes a dark red. He coughs, rubbing his throat as Avery shoots him a smug smile and Kayla guiltily looks at her hands. I sidle next to Avery as Wren uncomfortably works his way to the soda pitcher to stifle his coughing.

"Avery," I lilt. "Can I ask you a personal question?"

"No."

"Why did you invite Jack? He obviously doesn't like anyone here."

"Kayla refused to come unless I invited him," Avery says. "And I need her here or I'll never get Wren to—"

I lean in harder and she wrinkles her nose.

"Your moronic blabbermouth is infecting me. Get away," she says.

I back off. She's obviously plotting something devious. Jack's perfectly right about her being a weasel—a pretty weasel, but definitely a slinky little weasel. Jack bowls a spare. And he has perfect form, of course. He strides off the lane looking immensely smug and I slip a leftover cheesy nacho onto his chair the second before he sits down. He smirks at me, and I smirk back.

"Good work," I say.

"You don't need to tell me that. I always do well."

I make a gagging motion to Kayla, who giggles and sits beside him.

"So, Jack! Are you good at other sports? Like, baseball? Or basketball?" she asks, doe eyes wide.

"I played basketball in middle school."

"Oh! That's really cool!"

"I hated it."

"Oh," Kayla whispers.

I bowl my turn—a strike. To catch up, Avery bypasses everyone else's turn on the computer and I bowl a few more times. Strike. Strike. Strike. Strike. Wren cheers, and with every strike I hear Jack getting more and more irritated as he answers Kayla's innocent questions. Finally, when I turn around and sit for good, I notice Kayla's gone, the sound of wailing coming from inside the nearby girl's restroom. Avery looks impressed, as much as a china doll can form emotions like impressed, and Jack's white-knuckled fists are on his knees.

Wren high-fives me. "You were awesome!"

"Thanks!"

"I've never . . . Seriously, I've never seen anything like that! You have to teach me your secret."

First of all, don't be such a huge dork.

"Uh—"

Second, why is Kayla even hitting on Jack? Wren is way, way cuter and way nicer.

"Um, Isis . . ." Wren clears his throat, flushing red.

I blink. "Hm? Did I say that out loud? Oh dearie me."

Wren laughs, and Avery snorts. Jack stands abruptly and pushes past me, grabbing his bowling ball and striding down the lane with newfound verve.

"Got another stick put up your butt? I didn't know another one could fit, you're so tight-assed!" I call.

"Be quiet," he snaps. I turn back to Wren, who's gone a little white.

"Everything okay?"

Wren nods. "Yeah. It's just . . . been a long time since I've been around Jack like this. I didn't know he was coming, otherwise I wouldn't have—"

"Yeah, me, too. Too late now though, huh? No choice but to beat his ass and send him back to the eighth circle of hell from whence he came."

"Of course. I never back down from a good game of bowling."

"Awesome. It's you and me against the legion of darkness, then. Look, I'd better go check on Kayla. Be right back."

The girl's bathroom smells like hairspray and hand soap and boy-inflicted misery. I follow the scent to where Kayla is at the mirror, redrawing her makeup.

"Is everything, uh, mildly all right? Since I know it's not okay. Since this is like, the four millionth time that jerk has made you cry."

Her lip starts wobbling, and she drops her eyeliner and runs into my arms.

"He told me . . . he told me Wren and I would make a better match. He shoved me onto his ex–best friend, Isis!"

As she's sniffling into my armpit, I feel my eyebrows raise. Hmm. Pigs are flying like jet planes right now and the moon must be blue, because Jack might actually be onto something. But I can't say that in front of Kayla.

"Do you . . . do you like Wren at all?" I ask softly.

"He's a nerd!" she wails. "A student council nerd who spends all his time with homeless people! And he's not even close to Jack in terms of looks!"

"Ah yes, the great dilemma of looks over personality. We

can't have it all! Nobody's perfect! We're all shallow even if we don't admit it! Cities will rise and fall and the universe will collapse from its own inevitable heat-death!"

"W-What?" She sniffs.

"I'm saying Wren is actually not that bad."

"Oh. Okay. That was a lot of words."

"Look, you're gonna fix your makeup, you're gonna go out there, and you're gonna have fun. Don't let sourpuss-in-boots-that-are-cramping-his-toes-and-making-him-a-whiny-baby get to you! You're beautiful—"

She glares.

"—uh, not beautiful! You're funny! You're adequately able to function! All good things on the dating checklist. Either Jack will wise up, or you'll find someone else."

The beginning of a wail escapes her lips, and I retreat.

"You will NOT find someone else! If you like this guy so much, shit, why don't you just ask him out?"

"You don't think I've tried that? I've asked him out fifteen times this year!"

"How?"

"Facebook."

I slap my palm to my forehead. "I mean a real sort of ask, like walk up to him and form words."

"What if he rejects me?"

"You will then say, *Gosh, you're really pretty and all but I have to inform you that if you don't accept my date proposal my friend Isis is gonna come over here and do her freaky thing and trust me no one wants that.*"

"You've been doing your freaky thing forever on him, though."

"True."

"It's fine, I'll figure it out, okay? You're right—the first step is to fix my makeup and go back out there!"

She turns to the mirror to retouch her delightfully trashed movie star face and it's that exact moment I realize it's time for an intervention. I march back outside, down half an entire cup of soda, and plop next to Jack.

"Kayla stares at your butt a lot," I announce.

"Yes," he agrees.

That's it. One word. *Yes.* I swell with indignation, but before I have the chance to explode all over him, he adds, "It tends to happen a lot."

I suddenly become aware of how weary and adult-like and around-the-block Jack is and proceed to ask him a completely innocent, nonpersonal question.

"Have you ever had sex?" I blurt.

Jack closes his eyes.

I immediately start backpedaling, past what I just said, past the day I learned what the word "sex" meant, and for good measure, past my own date of birth.

"Just, wow. You don't have to answer that. Actually I only brought it up. Because. Uh. It's a survey! For . . . sex ed! And the teacher was all like, interview one person who you totally think is a weirdo and has never had sex ever because they are a dork and get back to me with a ten-page report on Monday. So."

"I tend to keep my private affairs to myself." Jack sighs. Kayla comes out of the bathroom and bowls her turn, giving Jack serious goo-goo eyes.

"So that means you have!"

He glares at me with much fervor. At least nine fervors.

"Sorry. You're an escort. Of course you've had it. Was it weird? Sex? Is it weird?"

Jack sighs again, and I push on.

"Because! You know, I've thought about it." I lower my voice. "*Sex. Seeeeex.* I mean, why the hell am I whispering? SEX! SEX!"

Kayla drops her ball. Wren looks to be in slight pain. Avery pretends not to know any of us and mutters, "Freak," under her breath.

I point at her. "I heard that!"

She scoffs and adds more booze to her soda. I shake my fist at her and spin around to face Jack again.

"I cannot, for the life of me, recall what we were just conversing about! Alas. I will forever remember this moment we spent together affectionately and *oh God I remember now you pervert!*"

"*You* were the one who shouted 'sex'!" he hisses.

"You were the one who was born, so really I think that's the root of the problem."

"The root of the problem is you. Are fucking. *Insane.*"

"That's not the point!" I slosh my soda in the general direction of everywhere. "The point is, do you see that fine piece of ass over there who happens to be my kind-of friend? Because she's really into you and she's the prettiest, nicest goddamn girl in school and I only barely approve of you and if you crush her pure maiden heart I will pull your pancreas out through your nose and feed it back to you in a drip inserted into your anus, is that clear?"

He opens his mouth, and for once, nothing snarky comes out of it. He leans back and folds his arms over his shirt.

"What if I pay you?" I whisper. He smells like spices and soap and honey again, and it's extremely unhelpful-slash-gross.

"Pay me to what?"

"Pay you to take her out. I've got some saved up, I can — "

He laughs, in that you-can't-afford-me way.

"Two hundred. Just to take her out and be nicey-nice like I saw you be with Alice."

He glowers, icy eyes freezing my insides. He musses his hair up in frustration and makes a half snarl in the back of his throat.

"Fine. I'll go out with Kayla for two hundred."

I make a quiet hiss of victory. "Where?"

"Saturday. The Red Fern, at seven. It's a Thai place downtown. I don't care if she's allergic. That's the only place I can go where they won't recognize me from my escort work."

"Cool. Obviously I will also be going along."

"What?" he snaps.

"To make sure you're nice." I smile. "Gotta see I'm getting my money's worth! She needs this more than you know."

Jack and I are the highest scores in the game, and at the

tenth round, we're tied. He bowls a double strike. I have to get a turkey, or it's over. I hold my ball up and breathe, trying to tune out Kayla's crazy loud cheering and Wren's sensible encouragement. Avery even snarks at me not to mess up. I get a double, and on my final round I eye the lane like it's a live snake. *Don't bite me, lane. C'mon, we're friends, even if you're a reptile and I'm a mammal. Friendship knows no racial bounds.*

I slip, and the ball plunks into the gutter and rolls happily away. Jack and I are dead tied. Wren and Kayla pat me on the back, and Avery tips her head back and downs more booze as she puts her shoes back on.

"Might wanna lay off on that," I say.

"Mind your own business," she snaps.

Kayla pokes her head between us. "Don't worry, I'm driving her."

"Driving me insane." Avery sighs.

Jack and I are the last two to put our shoes back on. He sighs and shrugs. "Neither of us won, but I might as well have. We both know I bowled a more tactically sound game. Your style is a huge illogical mess."

"Yes, my style sucks. But at least I didn't bowl half a game with a nacho stuck to my ass."

I smirk as I saunter away, leaving Jack to feel the back of his jeans wildly. I hear a swear and feel a sharp something ping lightly off my head.

The counter guy burps. "Uh, that guy just threw a chip at you."

"He's mad I won, good sir." I sigh happily. "And he's mad because he realized I'm going to keep on winning. It's what I do."

chapter nine

JACK HUNTER IS MOVING toward me without a shirt on and it is half glorious and half heart-attack-inducing and something in my stomach gurgles like I want to vomit. He smiles, but not like he smiled with Alice. He smiles like he means it, a soft, golden curve of his lips, and it somehow makes him look even stupidly handsomer.

"Jack," I start, my throat tensing up. "You're half naked!"

For some reason I'm wearing a low-cut bodice but I can't remember how I got in one of these. It's something straight out of the cheap romance novels I caught Jack checking out in the library.

Jack leans toward me, the smell of his honey-spice cologne wafting up, his bright blue eyes piercing into me as he leans down and nuzzles my neck. His lips are soft and warm as he says in a low voice, "Would you like help with the other half?"

And then suddenly the room is red, and there are roses everywhere, and the escort club receptionist I called is sitting behind a desk watching us but for some reason she looks like Kayla, who frowns, sees Jack kissing my neck, and keels over, dead.

"Ahh!" I bolt upright in my bed, sweat cooling on my forehead. It's the middle of the night. I'm in my own room in reality, hugging the stuffing out of Ms. Muffin. Jack's abs have disappeared into thin air, and Kayla is not dead. At least I hope not. I reach up to feel my neck and squirm—it seemed so real! I get up and douse my neck with hydrogen peroxide for good measure. Dream Jack or no, any and all Jack-touching needs to be disinfected immediately, lest I catch his fathead shitbaby germs.

The next morning at school, I have to make sure Kayla is not, in fact, dead, because my entire world is ending and I need to talk to her about it. She's standing under a tree talking to Avery, but I have to make doubly sure she isn't dead, so I inch up and poke her. In the butt. Several times.

"Isis! What are you doing?"

"Oh, thank God, Kayla. Your fabulous ass is intact! The stability of world peace depends on that ass."

"Get out of here, creep," Avery sneers.

"Good morning, Avery-bo-bavery," I chirp. "How are the pills treating you?"

The other girl she's talking with looks confused. "Pills? What pills? You have pills and you didn't give me any, Ave?"

Avery is too busy glowering at me to stop me from dragging Kayla away to a different tree.

"Isis, are you okay?"

"Kayla, do you think Jack is sexy?"

She makes a dying pig squeal and I shake her out of it. Politely.

"I had this nightmare wherein I thought Jack was sexy and you died."

"O-Oh. Well. I'm not dead! So that's good, right?" Kayla smiles.

"Oh Kayla, you gorgeous, sugary, incredibly fluffy butterfly, you are of no help to me right now and you have a date with Jack on Saturday at the Red Fern at seven I arranged it and I must go."

I leave her to chemically combust, and decide to track down the one other person in this school who'd have the patience to listen to my woes about Jack.

I find Wren in the student council office, filling out extremely interesting paperwork. He's buried behind piles of the stuff. I can barely see tufts of his black hair poking out. I reach into the paperwork pile and shove the two halves aside. Hundreds of them fall off the desk and to the floor. Papers drift through the air like snowflakes. Fat, boring-ass snowflakes. Wren looks up, face slack with shock.

"Whatcha doing?" I ask.

"Dividing up funding for the other clubs," he whispers, clearly distraught. A paper plops onto his head and slides off dejectedly. I'm respectful for three seconds.

"So anyway, I had this nightmare in which Jack was sexy and Kayla died."

"I'm . . . sorry to hear that?"

"Don't you see? Jack cannot be sexy! I can't even think that subconsciously, or else the war is gonna be lost! The countless troops living in my brain are going to lose morale if they spot a kernel of potential sexiness in Jack. They'll get confused! I can't like him. Not even one bit. Or the whole thing falls apart!"

"Might I suggest—"

"And that's not even taking into consideration my timer!" I crow, bending and picking up the papers for him. "Three whole years, Wren! Three freakin' years of not being a moron. I can't . . . I can't break that! I'll never be a moron again. I won't! Sexy thoughts lead to sex and sex leads to love. Or is it the other way around?"

"I'm pretty sure it's—"

"I can't do it, Wren!" I wail. "You have to help me! If I start to like Jack, and Jack sees that, he'll shoot me down because A. we are slightly at war and B. I'm a fat ugly cow and then my timer will get reset and I'll lose three years and I promised myself I wouldn't do it again, Wren, I promised!"

I slam the stack of papers back on his desk, my voice trembling.

"What do I do?"

He sighs. "Look, Isis, I don't know exactly what's going on, but if the thought of liking someone freaks you out to the point of tears, I don't think it's good for you. You should stop."

"I'm trying!" I shout, then whimper. "I'm *trying*."

Wren sighs, getting up and putting an arm around my shoulder.

"It's understandable. He's a good-looking guy. Maybe that's it. Maybe you like him only for his physical traits. We're teenagers. That level of libido is normal."

"Oh God, you used 'libido' and 'teenagers' in a serious sentence; what are you, eighty with a PhD?"

"And," Wren says sternly to drown my groaning out, "he *did* kiss you."

"As a joke."

"Yes, well . . ."

"It meant absolutely nothing."

"Yes, but you have to consider that even though your brain knows that, your body may not. And . . . your heart might be a bit confused, too."

"Pffft." I buzz my lips. "What heart? That thing I got rid of three years ago? Last I checked, it's impossible for organs to properly function outside of the body. Unless you put it on a pump. But that's gross and I definitely did not put my dumb little heart on a pump. I threw it out the window when I was driving to Walgreens —"

"Isis!" Wren grabs me by the shoulders, gazing into my eyes with that unblinking stare. "Listen to me for five seconds!"

I'm stunned into being quiet. Wren, realizing this is a once-in-a-lifetime occurrence, barrels on while he still has the floor.

"It's okay to like someone," he says. "Even if it's superficial. You don't have to let what my cousin did in the past define you. I know he probably did something horrible. He used to put frogs in the microwave and laugh about it. I know what he's like. I know he hurt you. But if you're feeling things for someone again, it's good. It means you're healing. You have to let that happen."

"I don't like Jack," I whisper. "I don't."

Wren hugs me. I rip out of his grip and put on my brightest smile.

"Seriously, I don't! Just ignore everything I said, okay? Jack's just really fun to pick on, you know? I'm just getting that confused is all."

"Isis—"

"Whatever Jack did must've been really bad if you turn pale every time I mention it and Avery has to go to a shrink, huh? He's probably as bad as Nameless!"

Wren immediately clams up, mouth closing and fists balling.

"Plus Avery was drinking the entire time at the bowling alley, while he was there. And you only looked at him twice, so. Yeah. I think it must've been really, really horrible." I tap my chin thoughtfully. "It has something to do with Sophia, doesn't it?"

"Stop."

"Did he do to her what Nameless did to me? I just have to ask Sophia, and—"

"I said *stop*." Wren's voice is so soft and dark I can't help but shudder. He adjusts his glasses and looks to me with those piercing hazel eyes. "Don't hide behind what he did, just because what I said to you hits too close to home. Jack's a better guy than Nameless, I promise you. It just takes a while for people to see that."

"Avery said he's dangerous when people start getting to know him."

Wren sighs. "He's dangerous, period. There's a reason he keeps people at arm's length. He might seem heartless, but he doesn't want to hurt anyone again."

"*Again?* So that means . . . he hurt someone. Did he hurt Sophia?"

Wren flinches. "Look, I'm sorry, Isis, but you need to leave. I can't talk about this right now. Leave, please."

I glare furiously at Wren, then turn on my heel and slam the door behind me. So much for Wren helping me. I'm on my own, and the terrifying thought that I might not absolutely hate Jack Hunter's guts is looming over my brain like a guillotine. And the mystery of Sophia is getting deeper and extremely annoying-er. I have to find that girl, and pronto, if I want any answers.

But do I? Is digging around in Jack's past really going to help me in not liking him? Of course it will, what am I saying? He clearly hurt Sophia. If I learn just how badly, I can knock this funky idea out of my brain that I think he's cute at all. It's the perfect tactic. And until then, I'll quash whatever idiotic feelings are brewing for him under seven tons of lead bricks inscribed with the word "NOPE." I have a war to win, a date to get ready for, and an arrogant asshole to finally force into apologizing to the only friend I've made so far.

Jack Hunter is not sexy.

Jack Hunter is on my shit list, forever.

And just to let him know it, I sneak into the agriculture building and scoop a plastic Baggie full of goat-and-chicken-and-God-knows-what-other-animal-poop compost, and lob it on his windshield. It's satisfying for all of two seconds before I realize it's just poop. It's not me. The true me wouldn't do something so basic, so kindergarten. But I've been shaken. Something in me is wrong, a loose puzzle piece, so I'm lashing out like a knee jerking in reaction to a doctor's tap.

The poo splatters on a new Drama Club Wailer Girl love note tucked under the wipers, and before I can do any deeper, extremely helpful soul searching, campus security yells after me. I run. There aren't many people in the halls, but I almost run smack into Knife Kid as I turn a corner.

"Hi," I say breathlessly. "Can I use your jacket?"

"Uh . . ." He looks down at the military-inspired green jacket. "Sure. Just be careful. It's vintage. See the holes with dark stuff around them? Those are stab wounds from Vietnam—"

"Fascinating. Thanks!" I grab it and put it on, running as the sound of footsteps gets loud behind me. I pull a hairband off my wrist, put my hair into a bun, and roll up my jeans. The first person I see around this corner has to cooperate with me, or I'm done for. I have to pretend I've been talking to him or her for ages, and I have to face away from security, so they only see my back. I turn left and race down the hall, my heart singing when I see someone with her head in her locker. I pull her arm and slam the locker shut.

"Quick," I hiss. "Pretend we've been talking for a long time, and if security comes by, point in another direction."

"Why should I?" Avery glowers. My gut sinks, but she's the only one around.

"C'mon, please!"

"You'll owe me."

"That's great! Sure! I love owing the devil favors!"

Security comes barreling around the corner, and Avery raises her voice.

"So I was telling him not to call me again, but he just couldn't get the message, you know? Anyway, do you have calc or English after this?"

"Which way did the running girl go?" a balding officer pants. I pull my jacket slightly over my chin. Avery looks him up and down and jerks her thumb behind her.

"Thank you," the other officer wheezes. They take off down the hall, potbellies swaying. When they're gone, Avery smirks.

"You'd think they'd be able to remember what a girl with purple streaks in her hair looks like. Idiots."

"Right, so, what do I owe you? Let's get this over with, Shelob."

"Are you comparing me to a giant spider?"

When I nod, she looks mildly impressed, and then suddenly points at me, all business.

"You're going to help me break into Jack's house after school today."

"Wow, uh, normally I would be one hundred percent down for criminal robbery, but I'm sort of having a crisis pertaining to him, and—"

"Wow, duh, I don't care. Should I call those fat-asses back? Oh, boys! I've got someone here—"

"Fine!" I hiss, clamping a hand around her wrist. "Just tell me what to do."

"Meet me in the parking lot after school. You'll be driving. Are you in any AP classes?"

"Yes."

"What am I saying, of course you are, you're ugly. Bring some unfinished homework from one of those classes."

And that's the story of how I was recruited to become a cat burglar by Satan.

θ ο °ο

Jack's house is fancy and huge—a gravel roundabout at the front cleaving the verdant lawn in two. Rosebushes and massive lilies and apple trees crowd around the house. A hummingbird feeder glows red with sugar-juice as tiny jewel-toned birds flit around, sipping nectar. A gardener waters the roses carefully, his head bobbing as he nods at each one, satisfied they're growing well. I park across the street like Avery tells me to. She grabs both sides of my face and forces me to look at her.

"Pay attention, weirdo."

"Paying a thousand attentions," I squeak.

"You are Jack's project partner for AP bio. You've brought stuff to work on with him. He's not there right now, and I know this for a fact, because he's visiting Sophia. His mother is disgustingly sweet. She'll let you in with no problem. Ask for the bathroom. Go upstairs and enter the second door on your right."

"I'm gonna puke."

"Save it for when you get out of the house!" Avery snaps, and lets go of my face. "It's just Jack's mom, and his room. It's not him. I'll keep watch. If he comes home early, I'll text you, so put it on vibrate and get the hell out of there if you feel it go off. If he catches you snooping around . . ." Avery shudders. "What he did with your butt crack picture will look nice in comparison. Got it?"

"Got it!" I salute.

"What are you looking for?" she quizzes me.

"A cigar box of letters."

"And which letter will you take?"

"The most recent one."

"And what will you do when you get it?"

"Get the hell out of the house and definitely never open the letter even a centimeter."

"All right. Do this, and we're even, you hear me? I don't talk about you chucking shit, and you don't talk about me going to the shrink's."

"That sounds fantastically equal and all, but you're forgetting the slight problem of *he'll notice a letter is missing because he isn't dead-ass blind and he'll ask his mom and he'll know it's me and then I'll get maimed.*"

Avery's frown deepens. She pulls her red hair back and puts it up in a messy ponytail.

"I don't care," she finally says.

"I care extremely a lot!"

"I'm not gonna risk his wrath. But you're already risking his wrath with this stupid war you two have going on. I need to know what's in the letter, do you understand? If I don't find out—"

Avery squeezes her doll-like eyes shut.

"Sophia doesn't talk to me anymore, or let me see her. It's my fault. What happened back then was my fault, and Jack cleaned it up, okay? But she blames me. And she's right; I deserve the blame. I was stupid, and I did something I regret. I've been working for years on apologizing. Years, weirdo. Five fucking years to work up the guts to say sorry. But if I don't see what's in that letter, I might never get the chance to."

I watch her face carefully. She's not lying. Her face is something other than disgusted—it's pained. Her expression is the same as when we met on that sunset bridge. A torrent of emotion is warring inside her, and it hurts like hell.

I might not like her. I might think she's a jerk and a weasel. But I know the feeling.

I get out of the car and shut the door behind me.

The Hunters' gate is intimidating—all wrought iron curves and curlicues painted a fresh white—but it's open. I stride up the driveway and smile at the gardener, who tips his hat to me. Wren wasn't kidding when he said Jack's mom got a large settlement sum—the Hunters are loaded. Jack is loaded. So why the hell is he escorting when he could just ask his mom for money? Unless he doesn't want to. God knows I know that feeling, too; I hate asking Mom for money. I hate asking anyone for help, period, and as much as I think he's a small, ugly snarkmancer, I know he's just like me in that regard. He does stuff on his own, always. He works alone, always.

I ascend the steps and ring the doorbell, and a woman in a canary-yellow sundress answers. She's so beautiful I'm struck dumb for approximately point five seconds. Her hair is soft and tawny, kept short and bobbed. She's maybe forty, with a brilliant smile and delicate ivory skin. She's holding a glass of dirty water in one hand and a dripping paintbrush in the other. Her eyes are the same almond-shaped, piercing, lake-ice blue as Jack's, but hers are joyous, whereas Jack's are always dimmed by boredom.

"Hi! How can I help you?" She beams, slopping a bit of water as she balances the door open with one foot. Her socks are rainbow-striped, and it somehow puts me more at ease.

"Uh, hi, Mrs. Hunter? I'm Jack's lab partner in AP bio, Isis Blake. We were supposed to work on a project together today?" I brandish the papers. Her face falls.

"Oh, shit! I-I mean, darn!" she corrects herself quickly. "You know what? Jack left a while ago, but he'll be back soon. Why don't you come in and have some tea. Do you like tea? Or are you a coffee person? I can make coffee, just be warned it tastes like ass and looks like ass—I mean, butt."

I laugh, and her concerned face at swearing in front of a teenager melts to sheepish amusement.

"I'm sorry. I hope Jack warned you I have a bit of a potty mouth. It's my one fatal flaw. Well, that and my uncanny ability to burn everything I touch on a stove. I promise I'll be on my best behavior."

"It's fine." I smile wider. "Adults who don't swear make me uneasy."

"Me, too," she agrees breathlessly. She struggles to hold open the door, so I open it for her. "Thanks. Come on in!"

I can't help the whistle that escapes my lips when I see the foyer. A massive flight of stairs leads up, the carpets are rich and red and probably Turkish—the country Turkey because turkeys can't make rugs—and there are hardwood floors and huge french windows letting in light and everything smells like lavender and is that a picture of Jack in his diapers oh my God he looks like a fat little Buddha.

"He looks like a fat monk," Mrs. Hunter says, hovering over my shoulder.

"I was— I was just thinking that!" I say. "Like a Buddha or something."

"I used to call him all sorts of names." She sighs. "He was too young to understand them, of course, and I was so sleep-deprived because of his crying I was ready to strangle someone, so instead of going crazy, I'd threaten him in a sickly sweet voice and he'd just smile and coo at me. Horrible of me, I know. Maybe that's why he's turned out the way he is."

"Weird?" I offer.

"Oh, definitely weird. Weird is a Hunter specialty." Her eyes twinkle as she leads me into the airy, bright kitchen. "He was such a happy baby. But I worry now. He's become mostly just sad."

She shakes her head as if to clear it and fills a kettle with water. "Is mint tea okay?"

"Yeah." I settle on a barstool. "I mean, I don't want to intrude, you seemed really busy ..."

Mrs. Hunter laughs. "Busy? Not to be modest, but I can afford to never be busy, ever. Though I admit, I miss the office sometimes."

She places the paintbrush and the water down, and it's then I notice the canvas in the room, facing some windows. Paints smear over a pallet, dozens of paintbrushes sticking up here and there in jars of half-dirty water. The painting itself is pretty—a horse of some kind. Mrs. Hunter rushes over to it and turns the canvas around.

"Oh no, no, no! It's not finished yet! You can't look."

"Right, sorry."

"No, I'm sorry. It's me. I have this stupid thing where I get nervous when people see my unfinished works. Not that they'll be any good when they're finished, either."

"That one was beautiful, though."

She flushes. "Thank you. I started taking classes a month ago. I liked them, but I dropped out because all the teacher wanted me to paint were ugly, soulless little watercolor land-scapes. No feeling! No passion!"

"Horses have tons of passion. Like, seventeen whole passions."

"Exactly!" She claps. "You understand. It's more fun to paint them than a bunch of boring trees."

A tiny whirling dervish of canine madness streaks into the kitchen, making soft *whoof* noises at me and wagging his tail. He's pitch black, with cute button eyes and a damp nose he mashes against my ankle in an attempt to either gauge how long it would take for him to chew through my Achilles tendon, or to discern what other dogs I'd passed on the street in the last seventeen years of my life.

"Darth! Down!" Mrs. Hunter snaps. The dog obediently wags his butt hard and jumps onto the barstool next to me. Mrs. Hunter grabs a dishrag and whips it at him, and he jumps off and excitedly barks before doing several determined laps around the kitchen for no apparent reason.

"He's so cute!" I say. "Darth is his name?"

"Short for Darth Vader. I mean, he's all black, I'd just seen *The Return of the Jedi*, it made perfect sense at the time!"

"It's way better than Fluffy."

"Right?" She smiles. "He's a mutt. Half Yorkshire terrier and half sugar-high chipmunk."

I laugh. Jack's mom is officially cool. Or at least she's trying hard to be, and in most adults that would make me roll my eyes, but in her scatterbrained way it's endearing. The kettle dings, and Mrs. Hunter pours two cups of tea, then slides one to me.

"Your kitchen is amazing. The whole house is," I try.

She sips and smiles. "You think? Truth be told I don't use the kitchen much—it's Jack who does most of the cooking. I just burn things and get paint everywhere. It makes him so mad."

She laughs, and I laugh trying to imagine Jack's screwed-up, exasperated face as he cleans paint off the counters. I burn to ask her a bunch of questions about Jack. Here she is, the woman who carried him for nine months and put up with his crap for seventeen more years. She knows everything about him, I bet—how often he wet himself, what he was afraid of as a kid, what stupid-looking costumes she forced him into for Halloween. And for some reason, I'd really like to know that, too. And not just to use as blackmail material.

I shake my head. Focus. Focus! She probably knows about Sophia. My fingers twitch around my cup. *Shut up, reflexes. This is no time to act up. Keep those wanton desires for knowledge inside, where she can't see.*

"So you and Jack must be friends, then?" Mrs. Hunter clears her throat. Darth Vader, finally exhausted by his valiant efforts to sniff every part of me, plops down at her feet.

"Ah . . . hahaha." I laugh nervously. "Not exactly."

"I understand. He's really hard to get along with, very withdrawn, a little snappish sometimes. He wasn't always like that, but somewhere around middle school he started changing. Hormones, I guess. And without a father—"

She cuts off, staring at a space over my shoulder for a few moments. She shakes her head and sighs.

"I'm sorry. I'm babbling."

"No, it's okay," I rush to say. "I mean, it's not okay he doesn't have a dad, or that your husband died— I mean, uh . . . *crap.*"

"It's all right." She chuckles. "No need to be careful on my part. I miss Oliver, God knows I do. But after fifteen years, I can say his name without breaking down. That's an improvement, right?"

"Definitely." I nod. "I've . . . I've got someone like that, too. Someone whose name I can't say."

"Oh, honey, I'm sorry. Losing someone is so terrible."

"I didn't lose him, he . . . he drove me away."

It's a personal thing to say. But Mrs. Hunter's gentle presence makes me feel like I can say anything. She puts her hand on mine and pats it.

"What idiot boy would break such a pretty girl's heart? One who doesn't deserve you, that's who."

I pull my sleeve down over my arm and force a small smile. Pretty. She said it so offhandedly, like it was true. But it's not. Of course it's not.

"I have to use the restroom," I start. "Where . . . ?"

"Oh! Sure." She gets out of her chair and gestures. "Right down the hall, through the living room, and to your left."

"Thanks."

I trot down the hall, making a show of walking with loud footsteps so she thinks I've gone down it all the way. I climb the stairs as silently as I can and inch the second right door open, sliding through when it's just big enough to accommodate my butt.

Jack's room is dim. The walls are painted dark blue, and dark blue curtains hang over the massive windows. The carpet is black, and the bed is king-size and done neatly in all blue, too. But the blueness isn't what weirds me out; it's how clean it is. There's not a single piece of dirty laundry lying around. His desk is organized neatly—pencils in a cup, even. His bookshelf isn't alphabetical, but there are tons of impressive books on it; classics, some manga, and a small section of books fitted with paper-bag book covers. I pull the cover off one and snigger. Romance. He's got a little section dedicated to it, and probably covered them so his mother wouldn't see. They must be Sophia's favorites. There's a TV and a PlayStation in the corner, and an Xbox. His computer is a laptop, sitting on his bed as if he just closed it to leave.

And the smell of him is everywhere.

It's the smell of sleeping and studying and reading, of skin cells and rumpled clothes, of being a teenage boy but being a weird, clean one, who bathes with a particular type of soap and uses a particular cologne made of mint and honey that overlays his sweat. I don't even know if it is cologne anymore. It might just be how he smells, naturally. But it's everywhere, and it's intoxicating. My hands are sweating more and more with every inhale. It's toying with my nerves—I feel like any second I'll turn around and he'll be standing there, glowering and plotting my ultimate demise.

I wonder if his mom knows what he does for a job? Even if he wanted to have his own savings, which I respect, he could just get a normal part-time job like the rest of us. He didn't have to go straight to escorting. With his looks, anybody would hire him. He could model! He could act! He could sell chicken wings and rake in the dough as ladies flocked to the counter daily just to see his face. Why escorting? I know it's good money, or so I've researched. Arguably, sex workers (or sort-of sex workers, in Jack's case) get way more money than any vanilla job on the market, except for, you know, stockbrokers and doctors and the like. Jack isn't stupid—if he chose escorting, it was probably for that reason. But why would he need a lot of money, fast?

I shove the confusion into the time-out corner of my brain. *You are being incredibly risky, Isis. You are asking big huge why questions while in the heart of enemy territory and last time I checked that gets people shot and killed. You're the general! The war depends entirely on you! If you're captured, it's over!*

Determined, I clench my fist and look around the room. Avery said it would be somewhere obvious, but still hidden. Thanks, Ave. That is basically extremely useful advice. I check under the bed, in the desk drawers, in his closet. Nothing. I'm running out of time. If I don't get back downstairs quick, Mrs. Hunter will know something's up and come looking for me. There's only one place left—his dresser. I inch the drawers open and rummage through all of them. Except the under-wear drawer. That thing can go to hell. At least he doesn't fold his clothes precisely, because frankly, the serial killer level of this room doesn't need any further reason to go up.

And that's when I find it. Mashed behind a bunch of shirts is a hard wooden box. I pull it out, the sweet smell of to-bacco wafting up from the intricately carved Cuban cigar box. It was his father's, or so Avery said. I briefly wonder how she knows so much about Jack when they don't speak at all. They obviously knew each other in the past, but how well? Probably very well.

Whatever he did must have been unforgivable, if Avery and Wren are so afraid of him now. But Avery did something awful, too.

Just what the *fuck* happened among the three of them?

I shake that thought out for the millionth time and open the box. Inside is a stack of carefully arranged letters, each on the same pink stationery with clouds around the edges. I take the topmost and open it slightly to check the date to make sure it's the most recent. It is. I shove the box back behind the shirts and hesitate before closing the drawer. Who even writes letters in this day and age? It's so old-fashioned and, as much as I hate to admit it, romantic. Finally, I have something from Sophia in my hands. The illusive, mysterious Sophia is right here, waiting for me to read her words. It would be so easy to just pry the letter open a little more. Just one sentence. One sentence never killed anybody. Except it has, probably, somewhere down the line of thousands of years of human existence, but like hell that's gonna stop me.

The handwriting is curly, elegant, and very girlie.

Dear Jack,

Can you believe it's October already? I put up a string of orange Christmas lights and paper bats over my bed. You'll see it when you come next time—it's really getting me into the spooky vibe. The nurses are saying we'll carve a pumpkin and put it on my windowsill. I'm going to give it a Fu Manchu mustache and call it Mr. Miyagi. Or I'll make it Hello Kitty. Which do you think would scare more people on the street below?

I'm doing well! Dr. Fenwall thinks I'll be well enough for a day out after my next round of treatments. We should go somewhere you want to go this time. And don't argue! I dragged you to the carnival last time and I know you hate it so you can drag me wherever you want and I won't complain at all! Promise. Okay, maybe a little whining. But only when my feet start to hurt or I see something cute I want. ;)

She really is sick. But she sounds so cheerful and sweet, I can't help but like her already. And Jack at a carnival? I can only imagine the intensity of his glares whenever someone would try to offer him cotton candy or pull him into a game of ring toss. And on the Ferris wheel? I scoff. He'd be bored the whole way through. He's a party pooper like that. Still, Sophia seems to really like him. She sees beyond it, somehow.

I know you've been feeling down lately and working extra hard for me, but don't worry. Dr. Fenwall says he's talked with the billing department, and they've got a grant just for people like me. So it's okay if you

don't work for a while. I'll apply to it, and I know
I'll get it. That way you can just relax and have fun
instead of worrying all the time.

I munch my bottom lip. Working? Is that why . . . is that
why he works as an escort? To pay her hospital bills? Can't
her parents pay them? Does she have parents at all?

Anyway, I'm so happy to hear about the new girl.
Isis, you said her name was? I know, I know, you
hate her and you can't see why hearing about her
makes me so happy, but I am!

My heart jigs around in my chest. She's talking about me!

But Jack, really. When was the last time someone
affected you like this? You never talk about your
classmates. She's the first one you've mentioned to
me. She must have made quite the impact on you. She
sounds like so much fun. I'm so, so happy you've met
your match. Yes, you heard me. Match. She's kicking
your butt, and you better step up if you want to
win!

That's why I'm happy. You have someone to fight
against, and I know how happy that makes you, in
a weird, competitive, perverse way. You always used
to complain about how everyone at your school was
so stupid and boring. You don't have many friends.
And I prayed every day you'd find someone who'd

give you a run for your money, who'd make you feel alive again, who might pique your interest enough for you to become friends. Well! There she is! You can thank me later. You'll let me meet her, won't you? I'd really like that.

Anyway, I better finish this and send it off. Naomi poked her head into my room and caught me writing this at four in the morning. Heehee.

I miss you every day.
Yours,
Sophia

I close the letter and wince. I feel like I've violated some sacred barrier by reading it now that I've finished it. I have to get back downstairs and leave. Holding this thing in my hand is making a sick guilty feeling pool in my stomach with every passing second.

I take out my phone. If I snap a picture, Avery can see the letter without me taking it. It's the perfect solution. If I can put the letter on something flat—

I whirl around and collide with someone's hard chest. Frigid blue eyes blaze with the coldest fire I've ever seen, the face they belong to carved in shadow and rage.

I squeak and shield myself. "Leave a pretty body for my mom."

chapter ten

I KNOW TWO THINGS for certain:

1. *I'm not going to escape this house alive. I have good reason to believe this. Predominantly, the way Jack Hunter has been handling a butcher knife for more than fifteen minutes.*

2. *I smell like dog poop. Possibly because as Jack marched me into the kitchen and sat me down, Darth Vader pooped on me. But not before I tied a ribbon to his tail. The savage Sith lord is currently chasing himself in endless circles in the hall. I snicker.*

Jack hasn't said a word since he caught me in his room. He instantly plucked the letter from my hands, grabbed my wrist, and marched me down here and told me not to move or speak. Feeling all kinds of hells guilty, I do neither, and simply watch him mess about in the kitchen with cold, precise movements.

Jack cuts mushrooms and asparagus with practiced ease. He's already chopped some beef and seared it with a delicious-smelling sweet soy sauce. He throws the vegetables in, and begins chopping bean sprouts and red bell pepper. When Jack's back is turned, I grab a pepper piece and munch, then make a face and put it back. Jack absently grabs the same piece, not knowing I've bitten it, and bites the same end, chewing thoughtfully as if to gauge the taste.

"Ew, gross!" I say. "Now your germs and my germs are fraternizing and making germy little babies!"

He glares at me. I weigh the pros and cons of an early death and shut my mouth.

"Did you want jasmine rice or white rice, Jack?" Mrs. Hunter's voice stabs through the tension in the kitchen as she walks in with two bags of rice, one in each arm. She sees me and smiles.

"Oh! Hi, Isis. Are you joining us for dinner?"

I shoot a look at Jack, who coolly ignores me and chooses the jasmine rice bag.

"Uh, yes? Provided I won't be taken out back and shot afterward?"

Mrs. Hunter laughs and settles beside me, and Jack just dumps the rice into the rice cooker on the counter.

"How was Sophia?" she asks her son.

"Fine," he says tersely. "They've decorated for Halloween."

"You should make her that pumpkin pudding you made last year. She'd love it."

Jack's hand goes still as he flips the stir-fry. It's a quick stutter-stop motion, but he continues when the meat starts to burn.

"She can't eat."

"Oh no, is she not feeling well again?" Mrs. Hunter sighs. "I'm sorry, honey."

"It's fine. She'll get better," Jack says with hard conviction.

Mrs. Hunter looks to me. "Jack and Sophia were friends from a very young age. She's such a sweet thing, but she's bedridden in the hospital. Some degenerative neurologic disorder. It's so sad."

"She's fine," Jack insists coldly. "And you don't need to tell that girl. She already knows."

Mrs. Hunter looks to me with surprise. "You do, Isis? Jack's kept it under such tight wraps I didn't know about it until a few years ago. I'm surprised he'd tell you."

"I didn't. She snooped."

Shame washes over me, hot and red, but I push it out. "Excuse me if I go around looking for your weaknesses when you posted mine all over the school," I hiss.

"Being fat is not your weakness," he snaps. "We both know it. You disproved that with your trashy outfit the next day. And I never asked Evans to do it. He went overboard. I never expected he would do something of that magnitude, and I never expected you to sneak into my house to try to get leverage."

"You used to be larger?" Mrs. Hunter gasps. "I bet you were just as pretty then, too."

Her compliment tears me out of my anger, but not for long.

"I'm sorry if I try to defend myself when you back me into a corner, jackass!"

Mrs. Hunter watches us snarl at each other, her head

going back and forth like she's watching a Ping-Pong match. With swords. And a flaming meteor as the ball. Darth Vader, hearing our rising voices, runs in and starts barking.

"I never backed you anywhere. Evans did," Jack snaps.

"This is our war. Take some responsibility for your fucking actions!"

"So you decided it was all right to come into my house," Jack's voice rises minutely. "Go through my things, and read my personal letters? You were looking for ways to hurt me. But it's not just me you'll hurt, is it? You'll go to Sophia and hurt her, too, just to get back at me."

I flinch. "I wouldn't—"

"You would. You're ruthless and maniacal and stubborn. I was wrong. You really do hate me. You'll do anything to hurt me because you hate me. You hate me so much you declared a petty little war on me."

"You declared first!"

"You've hated me from the second you saw me, and I can only assume it's because I remind you of someone who hurt you."

"Jack!" Mrs. Hunter looks shocked. "That's a horrible thing to say!"

"Did *he* say you were fat?" Jack asks coolly. I go still, but he presses on. "Did Will say you were fat?"

"Shut up," I growl, a roiling nausea creeping into my stomach.

"No," Jack says lightly, as if to himself. "It must've been more than that. Did he call you stupid? Prudish? Ugly?"

Ugly.

"I said shut the hell up!"

"Jack, I don't think—" Mrs. Hunter is cut off as Jack takes the stir-fry off the stove and turns, leaning against the oven and looking at me with sharp, chilly anger in his eyes. But something behind those fragments of ice suddenly goes soft. Sad warmth is in them, buried deep and buried well.

"Did he hit you?"

"Jack, that's hardly—" Mrs. Hunter starts. I stand so fast the barstool screeches and tips over.

"I'll kill you," I grit.

"Is that why you hate me? Because you think I'm like him?"

"Shut the hell up!"

Jack's voice becomes even softer. "Did he force you?"

Nameless rings in my head. *Maybe I'll love you, if you just hold still.*

"Jack!" Mrs. Hunter snaps. Darth Vader's barks turn shrill.

"I swear," I spit through my teeth, digging into my lips so hard there's blood. "I'll fucking kill you if you keep talking."

"Is that why you hate everyone? Because he hurt you, badly? Because you trusted him, and he took that and set it on fire?"

"Jack Adam Hunter, I want you to stop speaking *right now.*"

Jack smiles, brittle. "That's what happens when you trust someone. You get hurt."

I lunge for him, but I'm too slow. A slap resounds, and

Jack's head whips to the side. The silence in the kitchen puts on pounds, tons. Darth Vader chokes off a whine and goes quiet. The hissing of the rice cooker is the only thing that dares to make noise. Mrs. Hunter puts her hand down, face contorted with equal parts fury and regret.

"You will not"—her voice is slow and deliberate—"speak to Isis again while she is here today. Is that understood?"

Jacks eyes glint with shock and confusion. But he steels himself quickly and strides out of the kitchen without another word, without a glance at me. When he's gone, Mrs. Hunter turns to me.

"I'm sorry, Isis. He's . . . I won't make excuses for him, but he's not the best at recognizing when he's hurting people beyond repair."

"I'm fine," I manage.

"Sweetie," Mrs. Hunter says softly. "You're not fine. You're crying."

I raise my hand to touch my face. It's wet and cold.

Mrs. Hunter comforts me when I falter, hugging me. Every inch of my body shakes, and I break into choking sobs in her arms.

⊙　○　°°

Mrs. Hunter holds me until I calm down, and then she insists I drink a cup of mint tea. It's sweet and warm and opens my sad-clogged lungs. I thank her. She doesn't bring up what just happened, and she doesn't ask questions. She just busies herself with the tea and drinking her own cup of it. Avery's texts asking me where I am and what's going on vibrate on my phone, but I can't bring myself to answer them. Not when the awful word is ringing in my head.

Ugly. I finger the thing under my sleeve. I can feel the outline of it on my arm. It hurts, burns, and smolders, just like when I first got it.

Ugly ugly ugly.

Jack doesn't come down.

I leave after thanking Mrs. Hunter, making some excuse about my own mom needing me at home. Avery is in the car, still waiting, tapping away on her phone. She looks to me, irritated.

"Why didn't you answer my texts? What took you so long? Did you get it?"

"He caught me."

"He *what*?" Avery snarls. "But— But I didn't even see his car pull up!"

I jerk my thumb behind me. Avery turns around and her eyes widen at the black sedan parked almost a block behind her.

"He saw my car," I say.

"Why is his windshield streaky and brown?"

A single peal of watery laughter escapes my throat, but it cuts off quickly. Avery looks confused, and then shakes her head.

"What happened in there? You look sick."

"I don't want to talk about it," I say in a low tone, and

start the car. Avery must see my red eyes or snotty nose or the way I move like I'm drained of all energy, because she doesn't push me to stay or go back and get it. Even ruthless popular girls have a heart, I guess. The highway flashes by as I take her back to her house.

"I read the most recent letter," I say dully. Avery's eyes flash.

"Anything . . . Did Sophia say anything about a surgery?"

"No."

Avery exhales, a deep and worried thing that leaves her in one breath.

"Neurological, right?" I ask.

"Yeah. She didn't show any symptoms until after that night in middle school—" Avery squeezes her eyes shut. "It doesn't matter. Just forget about it."

"What did he do, Avery? For Christ's sake, what the hell did Jack do that makes you and Wren so scared of him? He's just a guy. A teenage boy."

Avery turns her eyes to me, something hard and unknowable in them.

"No, weirdo. He's not just a teenage boy. I know teenage boys. He's not one of them. He might look like one, and his birth certificate might make him one, but he's older. You feel it, right? Even you can't be that thick."

"Feel what?"

"The difference in him."

She looks out the window, and I pull off the highway. The trees flash by, green reflections in her eyes as she speaks.

"He's not like the rest of us. And he never will be."

Of course he's not like the rest of us; he looks like he belongs in an American Eagle ad in a magazine. He's got no heart—or at least, no heart for anyone whose name doesn't start with Soph and end in ia. Of course he's not like us; he's the Ice Prince.

Avery throws her phone in her purse in frustration. "Damn."

"What?"

"I can't get hold of Kayla."

"She's probably busy slathering mud on her face and putting cucumber slices on her eyes or whatever it is you pretty girls do to primp. She has a date tomorrow night."

"What? With who? It better fucking be Wren."

"Wren? Why?"

Avery tries to play it off. "N-No reason. It is Wren, right?"

"No. It's Jack."

"I told her—Wren!" Avery snarls. "Wren, Wren, Wren, and then after Wren she could uselessly go after Jack all she wanted."

"What are you talking about?"

Avery shoots me a look. "You saw how they got along at the bowling alley. Even Jack noticed. Outside of school, where she isn't popular and he isn't a dork, they're great together. Wren's had a crush on her forever."

It dawns on me then.

"You're using Kayla!" I snarl. "Oh my God, you're using her to get the funding for your French club trip to France or whatever! You're *using* your friend!"

"It's not just for me." Avery glowers a hole into my windshield. "Kayla will go. And so will Sophia. It's the last chance I have, all right? The last chance I have to . . . to make it up to her. The surgery might not be now, but it'll be soon. Jack told me. And she might not make it. I might not get to see her ever again."

"That doesn't excuse the fact you're forcing Kayla to flirt with a guy she doesn't like to get what you want—"

"Did he tell you?" Avery interrupts me. "Did Jack tell you how long Sophia has, even if she makes it through the surgery?"

I swallow, hard, and for once my famed motor mouth comes to a standstill. Out of gas. Out of things to say.

Avery looks out the window at the passing forest. "We pretended when we were kids that we lived in France. Princesses. That's what we'd play in her backyard. Princesses of France. And she's got a book—I'm sure she still has it. We put it together. Maybe she burned it. A scrapbook of the things we wanted to do when we grew up. It's full of French stuff. She was taking French, right before—"

She cuts off as I pull into her driveway. Her voice shakes when she continues.

"The school funding is the only shot I have at bringing her to France before—before she can't go anywhere anymore."

"Avery, can't you please, *please* tell me what happened to you and Sophia and Jack and Wren in middle school? Please?"

Avery's green eyes flicker over me, as if she's judging my worth. "You're like him, you know."

"Say what?"

"You're like him," she repeats. "Jack. You're different. People can feel it. That's why you two are at odds, probably. You're so similar. Like two magnets repelling each other."

"Avery, what happened?"

"Back then I still liked Jack. I was like Kayla—obsessed. Sophia and Jack were . . . It was obvious to everyone they were in love. Meant to be together. I couldn't stand it. So I arranged it. I bribed some of the guys who moved crates in my mom's shipping warehouse. Dock workers. Huge idiot guys who'd just go out and get drunk all the time. I bribed them. Money talks loud. I did it. I was a stupid kid and I did it, and now I pay the price for it every day."

I go still. Avery smiles at me, all bitter self-hatred and shadow.

"I told you, weirdo. I'm not good. And I never will be again."

My stomach curdles. But before it can shrivel in on itself, Avery opens the car door and walks out. Into her house. Away from me. Away from the truth.

When I get home, I throw together something easy—ham sandwiches. I take one to Mom, who's reading in the living room, and she smiles and hugs me.

"You look so sad today, honey. Are you all right?"

I force a smile, but today it feels brittle. The conviction isn't behind it. Nothing is behind it, just empty lies and too-full pain.

"I'm fine."

"New school, all that new homework, new friends. And

then me on top of it all! It was definitely not as stressful at
your aunt's. You must be exhausted."

I shake my head fervently. "I'm happy to be here. Honestly. I'm just happy I can be here to help you."

She gets up and kisses my head, murmuring into my hair,
"I'm so lucky to have you."

As I'm leaving to head upstairs, Mom calls me back.

"I saw that girl again today. The one with red hair. I finally remembered where I saw her—she goes to my clinic.
I've stood behind her in line at the receptionist's. She's pre-
scribed the same medicine I'm getting."

"For . . . ?"

"Depression."

She says it delicately, softly, but it's so much better than
what she used to do—pretend nothing was wrong with her
at all, that she didn't need meds.

"She goes to my school," I say.

"I know. She's so young to be on medication. It's tragic."

"I'm gonna go upstairs and finish my applications."

"All right, honey. Good luck! Knock 'em dead."

I escape to my room and shut the door behind me. The
most popular girl in school takes antidepressants instead of
molly or coke or the usual party drug suspects. The most
popular girl in school set in motion a chain of events years
ago that echoes still today.

I'm getting closer to finding out what happened, and winning the war once and for all.

But do I still want to know? Do I still want to war? Jack

defeated me totally today. He pulled out my every secret and laid them bare, chiseling them with a hammer of cruelty. I came to Ohio to escape, to get a fresh start, not to have everything brought up for people to see. He knows. And he could use it against me at any time. How could I have ever thought I liked him? There's nothing there in my heart for him but cold grief now. Grief and anger. I should've been expecting his savagery when I dabbled with Sophia's letters. Avery warned me. She warned me he gets touchy when people reach into the past, and I ignored it. I should've told her to get the letter herself. I should've never started this war.

That's what happens when you trust someone.

I should've never trusted Nameless.

I was an idiot for trusting Jack with my feelings that night at the party.

I clutch at Ms. Muffin and curl up on the bed.

Ugly.

Ugly, ugly.

Is that what you thought this was? Love?

Dark hair. Dark eyes. The smell of a cigarette. A crooked smile that used to make my knees quake and my head go fuzzy, becoming something sinister and evil.

I don't fall in love with fat, ugly girls. No one does.

Ugly.

Ugly.

Ugly girl.

Ms. Muffin's black beady eyes watch me with no pity.

Maybe I'll love you. Maybe, if you hold still.

chapter eleven

I WATCH ISIS LEAVE through the front door. Her thin shoulders are hunched. She's sniffing away the remnants of tears, fists clenched at her sides.

She broke into my house. She's inching herself closer to Sophia to hurt me. She is a nuisance. I should feel nothing for a nuisance like her. Especially not the gentle flame of sympathy that licks at the back of my mind. An urge to prove her wrong, that I'm not like the scum who hurt her. An urge to rip the bastard's balls off and stuff them down his own throat until he chokes.

An urge to protect her.

I scoff and turn away from the window. Avery's sitting in Isis's car. It's typical of Avery to get others to do her dirty work for her, but Isis still agreed to it. She's half at fault.

Avery deserves nothing, no part of Sophia. She doesn't deserve to even read the words Sophia writes.

I sigh and run my hands through my hair. I stink of the dog shit that someone—Isis, probably—threw at my car.

I ran it through a car wash, but it was stubborn. Just like Isis. The girl's a mystery. Most people fall open like books for me to read within a few minutes. Stray animal hairs on their jacket—pet lover. Over-sympathetic. Yellowed teeth—coffee or cigarettes or bad hygiene. All signs of an addiction to punishing oneself. Everyone is simple. No one bothers to hide themselves well. They put on perfume and makeup and designer clothes, but it's a superficial shield that I can read. It takes me minutes to know who they are—if they're particularly difficult, a few hours. People in Northplains, Ohio, aren't exactly complicated and duplicitous. They tend to stick to malls and keg stands, gossip and football games.

But then she came. The new girl—a complete mystery. Most new people settled quickly, but not her. She stood out, with no friends except overeager Kayla. She joined no clique, treated everyone with the same brusque, jovial, self-effacing humor. She isn't afraid of being alone.

She never dropped her guard, her smiles, and her jokes. It's an act, a thick, hard shield forged after years of pain. I know that now. But still, she didn't falter beneath it. She held it up even as I kissed her, even as the pictures of her old self circulated and the whispers about her turned vicious. She held strong. She took the blows, and she struck back at me with more fervor than ever.

The one exception was at the party. Maybe it was the booze, maybe it was just the night air. Maybe she felt it was simply the right moment. But that was the first and only time she's let the shield down. She showed me a glimpse of who she really is; the flippant devil-may-care new girl with a penchant for practical mischief has a heartrendingly tender center, still untouched by the world and its cruelties. With such a strong shield, I expected her to be empty on the inside, hardened all the way through. But when she thanked me for kissing her, when she confessed to having given up on ever being kissed, I was almost afraid to look, as if my gaze alone would be pressing too hard on the gentle petal of a girl that was peeking out. A girl who expected nothing. A girl completely different from the seemingly confident one who strode the halls with snark to spare. A girl who thought so little of herself, she truly, honestly, purely believed she didn't deserve to be kissed. It wasn't even an option for her.

Will Cavanaugh has destroyed her.

She was probably a trusting, naive girl before him, like a daisy. And then he came, and pulled her petals off one by one, forcing her to surround herself with thorns to survive.

But he missed one petal. And she guards it with a tiger's ferocity.

I'd stolen a glance at something she works hard to pretend doesn't exist.

And in my anger at her interference with my life, I threatened the petal.

Part of me feels guilty. Part of me feels proud. I protected Sophia, who has no one left in the world but me. I'm her only protection against the same evils that've scarred Isis so deeply. Sophia came so close to becoming like Isis—angry and bitter and sad—that it gives me chills. Isis is what Sophia could've become, if I hadn't acted on that sweltering August night and protected her.

Isis justifies me.

She justifies what I did. She's the embodiment of the pain that twists girls into tortured things. Seeing her every day is proof I did the right thing. It silences the doubting voices in my head, if only for a few seconds. Wren's avoiding gaze and Avery's fearful one don't sting as much when Isis is around. I know what I did was right, and that conviction is stronger in me when she's near.

I wonder how Isis would've turned out, if I had been there like I was for Sophia. If I, or someone else, had protected Isis, what would she be like now? Would she smile more? Not that contrived kitten smile she makes when she's being sly or feeling satisfied, but a true, happy smile. She'd be just as batshit insane, of course, but she'd do her practical jokes and pranks out of joy, not because she's running from her demons. Not because they're the only things that distract her from the pain.

Her face when I asked her what Will did stabs me in the gut with regret. I regretted the words the second they came out of my mouth, but I couldn't stop them. Anger burned hotter than guilt. But now that it's gone, I feel cold and empty and exactly like the asshole she thinks I am.

"Jack?" Mom's voice wafts through the door. "Can I come in?"

"Yeah."

She opens it carefully and steps in with equally careful

movements. Blue paint is smeared on her cheek, her hair in a messy bun.

"I think—" She takes a deep breath. She's never been good at discipline. I've always had Grandfather for that. But when she's worked up about something, she never backs down from saying it. She's much like Isis in that regard.

"I think she was a really sweet girl. I really liked her. What you said to her wasn't fair. And it was cruel."

"I know."

"Then why did you say it?"

"Because I was panicking. She and I— Mom, she and I have this thing—"

"You aren't going out, are you?"

"No, Jesus no. I have to look after Sophia."

"I know, but, Jack, she doesn't really—" She cuts off, eyes darting around the room. "I love Sophia, I really do. And I know she loves you. But I don't think she loves you in a healthy—"

"I'll apologize to Isis."

Mom drops the train of thought I hate to talk about, and smiles.

"Thank you, sweetie." She comes over and pats my shoulder. "I'd hate to see you lose a potential friend. You have so few of them."

"That's because none of them were interesting," I say, and peer out the window one last time, to where Isis is pulling away from the curb. "Until now."

chapter twelve

I SLEEP FOR AN entire day.

And when I wake up I'm a new person.

I'm empty. I've cried out everything I had in me. I'm an empty shell waiting to be filled with what comes next.

Or I'm just being a total drama queen.

I'm not empty. I'm still a person. I cried over a bad thing that happened in my life, but I probably shouldn't have. Compared to Mom's crisis, mine was small. Compared to a thousand other girls' around the world, mine is insignificant. It wasn't bad. Not compared to everyone else.

It was just a couple seconds.

It wasn't years. It wasn't months, like Mom. It wasn't a family member. Wasn't someone I see anymore. It didn't even hurt. There was no blood.

It wasn't bad. Not compared to others'.

So I should stop crying.

Leo drank too much, threatened to kill Mom jokingly in front of me once or twice. But I always knew he wasn't joking. I could feel it in my bones. I remember they used to shout at each other until Mom was hoarse and Leo took off to the bar. He was awful when I was around, but on a sort of fake best behavior. I can't imagine how bad he was when I was gone, and how bad he was toward the end of their relationship.

Mom's trying her best, despite all of it. So I have to try, too.

I get dressed slowly, carefully. It's a fancy place, but not too fancy, so I choose a shirt and jeans. My hand hovers in my closet, right over the Chanel box with the beautiful pink shirt. The beautiful pink top that doesn't suit me at all. I could still wear it. I could wear it with a jacket over it so no one could see. Mom wouldn't see. No one would see how dumb it looks on me, but it would get some use, at least. It's an expensive shirt. I don't want it to go to waste.

I know this beautiful shirt doesn't suit me. But for once, for one night, I want to be pretty. Not hot, not fabulous, not loud or pushy or annoying. Just . . . pretty. Pretty and sweet and nice, like Kayla. Like so many other girls who are better than me at being a girl.

I pull it on, the chiffon like smooth flowers against my skin. I put my jacket on, and I plan to keep it on. No one else but me needs to know what I look like in the shirt. I check my makeup in the mirror. I look pale and exhausted. A bit of lip gloss and eyeliner can't hide that. I can't even meet my own eyes in the reflection. Everything is too fresh, too open and bleeding.

But Kayla's waiting for the date she's wanted her entire life. Mom's waiting for me to smile at her and tell her everything is fine. I have to be fine. I have to be the one person she can always count on, the one person who's always fine—the huge, sturdy, stable-as-hell rock in the confusing ocean of her recovery.

Mom looks up from her newspaper. "Going out?"

"Yeah, with some friends to the mall." I'm sure it'd go over fantastically if I told her I'm paying an escort to take my friend on a date and subsequently snooping on said date to make sure I get my money's worth.

"Have fun! And drive safe."

"There are leftovers in the fridge. If you need me, I'll have my cell phone."

She waves me off. "Just go!"

"Are you sure? Like, concrete-around-diamond sure you'll be okay?"

"I'll be fine! You're not the mother here, all right? So please, go have fun."

"I love you."

"I love you more."

It almost comes out. Right there, with her face shining with a smile, I almost tell her what happened. But I immediately do a one-eighty. If she knew, she'd be disappointed. She'd be devastated it happened to me. She'd coddle me and try to be strong for me, instead. But that's not what she needs right now. She can barely comfort herself, let alone me. She's broken. Trying to fix me would be stupid when she isn't fixed, either. It's better if she doesn't know.

I've kept it inside this long.

I can do it for a lot longer.

Because I'm strong. Because I'm Isis Blake, and she might not be pretty, or sweet, or well-mannered, but she's very, very strong.

∘ ∘ ∘∘

The sun is just barely kissing the horizon as it sets for the night when I park at the Red Fern. The dimming blue sky is marbled with peach-cream clouds and streaks of blood orange. It's like someone took a bunch of gasoline and poured it all over the sky, then lit a match. But in a beautiful way, not a generally deadly arson way.

The Red Fern is clean and quiet, with sleek polished tables and comfy chairs and potted palms and tropical flowers everywhere. The hostess flashes me a smile. I crane my neck over her and look to the tables. There he is, on his phone. I point, and she waves me past. I sit opposite Jack, who's in a dark shirt and jeans, his hair combed and slightly gelled to one side. He looks bored, slouching in his chair and eyeing everything with the air of someone who's seen it all before. He makes the place look like a photo shoot for Prada or something. Seeing him makes me queasy—how he ripped into me yesterday still fresh in my mind. But this is for Kayla. It's everything she's dreamed of. For her, it's better than an apology, so technically it's also what I've been fighting the war for.

Is this the end of it, then? The end of our battle of wits? Has he won?

"Here." I slip him the envelope of money. "Two hundred, as agreed."

He looks up at me. His icy eyes betray nothing of what he's thinking or feeling. I can't tell if he regrets what he said yesterday at all. He's an infuriating block of ice. He reaches over and counts the bills. Satisfied, he slips them in his pocket.

"If she kisses me, it's an extra twenty-five. If she tries to sleep with me, I'm leaving."

"Are we even talking about the same Kayla? Kayla's timid and virginal as hell. She won't even look at your crotch, let alone go near it. Which, in my opinion, is an obscenely good call, considering the only things that come from that anatomical area are more or less disgusting monsters."

"You seem better."

I scoff. "You don't know what better looks like."

"You're chipper enough to crack jokes. But then again, jokes are like armor for you, aren't they? Easy to hide behind. Easy to distract people with so they don't see how you're really feeling."

"I'm going to be over there." I point at a distant table, half hidden by birds of paradise. "And I'm going to watch your every move to make sure things go well tonight."

"Technically I'm working," he says. "Your vigilance is unnecessary. I'm very serious about my work, and I perform well."

"Oh, I'm sure you do."

I get up and go to the table and order a Sprite. Kayla arrives ten minutes later, and I feel my jaw do a little drop. Her dark hair is combed to perfection, shining in the light and curled over one shoulder. She wears a strapless bright green dress that complements her bronzed shoulders, and her black heels accentuate her long legs. Her eyes are bright and smudged with beautiful smoky makeup, her lips a dewy, pearly pink. She spots Jack and flushes as she glides over. She's a picture-perfect doll, an incredible work of art, the kind of girl poets and writers flip their shit over and write fever-dream books about. Even Jack—Jack, the king of the stone-faced and icy-hearted—looks stunned.

No wonder Wren's got a crush! Look at her! She's a perfect goddess! But Wren's a good guy, so I'm sure it's not all tits and ass with him. He sees how smart she is. Um. Smart at things that aren't school! Like, lipstick! I've seen her identify a lipstick just by smelling it! And she can touch her tongue to her elbow, and she makes incredible brownies, but honestly the only thing you need to know how to make when you look like that is pee and carbon monoxide—

"Miss?" I feel a light tap on my shoulder. My waitress smiles at me, pained. "You're, uh, disturbing the other customers."

An old couple and a family are glaring at me. Kayla and Jack are on the other side of the room, and they aren't looking back, so I'm okay, but I quickly whisper, "Wow, sorry, I was fabulously thinking aloud again, I do that a lot, look, could you get me the noodles? This noodle thingy right here?" I point at the menu. "Thanks, wow. Sorry. But it was probably fabulous so I'm not really sorry though, but still, sorry."

The waitress scuttles away, and I make a shooing motion at the old couple who're still glaring.

"Don't you have something better to work on?" I hiss. "Like golfing or eating prunes or dying?"

The old lady looks shocked.

"Okay, sorry, not dying. But seriously, prunes are good for you."

I peer at Kayla through the leaves. I can see the side of her face, and it's practically glowing. They've ordered, and while they wait they stir their drinks and Jack asks her questions. Kayla talks excitedly, using her hands, and Jack watches with an intense concentration so unlike his usual boredom. He smiles gently when she says something funny, and when she falls silent or talks slower, his expression is kind and caring. Sometimes he interjects slyly and Kayla laughs. It's like a totally different soul has taken over his grotesquely good-looking body. He's all business, and business means making women happy. He's totally capable of it, as long as the money's there.

Does Sophia know, I wonder? Her letter said she knows he works, but has he told her he escorts? He obviously gives the money he makes to the hospital for Sophia's bills, which makes me think her parents aren't in the picture at all, and I know for a fact government funding for sick minors is tight. He's so good at being . . . well . . . good. He's done this escorting thing for a long time. If Sophia knew where the money was coming from, I'm sure she'd make him stop. But he can't afford to stop, can he? Her sickness is bad, and according to Avery, only getting worse. Jack wants to provide her with the best care. He really likes her.

Loves her.

The food arrives, and they eat and talk. My own food comes shortly after and I shovel noodles into my mouth while watching them. Kayla's happier than I've ever seen her. Jack is being patient and humorous and gentle, everything Kayla wants him to be. He's mirroring her. It's not the real him, but she's so in love with it she can't see that.

It's sad.

Maybe that's why Jack's eyes look a little sad.

Or maybe he's thinking of Sophia, how much he wishes it were her across the table instead.

After dinner, they order dessert. Jack gets up to use the bathroom, and shoots a meaningful glance at me. He wants me to follow. I wait a few minutes, then get up and slink behind the mottled glass so Kayla can't see me. I push the door to the men's room open, praying no one sees. Jack leans on the sink, arms folded over his chest and all wisps of the gentleness he had with Kayla gone. It's back to cold Jack Frost.

"I called you in here in case you wanted me to change what I'm doing," he says.

"No, it's fine. It's good." I nod. "You're doing good. It's a little disturbing how good you're doing, actually."

"I told you not to doubt me."

"Never did. I just know you don't respect people."

"I do. If they pay me."

I laugh. "Jesus, you're a piece of work."

"And you're not? I've never met a more stubborn, jaded, cynical girl in my life."

"It's true. I'm very special."

He scoffs, but something in his eyes eases. For a split second, he's the gentle, patient Jack as he says, "You are."

And then he's leaning in, mint and shaving cream and coconut milk from whatever he ate, and he brushes his thumb over my stunned lips. He looks up into my eyes, and freezes, like he realizes what he's doing. He pulls away.

"What the . . ." he murmurs, looking at his hands like they don't belong to him. "You had something on your lip. Forget what I just did. Just—just forget it."

I watch in miraculous horror as Jack Hunter, Ice Prince of East Summit High, turns a soft shade of red, his cheeks blossoming with it.

"Are you . . . are you blushing?" I whisper.

"No! Can't you feel the air temperature? It's ridiculously hot!" he snaps. "I'm leaving and finishing the job. Stay and watch if you want, I don't care."

He's angry. And it's not cold anger—it's hot and instant and boils up and over his icy eyes and marble-perfect lips. He shoves out the door and stalks back to the table. I wait a few minutes, and then go back to mine. He's smiling again, but his face is still a little red, and his laughter is louder and more savage than it was. Kayla doesn't seem to mind, though. They go through almond ice cream with some kind of cookie in it. Kayla tries to feed him, but he refuses and shoots a look at my table that says, "If you make me eat that from her fingers it will cost more." I shake my head and he goes back to politely rejecting it.

Save for the little tantrum he threw in the bathroom (Jack Hunter! Tantrum! The words are opposites!), everything's been going great. Kayla hasn't cried or run away once. And as Jack pays the bill and offers Kayla his arm and she laces hers in his, I get the distinct feeling it's been the best night of her life. I pay my bill and wait, watching them out the window. They stand on the sidewalk, immersed in the golden glow of a lamppost above. Kayla is leaning into his arm, and she looks up and asks him something. He goes still, pauses, and then leans down to kiss her. It's slow and soft, and she melts into him. They look perfect—two beautiful people on a date, kissing beautifully. Usually people look like pigs half mashed into each other, all slobber and tongue, but Jack and Kayla are too pretty for that. It looks like a movie. It looks like they'll walk off into the sunset to live happily ever after.

And I feel . . . jealous?

I put my napkin around my throat and experimentally pull. It would be a great noose. Feeling jealous of love? Since when did that happen? When did I even care about it at all? I don't. It's a false promise, a fool's gold tale, something that doesn't happen to people like me. And yet here I am, jealous. Not of Jack, no. Of Kayla. I'm jealous of the sweet love that shines in her eyes. She can still feel love. She still thinks it's some wonderful, ascendant, pure thing. Even if it's naive, it's still a better way to look at it than the poisonous, to-be-avoided-at-all-costs bog I see love as.

I'm not fourteen anymore. I can't go back to that pure love vision. It's gone. Forever.

I'm jealous of Kayla, and how she's never been hurt.

Sure, Jackass has insulted her a few times with his extreme, tell-it-like-it-is rationality. Maybe Avery told her he's got a sick girlfriend in the hospital, and that hurt her. But she hasn't been torn apart from the inside out. She hasn't been laughed at, pulled at, pushed into.

She's still pure.

I let the napkin drop from my neck and slap my hand over my mouth to stop the sudden rise of vomit in my throat. It hurts. The wound is open and it's hurting again, and I have to get home. I have to find a dark room and curl up there and try to forget. I stagger out of the door, the bell over it tinkling behind me. I only hear it faintly. Everything is blurry and I can't breathe. I try to inhale but fire bursts in my lungs, rips through my body. I'm shivering. Maybe I'm dying. That'd kinda suck to die over nothing at all. To die over something as stupid and idiotic as love. Here Lies a Stupid Little Girl, Who Collapsed Into a Casual Ball of Panic and Pitiful Sobs at the Idea of Love. P.S. Cupid Won This Round, Sucka. That would be my gravestone, and pigeons would poop on it and teenagers would have sex on it, and when the world floods from global warming it'll flood and my pathetic fetal-position bones will float up and I'll wander as a ghost and wail in couples' ears—

"You." A voice cuts through my nausea. "Are you all right?"

I look up. A blurry Jack hovers over me.

I gracefully vomit on his shoes.

It takes me a cool ten minutes of puking in front of my mortal enemy to realize he's helped me into his car and actually what I'm puking off of isn't a curb but the passenger side of his black sedan. He sits in the driver's seat and taps on his phone the entire time. When there's a brief pause in my retching, he looks up.

"Are you done?" he asks.

I immediately try to bolt out of the car and run to my own so I can shove my head into the exhaust pipe and mercifully die, but he pulls my shirt and yanks me back in.

"Just let me die!" I wail.

"Not quite yet. I have uses for you."

"You're so creepy! You're so creepy and I'm so vomity and I mildly hate everything in this conceivable universe!"

"Kayla included?"

I stop wailing to glower at him. "Since I just paid you two hundred moolah to make her happy, obviously no, she is the one thing I do not hate. Her and like, pastries. And small kittens. But everything else can roast in Satan's left armpit!" I whip my head around wildly. "Speaking of, where is she?"

"Went home."

"You . . . you should go home, too." I inch my foot slowly out of the car door. "I'll just—"

I lunge to run away and drown myself in the nearby puddle of homeless person piss, but Jack yanks me back again, reaches over me, and slams the door shut. I pull on the handle.

"You child-locked it!" I gasp.

"Stay here until you feel better," he grunts.

"I feel fine! I'm at least sixteen fines," I assure him. "Look! I can breathe! I can use my legs!" I do bicycle motions in the seat. "I can head-bang!"

I bang my head twice and Jack has the fortunate intuition to roll down the window seconds before I vomit out of it. When I empty my stomach of the last remnants of my noodles, I gasp and pull my head back inside.

"What? Do you get off on watching my fantastic gastrointestinal fireworks? Is that why you're keeping me against my will?"

"You aren't well," he insists stonily. "Sit and relax until you are."

"Relax! Please, tell me, how the hell I can relax when the world's biggest snowman is sitting next to me, talking like he has a heart? It's out of character! It's . . . it's disgusting! You aren't Jack. You're some fucked-up alien from Zabadoo here to take his body back for your beautiful specimen collection, aren't you?"

Jack starts the car. I yank at the door handle twice as hard.

"C'mon, you piece of baby-proof shit! I'm sure babies have actually shit themselves trying to open you, but I won't! I just puked the next twenty-four hours worth of shit out! I'll get you open, I swear I will, or I won't and then I'll be captured by extraterrestrials and, well, it was nice knowing you but really I think whoever invented you made a huge error in judgment when they didn't take the Zabadoobians trapping a fabulous teenage girl in their car into consideration."

Jack takes a sharp left turn and the momentum squashes my face against the window. I quickly put my seat belt on.

"Where are we going?" I ask.

"I'm taking you on a date."

I immediately regret ever hiring him for tonight. And also living. Jack must see my panic, because he sighs.

"It's your first date, right?"

"Uh, yes? But, you don't really have to do that? Considering it's not something you want to do? And I don't really need one, or like, even really want one? Dates are for people in love and that's never going to happen for me again so I really don't think it's necessary."

"It's an apology. For how I acted yesterday. Nothing personal, and nothing romantic."

"Oh." I brighten, but some buried part of me sinks. I punt the feeling out of this universe along with the last of the Zabadoobians. "Right. An apology. Okay."

"You sound disappointed."

"I don't want you to be alarmed, but I think you might be

crazy. I am the opposite of disappointed. I am oppopointed. Disaposite. There is nothing I would like more than to go on a not-date with my worst enemy who just went on a date with my friend, which, by the way, I paid him to do."

"You're also babbling."

"And I'm babbling! How cool is that! Just drive so we can get this over with, you alien!"

He smirks and steps on the gas.

chapter thirteen

WE DRIVE FOREVER. FIVEEVER. Sixever. Sevenhundredever. We wind past decrepit buildings skinned with age and scabbed with graffiti. A murder of crows fights over a loaf of bread a homeless person scatters about. Huge neon signs in Korean and Chinese blare in all colors of the rainbow, the smell of fried chicken and sesame seeds pouring in. It's the exact opposite of the clean, fancy area of town I was vomiting all over.

"Are you taking me to a black-market butcher to sell me for body parts?" I politely inquire. Jack pulls into a parking space and takes the keys from the ignition.

"Get out. It's a bit of a walk."

He gets out and I follow his stride down the dark sidewalk.

"You know, if you wanted my liver, all you'd have to do is ask nicely. I'm sure we could work something out. With my fist in your face."

"Body parts aren't on the menu with you. Tonight, or any night in the future."

"Oho! Was that a double entendre? Thanks, but when you're as fantastic as I am you can't afford to sleep with nerds."

He suddenly veers right, into a tiny alleyway. So this is where I meet my end—in an alley of Chinatown, chopped up into little pieces and shipped to China to replace some old businessman's cirrhosis-infested liver. My eyes widen when he pushes open a tiny door and walks three or so steps down into a restaurant. A counter sits in the middle, glass cases holding gleaming ruby slabs of tuna and pale swathes of yellowtail. Sushi chefs expertly slice and dice and mash rice. Only a few people are at the bar, and the hostess, a short Japanese woman with a dimpled face, quickly darts to us.

"Jack!"

"Fujiwara-san." He inclines his head. She reaches up and, to my utter shock, pinches his cheeks like he's a child.

"Look at you! All bones, no fat! You haven't been eating!"

"I eat well enough," Jack insists, not even trying to push her away as she straightens his shirt collar for him. Her dark eyes lock onto me, and she smiles.

"Who is this? A friend? You've never brought any of your friends before. I was beginning to think you didn't have any!"

"She's not my fr—" he starts, then gives up. "Fujiwara-san, this is Isis Blake."

"Ahh, Isis-chan!" Fujiwara bows, and I bow back and almost take down the tiny bamboo plant on the counter. "It's good to meet you."

"Nice to meet you, too," I say.

Fujiwara turns to Jack. "Usual?"

He nods. "Please."

"Right this way!" she crows. She totters in traditional wooden sandals over to the bar, seating us at two stools. She's quick with the drinks—two cups of bitter yet refreshing green tea. She hands us the menus and pats my back, black eyes gleaming into mine. "Please enjoy."

"I will. Um. Thank you."

Jack peruses the menu in silence. The Asian couple next to us eat and laugh, talking with their sushi chef in Japanese.

"How did you find this place?" I whisper.

"Fujiwara's daughter was a client of mine," he says. "She brought me here once. It's got the best sushi in Ohio. You don't have to eat anything, if you don't want to. I'd guess you don't feel all that well after puking so much."

"Then why'd you bring me here?"

He shrugs. "I thought tea and a dark, quiet place would calm your stomach."

"Trust me, it's not my stomach that's the problem. It's me! In general! How awesome is that!"

"Not very awesome at all," he concludes.

"So . . . what about Fujiwara's daughter? Do you still see her?"

"She left. Got married, actually, to an American businessman, and went back to Japan." He opens his phone and pulls up a picture of a fat, happy Japanese baby in a Santa hat, showing it to me. "She sends me pictures of their son."

"Do they all do that?"

He turns off the phone. "No. Yukiko was special. She . . . understood me more than most do. She was the only client of mine who held my interest for more than five seconds. So we keep in touch."

"Did you have—"

"Not that it's any of your business, but no. She hired me to pose as her boyfriend so her ex would stop harassing her."

"Oh. That's actually pretty cool, that you get to meet so many different people."

He shrugs. The sushi chef says something to him in Japanese, and he talks back in surprisingly smooth-sounding Japanese. He looks to me.

"Do you want anything?"

My stomach politely reminds me it's empty again with a rollicking gurgle.

"This thing." I stab at the menu. "Whatever that is, I want two of it."

He snickers and says something to the chef, who nods and starts chopping fish and taking out rice. We watch him work, since I don't know what to say and Jack is quiet.

"They spend years washing rice," he says finally.

"What?"

"To be a sushi chef, you spend years washing rice. Two, at cheap sushi places. Ten at the expensive, traditional ones."

I suck in air. "Jesus! Just making rice? The entire ten years?"

He nods. I look at the rice with a newfound admiration. It's gotta be some damn good rice.

I sip tea and nervously realize I'm on a date with Jack Hunter. I then proceed to gulp tea and scald my voice box. I gasp, and Jack cordially hits me on the back a few times to make sure I'm not choking. The chef gives me a concerned look, but Jack waves it off.

"Why?" I gasp.

"Why what?" Jack looks to me, icy eyes piercing.

"Why me?"

"You've never been on a date." He says it like a fact, not a question. I glower.

"Duh."

"So. This is your first date. Consider it a learning experience."

"What am I supposed to do? Talk about my hair? Ask you about your job? My hair is flawless and I already know what your job is!"

"Normally, a male and a female on a date will talk about whatever comes up naturally."

"Uh, right, but you and I ain't exactly natural."

"An immovable object meeting an unstoppable force," Jack says lightly.

"Two unstoppable forces *crashing and careening off a cliff to their untimely deaths*," I correct.

"Oil and water."

"Oil and *firebombs*."

He raises an eyebrow in partial agreement and takes a sip of his tea. The sushi arrives, and octopus and eel and tuna melt in my mouth. Everything is so fresh and delicious I can barely stand it. I wiggle my butt and make contented humming noises.

Jack looks at me. "Are you having a seizure?"

"I'm happy! It tastes awesome."

"So you squirm and make tuneless little noises when you're happy?"

I frown and become self-conscious. I eat with more decorum, but Jack scoffs.

"I didn't mean— It's fine. It's just . . . interesting of you. Almost cute."

I feel an electric surge crawl up my spine and settle in my brain, buzzing. *Cute. Cute.* Jack just called me—

"In a deranged puppy way," he adds. The electricity leaves and I realize how stupid I was for thinking anyone would willingly call me cute. I'm not cute. Loud, sure. Rude, yup. Not cute. Never cute.

The sushi goes quickly, so we order seconds and wait.

"So, I mean," I start. "How did you get into, um. You know."

Jack sips tea thoughtfully, then puts the cup down.

"There's a surgery. It's expensive, and experimental. But it's got a decent success rate and it would give Sophia years to live. Maybe even get rid of the thing for good. I've been taking on double outcalls to make the down payment on it, and I've almost got enough. The two hundred you gave me for Kayla will put a nice dent in what's left."

"Happy to help."

He sighs and leans back. "I used to work tables. Waiting at a

French restaurant in Columbus. It was good money, and it kept her bills afloat, but then Sophia started getting worse. The surgery came from Sweden. My money was good, but not enough to pay for that on such short notice. And then one night, I waited on the table of the founder of the Rose Club. Blanche Morailles. She gave me a much better option, with higher pay. High enough to make the money for the surgery in a year and a half. I didn't know if Sophia would last that long, so I—"

Jack shakes his head. "She's been doing well so far. I've got another month to go, and then I'll have enough. She just has to hold on for another month."

I was right. He's escorting to get a lot of money, fast. For Sophia. All of the trouble—acting like he cares about other women, kissing them, sleeping with them. All for Sophia. I stir my drink, and Jack frowns.

"I know what you're thinking."

"Doubtful," I say.

"You think I shouldn't escort. You think it's bad, or unlawful, or whatever."

"You . . . you have to *sleep* with people—"

"I've told you, it only happens rarely. And it's not as if I'm forced to do it. I'm free to refuse whenever I wish."

"Then you should always refuse."

"If I do it, they're pleased. They give me more money. More money means more funding for Sophia's surgery sooner. It's simple. Sleeping with people is easy," he says tersely. "It means nothing. It's a mechanical action. It requires nothing of me I am hesitant to give. The women are usually considerate, and well-spoken, and gracious. Sometimes they're difficult, or into darker things, but I adapt."

"They use you."

"And I agree to it. So they don't really use me. If anything, I'm using them equally. It's not all one-sided. It's a mutual agreement. And as far as escorting businesses go, it's a good one. No men. Blanche doesn't make me take male clients, and for that I'm grateful. It's a good deal. A fast job that can save Sophia. So I'll keep doing it, for however long it takes."

"Why not just ask your mom for the money? She's got a lot, and I'm sure she'd want to help . . ."

"No. I have to help Sophia on my own. She is my responsibility. No one else's. I can protect her myself."

His voice finishes with a hard, determined edge. Our next round of sushi arrives. We eat in total silence.

"Are . . . are you okay?" I ask.

"I'm fine," he says, face icily passive.

"Yes, well, it's a little hard to tell, considering I've seen constipated rocks display more emotion."

"I don't need a moron asking how I feel."

"I'm just trying to be nice! You're such a fat doodoo shitbaby!"

"Occasionally I have fantasies of intellectual conversation." He sighs. I'm so angry I start up from my stool only to bump into Fujiwara, who's behind me carrying a tray of tea. Boiling tea. It spills all over me, drenching my jacket. I yelp and unzip it quickly, throwing it to the ground.

"Oh, Isis-chan, I'm so sorry!" Fujiwara cries. "I'm so, so sorry, I didn't see you, it's my fault."

"It's okay!" I assure her. "It's okay, really, I was the idiot who didn't look—"

"No, no, it's all my fault—"

Jack stands, and together the three of us pick up the teacups and help Fujiwara mop up the mess, even as she refuses help and apologizes in an endless stream. She mumbles something about making up for it, and disappears into the double doors of the kitchen. Jack and I sit down, and the bar settles, and it's only thirty seconds of having my jacket off before I realize what a horrible mistake it is.

The pink shirt. I'd forgotten all about it. It shimmers and quivers with my every movement. My shoulders are exposed. You can practically see through the translucent material to where my polka-dot bra is. I look stupid. I can feel everyone staring at me and I know they think I look stupid, and ugly, and that it doesn't suit me.

Jack's gone still, frozen halfway while raising his teacup to his mouth. His eyes are on me, on every part of me as he looks me up and down with a slow, deliberate gaze.

I start to pull my wet jacket back on, but Jack's hand stops me. "What are you doing?"

"It's not right," I hiss. "I didn't mean to— I wasn't supposed to take it off. It looks stupid on me—"

"No," he interrupts. "Not at all."

"Just—" I reach for my jacket.

"It's beautiful," he says softly, then clears his throat. "You look . . . beautiful."

An iron fist squeezes my heart, my throat, my stomach, and then lets go, a bittersweet burn spreading through my body like fire. I savor it one moment, and then suspect it the next, and then I realize what's really happening.

"I get it!" I smile. "You're still in escort mode from all that time with Kayla! It was only a few minutes ago your date ended, after all."

"What? No, I—"

"It's okay, really! You just forgot to flip the switch back from escort you to regular you. Totally understandable. Work and life are hard to compartmentalize. Thanks for the compliment though. I bet I'd have to pay at least ten bucks to hear it if I were a client, huh? But I got it for free. Score!"

"Isis—"

Jack's cut off by Fujiwara crowing apologies as she comes between us with a tray of tiny tea cakes, cookies, and a few scoops of green tea ice cream. I pull my jacket on and zip it all the way up to my chin. I chat with Fujiwara excitedly the entire time I eat dessert, talking about how good the sushi was, and where she gets her fish, asking the best tips for getting green tea stains from jackets, and thanking her for the sweets. Jack's silent, picking at the cookies, and Fujiwara brings him the bill.

"I'll pay half," I offer, leaning over to look at the price tag. My eyes practically bug out. Jack waves the envelope I gave him the money in.

"You already have."

We drive back to the Red Fern parking lot in silence. I busy myself with my phone, trying not to see the white knuckles Jack has on the steering wheel.

"You must be tired," I say when he pulls into the parking lot and I get out. "Get some rest, okay? And thanks for the practice date! Not that I'll ever need to practice, since, you know, it's never going to happen, but it was a nice thought. I had fun. Sort of."

"You'll have more fun," Jack says, hands in his pockets and a faintly pained look in his eyes. "You'll go on more dates, with other guys. Good guys. And you'll have fun."

I shake my head. "I won't. I told you—that kind of stuff isn't for me."

"It is," Jack insists. "You'll fall in love someday."

I laugh. "Nope. Never again. It's been three years, and it'll be a hundred more. Drive safe, okay?"

I whirl around and start walking to my car. I swear I feel fingers glance over my hand, but they pull away just as quickly. Or maybe it was the wind. I don't look back. I drive home. When I check on her room, Mom is mercifully asleep, safe and sound. I pull the shirt off as soon as I can and throw it in the closet to rot.

Beautiful.

⊙ ⊙ °⊙

Part of me wanted to grab her. To pull her back. To hold her. Another part of me knows she'll hate the first guy to do it after so long.

And the third part of me is afraid. Afraid at her conviction. Afraid of how convinced she is that she'll never love
again. Afraid of how pretty she looked in that shirt. Afraid
of how sad she sounded when she convinced herself I didn't
mean what I said.

I am afraid of the things I am beginning to feel.

Because I haven't felt anything new, for anyone new, for
so long.

I might not be able to convince her that the world isn't
devoid of gentleness. But I can at least make her smile, if
only for a moment.

◉ ○ °◦

I wake up to Kayla's texts filled with smiley faces and exclamation marks, describing her date—how kind Jack was, how
good the food they ate was, and how he kissed her like he
loved her. She's going to ask him out again on Monday, and
she thanks me a million times for whatever I did to get him
to go out with her.

Mom's at the table, sipping coffee.

"Sleep well?" I ask.

Mom smiles and nods. "Pretty well. You must've gotten in
late, I didn't hear you. Did you have fun?"

I recall the sushi place, and how delicious it was. I remember the tea and puking and Jack's soft eyes—

Beautiful.

"Yeah." I force a smile. "It was fun."

"Boys?"

"Just one."

Mom quirks a brow, smiling. "Oh really? Not a dozen guys this time? Just one? He must be special. Care to tell me about him?"

"Nothing happened! I just— There was a guy."

"Booze?"

"Not even a bit of sake."

"So it was a sushi place? With a boy? Sounds very suspect, young lady. Did you use protection?"

"Mom!" I snap, my face heating. "I've told you repeatedly: boys have cooties and bad hygiene. No one likes them except other boys and people with no sense of smell."

"So I can expect you to bring home a girl one of these days? I'll try to act shocked." She smiles.

"I'm not bringing anyone home!" I wail. "I know it's hard to believe, but some people my age aren't entirely obsessed with the idiotic game called dating! Some of us have lives! And generally higher goals than messing around in the mud with our peers. I've got colleges to apply to! And friends to hang out with! And an entire life to plan!"

"Whatever you say," Mom singsongs. I get a pan and start the burner, taking out a few eggs and slices of bacon. I can feel Mom's eyes on my back, watching me, contemplating how much I've grown up or something equally annoyingly parental. The smell of sizzling bacon fat fills the kitchen. The birds chirp outside, sun streaming through the curtains. It's beautiful.

Beautiful.

My skin prickles as his voice reverberates in my head. It makes me fumble with the pan and nearly sends all of breakfast casually crashing to the floor. Goddamn him! Even if he didn't mean it, it still sticks in my head, like a grass thistle in my clothes.

And to put the shit cherry on top of a shit sundae, I can't even lash out at him over it. The war is over.

I know that from how happy Kayla seemed. With her now potentially satiated, I have no reason to attack him, other than general dislike and boredom. And those are petty. So petty I don't know if I'll have the heart to fight him with them.

It's over.

I'm supposed to be happy. I won, more or less. Or we ended on equal terms, with me slightly winning. Or am I losing? Did him calling me that awfully wrong word mean he won? Does it even matter who won or lost? It's over, and now I have nothing to look forward to. Nothing to scheme, nothing to plot for. Just emptiness where the war used to be. And somehow it hurts more than it should. I'd gotten so used to it, to exchanging barbed words with Jack whenever we passed in the hall or catcalling him with insults, that I've forgotten how to be normal. Do I just smile at him? No, that's repulsively, completely, definitely gross. All the other girls do that.

I spend the rest of the day finishing my college applications. I stare at them all—Seattle, Oregon—and secretly I know I'm only going to be sending off the one to Redfield. It's the closest. It's the only one that'll let me still look after Mom and get a college career at the same time. I don't have siblings; I'm the only person she has left. I can't leave her, hurt her like everyone else has. I dipped into my Europe traveling fund to pay for Kayla's date last night. I've pretty much all but given up on that dream, anyway.

But it's for the best. It's the right choice. Not the one I wanna do, but the right one. And that's all that matters.

I stare at the thing on my wrist. The pockmarks will always be here, burned into me by Nameless, by his cigarettes. Mom's never seen them. I've been careful, the same way people who cut are careful. I searched their forums for tips on how to keep things hidden—wrist bandages, long sleeves always, sweatbands, and thick, chunky bracelets. Kayla's the only one who's seen it. And she treated it respectfully, without asking questions or prying too hard. Kayla's my only real friend in this place.

She deserves to be happy.

chapter fourteen

JACK HUNTER SAID I'M beautiful. There is only one conclusion as to what must be done.

Jack Hunter's gotta die.

Or he can cry like a huge nerd.

I'm not picky.

He's stepped over the line one too many times. He's confused me too many times. The line between us is faded and scuffed and I'll have to draw it back on with paint, carefully, and it'll probably take hours and my back will get sore and honestly he had no right to kiss me or take me on a date even if they were fake and he certainly, absolutely, positively had zero right to call me beautiful without my express permission. It was uncalled for and mostly a huge fat lie, and lying is punishable by death. Or it should be. Uh, except for me. Because I've lied a lot. To Mom, to Dad. To myself. I should get exiled instead. To Maui.

I park and give an explosive sigh into my car. The war might be over, and I might be exhausted, but I have to get him back one last time. Just once, for messing with my feelings. Not that he did. Just, uh, he sort of kind of toyed with them, but I knew it was fake all along, so he didn't really. But still. The fact that he even said those lies to me objectively deserves some sort of minor capital punishment.

Also, because Jack is now going out with Kayla.

I get out of the car and make my way to Principal Evans's office.

The first day Kayla grabbed Jack's hand and he let her and they walked down the halls together, you could practically hear the hearts of a hundred ladies breaking in two. Poetry Girl burned her notebook. Drama Club Wailer performed the greatest tragic screaming monologue from Shakespeare the drama teacher had ever seen. The girl who's making the statue almost smashed it, but the art teacher convinced her to put it aside and finish it later, when she was in a better state of mind. A huge majority of lady teachers took sick leave. To go cry into tubs of ice cream and watch *Sex and the City*, probably.

I see the legendary couple as I walk through the quad before the morning bell. They're sitting on a bench. Kayla kisses him on the cheek, and he nods. Just nods, doesn't smile. Doesn't say thanks or kiss her back. It's like he's just tolerating her. But Kayla can't see that.

She gets nasty glares, so I've taken it upon myself to be her personal bodyguard. I just never say that out loud. It just sort of is. Homeland security for Kayla. And her fabulous breasts. Kayla's so wrapped up in love, she's all but oblivious to everything else, so that means I get to pull hair and wave warning fingers and punch a few harlots. Or five harlots. Evans isn't happy.

His secretary, now completely used to my venerable presence, waves me through. I throw my backpack on the ground and flop into a chair.

He folds his hands on his desk and sighs.

"The papers are right there."

I pull the stack of papers toward me and get out a pen. In exchange for not being suspended for punching people like I was at my previous school, I get to help Evans grade math homework. He somehow found out it's the one thing I'm good at, probably from Mrs. Gregory, the snitch. I knew I should've played dumb in her class. But now I get to sit here and grade these sheets while Evans pretends he isn't actually testing my abilities in the slightest. He usually drinks coffee and answers emails, but today he watches me work. I flip through papers, making tiny tick marks and writing the correct answer by each wrong one. The first day he offered the answer sheet to me, but I brushed it off. He later checked my work against it. After that he hasn't offered the answer sheet again.

"You are very good at this, Isis."

"Yup."

"Your SAT was rather miserable, though. Why is that?"

I sneer. "Well golly gee, Mr. E. Maybe it was because I didn't eat breakfast that morning! Or maybe it was because I had explosive diarrhea! Or maybe it was because I was going through a bit of an emotional crisis! I was eighty-five pounds heavier, with a boy—"

Ugly.

"—with some problems! Wow. A teenager with problems. Imagine that."

He glowers and takes a sip of coffee. We both know I haven't forgiven him for the picture incident, and I never will.

"You should take it again," he insists. "There's still time, before college applications are due. You could get a very high score."

"And make your school look even better," I mumble. Mr. Evans frowns.

"Come now, Isis. It's not just about our reputation. Any school would be happy to have a female who can do math so well and easily. And according to your report card, your English isn't bad at all. You could go to some extremely prestigious schools with those kinds of SATs. You could further your own life; make a great start for yourself."

"Redfield University is fine with me."

Mr. Evans laughs, and then when he realizes I'm not joking, his face falls.

"Isis, are you serious? I'm talking MIT, UCLA. Redfield is for people who aren't smart enough for anywhere else. You could go where you wanted! Wherever you wanted in the country! Possibly out of the country! There are programs in China, Brazil, Europe!"

I flinch at the last word and scribble an answer.

"I-I have no interest in traveling. It's full of rude people and food poisoning."

Mr. Evans falls silent and watches me work for a while longer. I press on, determined to ignore his gaze. Finally, he turns on his computer and starts answering emails.

Wren comes up to me at lunch. Kayla stopped sitting with me long ago, instead hanging with Jack at his usual empty table. She tries to feed him soup and he grimaces, but she laughs. She sees me staring and waves, smiling. Jack looks at me, and I quickly turn around and bury myself in my PB and J. Wren stares at the couple with his intense hazel gaze.

"It's true, then? They're really going out?"

"You just heard about that *now*?"

He shrugs. "I've been working in the council office most of the last few weeks. Crunch time is coming for the budgets, and I'm training Miranda to succeed my position when I leave next year, and the food bank was broken into last night, and they can't afford a new lock, so I called in some favors with Arnold's locksmith father—"

Wren sees my eyes glazing and sighs.

"Sorry. I'm rambling about completely uninteresting things."

"Duh. But that doesn't mean I'm not sorry. It sounds rough."

"It's just presidential duties." He smiles wanly. His eyes flicker over to where Kayla is laughing at something Jack said. His stare dulls, eyes almost ashamedly looking away.

"You like her," I say. It isn't a question. I expect Wren to get flustered or change the subject, but he just stares at Kayla again and nods.

"Yes."

"And Avery was pushing her toward you for a while."

"To get funds for her club. I know how she works. But I—" Wren looks wistfully at Kayla over my shoulder. "Kayla was paying attention to me on her orders. But I tried to push that out, and just focus on her attention. Kayla, talking to me and listening to me and laughing with me, when she'd never even given me the time of day before. I tried to . . . selfishly pretend she was doing it because she wanted to, not because Avery told her to."

Wren falls quiet. I touch his hand.

"Shit, dude. I'm sorry."

Wren smiles. "It's fine. I mean, it's not fine. But as long as she's happy—" He looks to her again. "Then I'll be all right."

"You're a good guy."

"No." Wren laughs. "I'm a stupid guy. And Jack's a frightening guy. So I'll watch from afar, and make sure he won't hurt her. Even if that's creepy and pathetic."

"It's not. It's sensible."

"Avery's pissed, too," Wren says, jerking his head to Avery and her tableful of likewise fashionably dressed girls. Avery glowers at Kayla, stabbing her salad with unnecessary enthusiasm.

"Why?"

"Kayla stopped talking to me. Fake-flirting. Avery came

to me this morning and tried to flirt instead, but I wouldn't have it. I guess Kayla refused to take Avery's orders."

I smile, pride welling in my chest. "She's getting stronger."

"Yeah," Wren murmurs. "But at what cost? What if Jack— What if he—"

Wren takes a bite of burrito and swallows nervously.

"What did he do back in middle school? Give me a hint. Just one tiny dust bunny–sized hint."

Wren's silent, glowering.

"Avery told me she hired guys from her parents' docks. She said she hated Sophia. What did she hire them to do? I know you know. I know you were there when it happened."

He flinches.

"Avery told me to film it. That's the only reason I was there. I was head of the film club in middle school. I had access to all the cameras, so she bribed me into coming to the park and hiding in the bushes with her and filming it."

"Filming *what*?" I whisper.

The lunch bell rings before he can answer, and he gets up and leaves quickly, shame crippling his face.

I walk alongside Jack and Kayla as they go to their next class. I zap a revenge-suspect with a glare, and she veers off course with her handful of shaving cream. *That's right, keep walking. There'll be no shaving-cream-on-Kayla's-lovely-face incident today, thank you very much. Or, if there is, I will shave you. Down to the bone.*

"You're making threats aloud," Jack deadpans.

"It's good for business," I chime. Kayla smiles, and links her other arm with mine.

"I've got two of my favorite people right here. It's amazing. You're amazing!"

I shoot her a sheepish smile and she ruffles my hair. How could I have ever been jealous of such a lovely girl's innocence? I'm ashamed of myself, a hot knot working its way into my throat, chock-full of guilt. She deserves a better friend than me. She deserves castles and kingdoms and all the fairy-tale endings that still exist in this meager world. All of them should be hers.

She kisses Jack on the cheek and goes into the chem lab. Jack and I stand outside the door, each with different classes, but a tense thread rooting us to our place in front of the mottled glass.

Jack speaks without looking at me. "You're happy."

"Generally, yeah."

"No. Not generally. Generally you're miserably sad and dour, hiding it behind the jokes and passionate outbursts. You're like fire. But it's a sickly fire. Everyone can see that."

I open my mouth to argue when he interrupts. "But when you're with Kayla, when she's happy and smiling at you, that fire turns. It goes from sick to full, healthy, lively. She makes you happy."

"She's the first friend I've ever really had."

"That's what I figured."

"Why are you cheating on Sophia with her?"

He doesn't flinch, but his eyes splinter with a fraction of pain. "I'm not cheating. I visit Sophia every week—"

"Are you Sophia's boyfriend?"

Jack's eyes grow dangerous. "I was. Once. She has no one but me now, so I am as much as I can be to her."

"Is that a yes?"

"What makes you think you deserve an answer?" he snarls.

"I'm just trying to look out for you, Casanova! What if I accidentally slip to Kayla who Sophia is? Kayla would be devastated, if she knew you were going out with two ladies—"

"I'm not," he says, all steel and glacier ice. "Sophia and I . . . it's complicated. But we're not together in that way. Not anymore."

"But you love her."

"I do," he replies without missing a beat. "I always will."

His conviction is so foreign to me. Guys don't have willpower. Not the ones I know. Except Wren, but he's an outlier. Regardless, even fewer of them love a girl deeply enough to keep loving her, even if they aren't together. Sophia and Jack's relationship must have been amazing.

A kernel of jealousy sprouts in me again. I'll never know what that's like, to love someone that much. Ever. I shake my head.

"But why go out with Kayla all of a sudden?" I ask. "I thought . . . I thought you didn't really like her? You kept saying she's annoying. So why go out with her?"

Jack fixes his icy eyes on me, hair falling into them a little. He doesn't answer, and pivots and strides away, the crowd parting around him. For him.

o   o   °°

Isis looked up at me with those warm, burning, flame-mahogany eyes and asked me, "So why go out with her?"

She's oblivious. I still don't believe it myself. But I know it's the right thing to do.

She has no idea how much Kayla's smile makes her smile. Unconscious, soft grins form on her face when she looks at a happy Kayla, and full-blown joy crackles across her features when she laughs with Kayla. Kayla reminds her of who she used to be, maybe—naive and innocent.

But as Isis cocks her head and waits for my answer, she doesn't realize in that moment she's just as innocent as Kayla. She's never been loved. She's only given love. She has no idea why someone like me would go out with her friend, if only to make her friend happy, and her happy in turn. As long as Kayla can kiss my cheek and talk about *Vogue* and Nicki Minaj with me, Isis smiles. Real, true smiles. Smiles free of pain or jaded bitterness. Isis truly doesn't believe anyone would like her enough to kiss her, let alone do something to make her smile. There's no coyness in her question. She simply has no idea what it's like to be loved.

Love? I frown and scratch out the notion with an imaginary mental pen. But as I walk away from her, the answer too hard to say, the urge to turn around and look at her just one more time before I go is overpowering.

It's evidence.

It's cold hard fact that mental pens don't need to scratch anything out.

When had it happened? How stupid and predictable was it? The new girl—the manic, rambunctious, permanently sugar-high girl—barreling into town like a whirlwind and demanding I pay attention. Demanding I fight. Demanding everything but the one thing that's begun to grow inside me.

I should burn it.

The plant is still young. It hasn't flowered yet, its roots haven't laced over my heart just yet. I can still stop it. It's not too late. Sophia is still a strong flower in my chest. She's the only one who should matter. Guilt sickens me. Sophia. I'm being unfaithful, aren't I? Escorting wasn't truly cheating—I loved none of the women. None at all. They were cows to be milked for money, and that was it. I love only Sophia. Sophia has always been there. Sophia is sick, and she needs me. I can't abandon her, or leave her. I'm the only one she has. It was never a problem, since no other woman ever held my attention. But now . . .

Something tears at me, serrated and sharp.

It's too late.

I'm an idiot, and it's too late.

Avery invites Kayla and me to her Halloween party on Saturday. I'm a little wary, since Avery smiled too much at Kayla when she invited us, but I'll go, if only to make sure Kayla doesn't meet any trouble. And with all the popular girls who've had a crush on Jack forever being invited too, I triply have to go. I will be the silent protector Gotham Kayla needs.

"You're going as that?" Kayla sniffs at my tight-fitting latex Batgirl costume. I wince and adjust a brewing camel toe.

"It's a symbol of my commitment to justice!" I crow, and whip out a fake bat-star from my utility belt. Kayla laugh-sighs and pulls my chin up. Her mermaid costume—a skirt with a tail—drags behind her, and her bra is shimmery and made of spray-painted seashells. Her dark hair is woven with smaller shells, and her makeup is green-blue and like-wise sparkly.

"Okay, just hold still and let me do your makeup, at least."

"Make me look like an actual bat."

"Ew! No!"

"Give me a huge proboscis like those weird bats in Africa."

"Ugh!"

"Smear my face in guano."

"Okay, that's it, you're being nasty and it's ruining your eyeliner so you need to officially stop."

I laugh and mime zipping my mouth shut as she works, fingers delicately smearing eye shadow and lip gloss and foundation on my face.

"They don't even put this much makeup on dead people for open-casket wakes," I complain.

"Hush. I'm almost done."

When she's finished, I open my eyes and look at a whole new person. Smoky eyeliner and pink gloss make me look—

"Beautiful!" Kayla claps her hands.

"Not ugly," I correct. "Your work is great, it's just my face. Sorry you didn't have something nicer to work with."

"Oh, shut up!" She smacks my shoulder. "Now c'mon. We're gonna be late."

She grabs her purse and keys and stops in the living room, tiptoeing into her father's study. She's only gone for a few seconds before she dashes out, a bottle of expensive-looking whiskey in hand and squealing.

"C'mon c'mon c'mon run run run!"

I shriek in the back of my throat for no reason and run after her out the door, my cape billowing in the cool October night. The sky is steely and filled to capacity with heavy rain clouds. As we pull up to Avery's jack-o'-lantern-lined driveway, a few fat drops of rain start to fall. Orange and black lights are strung everywhere inside; bowls of orange punch and pumpkin cookies and cinnamon cakes crowd the kitchen counter. Girls dressed as skin-showing cats and nurses and witches crowd the house, and guys in football-player costumes and president costumes and rapper costumes with ridiculous gold chains stride around. I high-five the guy who's dressed up as Pac-Man, because he's the only creative costume here.

As more people arrive, the line of booze bottles on the counter doubles, triples. As the night grows darker, the jack-o'-lanterns glow eerily on the porch, the wind howling through the trees outside. Guys scare girls and girls shriek, and someone starts the music when Avery finally comes down in a resplendent princess dress, complete with a tiara, perfectly curled red hair, and a fluffy blue ball gown.

"You look amazing, Ave!" Kayla shouts. Avery gives her a shark-smile and they hug in that cheek-kiss way popular girls do. Avery's eyes whisk over me and she laughs.

"What are you supposed to be? A drowned rat?"

"Batgirl, you heathen. Duh."

Avery sighs. "It's a good thing I invited you. After that fountain stunt, you're the girl to go to for hilarious entertainment at your expense. You don't mind looking like an idiot, right? Making a fool of yourself? Good. Do that tonight. A lot."

"You forget yourself, your highness," I sneer. "But I don't take orders from you. So you can shove that plastic scepter up your butt and painfully poop it out later."

Kayla barely manages to contain her laughter until Avery storms away, and then she explodes with it. "Did you see the look on her face?"

"It won't last. She feeds on pain and ineptitude and from the look of this crowd—" I glance around at everyone barely getting tipsy. A guy draws a penis on a jack-o'-lantern and a girl pulls down an entire string of lights by getting it caught in her angel wings. "That will be plentiful tonight."

I wave at Wren, who walks in dressed in green as Link
from the Zelda video games. He's even got a cool replica
plastic sword. He walks over and shyly blushes. "H-Hey."

Kayla sighs. "What are you supposed to be, anyway?"

"Uh, Link?" I inform her. "From Zelda?"

"Who from what? Is that a TV show?"

I roll my eyes at Wren, but he just laughs it off.

"Yeah, it's a TV show. It came out a long time ago, though."

"Oh, so it's like a vintage thing. Cool." Kayla smiles. A
second later she shrieks in my ear. "There he is!" Kayla
squeals. "Promise you won't drag him into a fountain this
time, okay? I want to spend some quality time together
tonight!"

I look to where Kayla is pointing—Jack just walked in. I
should've known; that's why all the girls in the room are whispering to each other and smiling coyly. My jaw would drop if
I weren't so exquisitely in control of my every facial expression. Jack's got a pirate hat on, but it's wrapped in a silk hand-
kerchief and has some fake dreads attached to it, woven with
beads. His loose white shirt is open, showing his collarbone
and just the top of his pecs, with a vest over it and a golden
compass hanging from a loop on the breast pocket. A fake
sword rests on his hip. His breeches are tucked into his black
leather boots, equally worn and dirty-looking, and his blue
eyes stand out like hard icicles with the smoldering eyeliner
smudged around his eyes. He's the spitting image of—

"Captain Jack Sparrow!" Kayla yells, and leaps into his
arms. He smiles at her, then nods at Wren and me.

"Link," he says. "May the Triforce be with you."

Wren looks nervous, but he smiles. "Yeah. And with you."

"Clearly Wren has the Triforce of Wisdom. I've got the Triforce of Courage, and you get Power," I say. "Or not. You don't get a Triforce at all. You're Ganon."

Jack smirks. "I could live with being a villain."

Wren looks impressed. "You play a lot of video games, Isis?"

"What else does a friendless chubby kid do?"

"So this entire time you've been calling me a nerd, but you're secretly one?" Jack quirks a brow.

"Isis just calls everyone nerds. It's her way of saying she likes you." Kayla smiles.

I flush. "Is not!"

"Is that the best comeback you've got tonight? 'Is not'?" Jack makes a *tsk* noise. Kayla leads him over to the kitchen and pours him some booze. He grimaces at it, but he glances at me and takes a swig. I go in and fix myself a rum and Coke, and stand by Jack.

"Do I drive you to drink or something? Thought the Ice Prince doesn't drink."

"I don't. Tonight's special."

"Yeah? Why's that?"

He jerks his head to Kayla, who squeals with a group of girls and points at Jack, then squeals louder with them.

"She's excited, cut her some slack."

"Excitement is not covered by my eardrum health-care provider."

"Every girl is excited by her first boyfriend. Let her enjoy it."

Jack's quiet. Someone turns on house music. The bass thumps through my chest.

"Did you?" Jack asks.

"Did I what?"

"Enjoy having your first boyfriend?"

"At first."

I stare at Kayla's smile, and smile into my own cup.

"At first it was great. It was really great. Held hands. Went on a picnic, once. He didn't like going in public with me much, since I was a whale. Didn't kiss, because I was too shy. Mostly we stayed at his house or my house. Talked. Watched TV. Once he brought some pot over and I almost vomited. It was the first time I smoked anything, ever."

"Rebel," Jack murmurs.

"I know." I laugh. "I felt so badass. All it did was make me hungry and then I slept for fifteen hours. It wasn't even fun."

"But you had fun with him."

I watch the dark soda bubble, fizz, pop. Soda can corrode stuff. Metal. Stone. I read that somewhere once.

"Yeah. I had fun. Except it wasn't real. He was pretending."

Jack's patiently quiet. I grin and shove my cup at him.

"I'm gonna go dance. Don't drug that or anything."

As I sway to the beat, getting lost in the vortex of heat and bodies that is the dance floor, my memories fall away. Music is the best medicine. It blasts away all the thoughts in your head if it's loud enough, and keeps them away if it's a good enough song. I don't ridiculous dance like I did with Wren, but I don't dance seriously. Can you even dance seriously? Whatever, that's a question for some tap-dance or jazz snobs. I just dance. Wildly. I throw my arms up and jump and twirl, the orange and black of the lights mixing with the alcohol in a pleasant haze. I can observe, however blurrily, the party from the inside out. Someone's throwing cooked spaghetti at a wall and watching it stick. Knife Guy sneaked his way in, dressed up as a serial killer in a blood-spattered apron and a fake cleaver, and he's talking excitedly with a guy dressed up as a samurai about the fake katana he's got. Wren's flitting nervously around Kayla, who's showing him all the framed baby pictures of Avery tucked behind the fridge so no one could see how embarrassingly fat and bald she used to be. Avery herself is grinding on some tall, dark guy from the swim team. A green alien costume guy slides down the banister on his belly and crashes into a wall, jumps up, and runs up the stairs to do it all over again. And Jack's looking at me. The music changes to some slowish hip-hop and the party rages on and Avery and the guy are kissing and Kayla and Wren have disappeared and I lean back, into someone's chest, and I don't care whose because I'm so tired and so drunk, and I hear the clinking of beads and look up and it's Jack.

"Shit!" I stumble away, tripping over a couple. The three of us fall in a tangle of limbs and wounded egos, and Jack pulls me up and holds my hand, tight.

"Try not to kill everyone."

"Let go of my hand before I scratch your eyes out."

"You're drunk. You're going to fall over again."

"I'm perfectly capable of balancing on my own!"

I wobble, and to keep myself from eating vomit-and-glitter-stained carpet, I grab Jack's arm. The shirt is soft and white under my fingers, but his muscle is taut and smooth.

"Either you go sit down—" Jack says warningly.

"No! I want to stay here with the music!"

"Or you use me as balance. But you're a little too drunk to dance with any sort of coordination anymore, and I don't think anyone else wants you grabbing all over them."

"Screw you," I snap. "You're just . . . you're just trying to smother me!"

"Yes. In your sleep. So you'll stop living and Kayla will be all mine," he deadpans.

I can't help the laugh that escapes. I sigh and lean back into his chest again. We stand like that, and he stays still, but I sway gently and he starts mimicking me.

"It's nice not to fall," I murmur.

"Generally speaking," he agrees. The music changes, and it's loud and annoying, so I leave. Somewhere quiet. Somewhere soft and quiet. I open guest bedroom doors until I find one that doesn't have a writhing couple on the bed, and close and lock the door behind me. I flop on the soft comforter. Fancy down comforter. Fancy glass lamps twisted like sea kelp. Fancy pictures of the ocean and fancy pillows that smell like lavender. I suck it in and try to make the room stop spinning. The music still thumps below. A weight is sitting on the bed to my side. Jack. I frown and squint up at him.

"Why did you follow me?"

"You dragged me with you."

I slump into the pillows again, my voice muffled. "Oh."

I watch him take off his hat, his normal golden-brown hair sticking up slightly.

"You look better without the dumb dreads," I mumble.

"I thought you liked Johnny Depp?"

"Is that why you dressed up as him? Because I like him?"

Jack makes a show of standing quickly and putting his hat on the farthest chair. "No. Of course not. It was just what I had in my closet from last year."

"There's a price tag on your vest."

The tiniest of cringes passes through him, but he hides it well and turns back to me, eyes all cold and dangerous-looking.

"I don't know what you're talking about."

"It's okay." I sigh into the pillow. "You don't have to get all defensive. If you did it for me that's okay. Weird, but okay."

The coldness fades from his eyes, and he comes back and sits on the bed.

"You're so conceited. Like I would ever pick a costume just for you," he scoffs.

"I know. I was kidding. I know you'd rather . . . rather throw me in a pit than do something for me. I wouldn't do anything for you, either."

Liar.

I roll over, my cape cocooning me like a burrito. I pull my mask off and throw it over the bed.

"I drank too much."

"I know. I'll get you some water."

Instead of fighting it like I know I should, I relent.

"Okay."

He comes back with a glass of water, and I drink greedily. Some of it slips down my chin and I make a face and wipe it away.

"I'm gross. Look at me, getting all sloppy in front of my mortal enemy. Unexecutable. Inexhaustible. Un . . . un . . . under the sea."

"Inexcusable," Jack offers.

"Yes!" I point at him. "Yes. That."

There's a shriek from downstairs and someone yells, *"Oh God, I'm bleeding!"* Life goes on.

"So if . . ." I sit up on my elbows. He's right in front of my face, sitting on the side of the bed, his knee level with my eyes. "So if Kayla makes you have sex, do I owe you money?"

He snorts and looks down at me. His fingers stop playing with the hem of his shirt.

"I'm not having sex with Kayla."

"But you're going out."

"Not really."

"You can't . . . you can't string her along like that. She really likes you!"

"And so do a dozen other girls," he says wearily.

"Yeah? Well, sorry we like you," I snap.

Jack freezes. I freeze.

"'We'?" he asks.

It all happens so fast, like a shooting star, a lighting bolt; all the feelings I buried, all the things I wanted to say, all my fears batter down the bomb-safe doors I'd been keeping over them, helped by booze and exhaustion and emotional bruises that left me soft and ripe for the picking.

"I like you."

I reach out for his hand, my own trembling. His fingers look so long and slender and gentle. They feel smooth and warm. I take hold of a few of them, like they're a lifeline. A raft in the sea. A rope in a deep hole.

"You smell good," I say. "And you're fun to pick on. And I like your mom. You're smart. Kind of dumb, but also kind of smart. I had fun. With the war. And the kiss. And the date. And you called me beautiful and it was nice. So even if we never battle again, even if you hate me forever for saying I like you, thank you. Thank you a lot—"

I never get to finish.

Jack leans down, his lips on mine, and I roll over and push myself up, and he pushes back, and I'm against the pillows and headboard and he's kissing me—

❍ ❍ °❍

—and this time she kisses back. This time she is not shocked into motionlessness. This time there is no one watching. This time she is hungry. This time, she darts her tongue out, kisses the corner of my lips, bites at my bottom one and pulls, hard, and I make a noise between a strangled groan and a hitching of breath. She's curious, and inexperienced, but curious and stubborn and looking for something, anything, to kiss, anything to put her hands on—

ⓔ ⓞ °ⓞ

—his neck tastes even better, and his throat is soft, and his Adam's apple goes up and down as he swallows nervously (nervously?) and I pull away and murmur happily against his skin.

"I can feel your pulse on my lips."

ⓔ ⓞ °ⓞ

—and she has no idea what she is saying and how it's wreaking havoc, how it sends a molten jolt of static electricity down my spine, through my stomach, and straight to my crotch. The thin pirate pants betray everything. My own body surprises me—I had no idea it longed for her with this buzzing, frantic intensity. It wants to taste her, tease her, fuck her with the slowest, softest, deepest mercy, the kind that'll curl her toes and make her beg. I press against her harder and wrap my arm around her waist and she giggles (giggles!) and my every instinct screams at me to move down her body, to pull the ludicrously hot latex suit off inch by inch and drag my mouth over her collarbone, her breasts, her stomach until she is screaming for me, screaming and panting my name and she forgets all about that bastard, all about pain, all about sadness. I want her. But more than that, I want her to be happy—

◦ ◦ ◦◦

—he pulls me down, lower on the bed, my head on the pillows, and he's suddenly on either side of me, straddling me, and I'm shaking and afraid but I'm not, not at all, my outside is betraying my inside, because my inside wants this more than anything, but he could hurt me, he hurt someone, this is wrong, he loves Sophia, not me, not me, not me, he could hurt me, he's going to hurt me again—

◦ ◦ ◦◦

—she's trembling. I kiss her neck, her shoulder. Her whole body is quivering uncontrollably.

"Are you all right?" I ask.

Her face twists, collapses, and she hides it in her hands.

"I-I'm sorry," she whimpers. "It isn't right. This isn't right."

Something in my chest cracks down the middle and tears in two. It feels right. God, this is the most right-feeling thing I've felt in months, no—years. I'd been stumbling through client after client, closing myself off and forcing my way through it all with mechanical responses and sickly pleasure. But just touching Isis now, I can't be cold. It's impossible. She burns it all up, all the resentment I didn't think I had, all the cynical professionalism that compounded on my fear for Sophia. I'd forgotten how to enjoy, and her every soft breath against my face and touch of her fingertips shows me how again, clear and bright and warm as a fire. It's right. Dear God, it's fucking *right*.

But she's scared. She's unsure. She's wounded in more ways than I can count. And she's drunk. I'm buzzed, but she's drunk. Doing anything now would be uncalled for. I back off immediately.

"You're right. I'm sorry. I didn't mean to—"

"N-No," she sobs. "It's my f-fault. I'm sorry. I'm so sorry."

"Hey," I say gently. "Hey. Look at me."

She quivers, cracking her fingers and staring up at me. Her eyes are red, tears wetting her cheeks and her mascara blurring, but not running.

"It's not your fault. Nothing is your fault." I get up and grab my hat from the chair. "Stay here and sleep it off. Drink that glass of water. Lock the door behind me and don't open it until morning. Understand?"

She sits up, sniffing. She doesn't nod.

"Understand?" I repeat. She shakes her head, purple streaks sticking to her cheeks.

"Don't go."

"It's better if I do. I make you uncomfortable."

"No!" she shouts, and then lowers her voice. "No. I— I would feel better if you ... if you stayed. In here. And made sure no one comes in."

"Kayla will get worried."

Isis's face falls. "Oh. Oh, you're right. You should g-go."

I watch her, her body giving a shuddering sigh, trembling constantly and shallowly. She clutches her own arms and rubs them like she's cold. I did this to her. I can't leave her. Not like this.

"Here," I say, and walk over. I pull up the comforter, and the blanket, and she eagerly worms her way beneath it.

"Are you sure that latex isn't uncomfortable?" I ask. She looks down, and I instantly regret saying it. "I wasn't implying you should take anything off. Just, it looks very tight, and that might be hard to sleep in. I didn't mean—"

"I know," she murmurs. "It's okay. I would take it off, but I don't have anything else."

"Use this." I pull my shirt over my head and hand it to her. She rubs her face on it like a cat.

"Oooh, soft!"

"I'll just. I'll be outside."

"No, it's okay, just turn around. No peeking."

"Never." I make for the door.

"C'mon, you big prude! You're an escort! Act like one!"

Admonished, I stare at the corner as I listen to the sound of unzipping and struggling. She grunts and curses. I smother a laugh, focusing on the whitewash of the room and the vapid painting of the ocean on the wall to scour my mind clean of the dirt it's currently shoveling into its mouth by the truckload—what are her breasts like? She isn't flat or small; her infamous tight outfit after the pictures spread had shown me that much. The latex revealed gently flared hips; good, strong thighs; a small waist I could fit in one hand—

"Okay. You can look."

I turn just as she's halfway into bed. She looks so much smaller in my billowy, oversize pirate shirt, so much more delicate. The swell of her chest is soft and considerable. With smeared makeup and only a shirt, she looks so vulnerable, so different from the persistent, confident hellion of the last two months. Her bare legs flash for an instant before she tucks them under the covers and pulls them up to her chin.

"It smells like you." She smiles sleepily at me. I tamp down the excitement that courses through me at her words, unruly and out of place.

"I'll be over here." I sit in the chair.

"Okay. Good night."

I flick the light off. "Good night."

She slowly, so slowly, stops trembling. Her breathing evens out. When the last tremors cease, I finally lean back in the chair and close my eyes.

chapter fifteen

MY BRAIN THROBS WITH a painful rhythm, trying to escape the household of abuse that is my skull. I crack my eyes open, light assaulting them. I wince and yelp, and pull the covers over my head. Whose bed is this? Why am I wearing this soft white shirt?

And then it hits me, and my brain melts out my ears. This is Avery's house. Avery's guest room. Jack's shirt. I'm hungover and wearing Jack Hunter's shirt. My breathing quickens, panic settling on my chest like a fat, evil little man. No one's next to me in the bed. It's completely made, so no one slept there. It was just me. I think. I frantically scrabble in my mind for memories of what happened last night, but it's a massive blank. I don't remember *anything*.

I ease out of bed and test my weight on the floor. My mouth tastes like sin on a hot biscuit. I go into the bathroom and rub toothpaste on my teeth with my finger. It'll do for now. I sniff at myself—I don't smell like sex. That's a good sign. But it doesn't mean nothing happened. I wish I could fucking remember! I pull the shirt off and put my costume back on. How did I ever manage to get this off? Or did I not take this off? Did someone else? Did Ja—

The door opens, and Jack looks in. He's shirtless, his stomach and chest torqued with fine definition. It almost distracts me from his worried face. Almost.

"You're up," he says.

"What the hell happened last night?"

"No time. Kayla needs you."

He ducks out of the door. Cold dread settles in my stomach, and I follow him down the hall. Candy wrappers and empty red cups litter the floor. The barest of sunlight streams through the windows—it's not full morning, but it's not night, either. I check my phone. Six exactly. Most of the party crowd's gone. Jack urges me to hurry, and waves me into another guest room at the end of the hall. Kayla's sitting on the bed, Wren beside her. She looks terrified and exhausted—her mermaid skirt askew and her makeup smeared. Wren offers her a roll of toilet paper, and she takes some and blows her nose with a loud honk.

I rush to her, kneeling and putting my hand on hers. "Kayla! What happened to you?"

"Avery." She breaks into a fresh wave of sobs. "Avery . . . my drink . . . she put something in my drink, Isis!"

I shoot a look at Wren. "What, like a date rape drug?"

He nods. "She couldn't move for a whole thirty minutes."

"Did anyone—"

Wren shakes his head. "Avery locked the two of us in here.

Barred the door with a chair and said we couldn't come out until we . . ."

Kayla wails, and looks to Jack lurking in the doorway. "Where were you? I was so scared! Why didn't you— Why didn't you—"

"I feel asleep in another room," Jack says softly, but doesn't move any closer to her. "I'm sorry."

Kayla puts her face in her hands and wails. Wren flinches. I rub Kayla's shoulder.

"Hey, listen. You were safe. Wren's a good guy, okay? You didn't need to be scared." I look up at Wren. "Right? You didn't do anything? Tell me the truth now, and I won't disembowel you."

"I swear to you, Isis. I would never—I'm not a monster." His eyes go wide. A surge of shame makes me back down.

"Yeah. I know. Sorry for doubting."

"Avery thought . . . I guess she thought . . ." Wren winces. "She thought I would."

"And use it as blackmail against you for those funds," I finish. He nods. Jack instantly springs into action after hearing that, walking over to the mantelpiece and shoving the ornaments there aside. He picks up a clock and smashes it.

"Jesus!" Wren shouts as we both jump. Kayla shrieks and covers her ears. Jack turns to us, holding a tiny black box.

"A camera," he says dully.

"For evidence," I mumble, slowly standing as the rage fans its flames higher in me. "That fucking bitch—"

"Don't!" Kayla clings to my arm. "Don't, Isis, please! She's my friend! She's . . . she's the only friend I have—"

"Wrong," Jack interrupts, voice hard. "Look around you. It's the people here now who are your real friends."

Kayla looks like he slapped her. She breaks into tears again, and Wren winces, unsure of what to do but so obviously wanting to help. He looks to me.

"Let's go. We have to confront her."

I scoff. "Confront her? That's a little mild, don't you think? I'm gonna rip her tits off."

Wren smirks and we stride down the hall together, leaving Jack and Kayla alone. We weave around groaning people waking up, puddles of vomit and sticky booze, and the occasional pile of shed clothes. We go to the second master bedroom, and Wren knocks. No answer. I motion for him to stand back, and kick the door with all my furious might.

Avery's room is painted pale purple, with a beautiful canopy bed in the center. She sits up from the pile of silky sheets, princess costume still intact, if slightly disheveled. She sees me, sees the look on my face, and tries to bolt for the window. I lunge at her, pull her back by her hair, and punch her hard enough to have her crashing to the floor.

"You really don't learn, do you?" I say softly.

"Wh-What—" She coughs. "What are you talking about?"

I lean down and grab a chunk of her red hair and pull. Hard. She screams and twists.

"All right, all right! I'm fucking sorry!"

"No. You aren't. But you will be."

"You aren't getting the funding, Avery," Wren says stonily. "Not now, not ever. I'm declaring the president of the French club unsuitable for duty. I'm putting a sanction on you. You're officially banned from joining any clubs and attending senior prom and graduation night."

"You can't do that," Avery snarls. "I've been homecoming queen for four years straight! I'm in the running for prom queen and everyone knows I'll fucking win. If you ban me, no one will come to prom. No one will come to your stupid little graduation night, either!"

"Do you really think you have that much influence over the student body?"

Avery scoffs. "I say jump, they jump. You know that."

"Do you think you'll have that much influence when we tell everyone you drugged someone at your own party? How many girls will trust you again? How many will brave the threat of being date-raped to come to your parties?" Wren coolly asks.

Avery's face goes white. I pull her up by her dress and sneer.

"If you so much as breathe in Kayla's direction ever again, I'll kill you."

Avery rips out of my grip and points at Wren. "You did it! Don't lie, you sanctimonious bitch! You're a sniveling little coward opportunist and I know you slept with her!"

Wren smiles, hell-bent gaze turning more determined, more fixed and just slightly amused.

"I'm not that boy in the forest anymore, Avery. I'm not

someone you can force into doing what you want. We're older. And I'm never going to let you hurt another girl again."

Avery takes a step back, shocked. She looks down at her hands, turns them over.

"That's right," Wren says. "You were so caught up in getting those funds, you didn't realize you were doing the same exact thing you did to Sophia. You did it again. You haven't learned at all. And you'll probably do it again, and again, until you kill someone or someone kills you for it."

"I was doing it for Sophia!" Avery screams, livid. "Those funds, the French club trip, it was for Sophia! She doesn't have long, Wren, you know that! You fucking know that!"

"So you'd hurt someone else to help her?" he asks.

"I'll do anything to help her," Avery says through gritted teeth. "Anything."

Wren smiles. "It's too bad you can't wring the money from your parents. Then again, they're too smart, aren't they? They raised you, after all. You're their spitting image, and they keep perfect record of their money. They'd track where it went, who was invited. They'd find Sophia's name, and dig around in her background. And then what you did would be brought to light. It'd explode in your face. The whole town would know. Maybe it's time the world knew."

"You wouldn't dare," she snarls. "You and Jack would get dragged down with me."

"Maybe. But I'm sure in court Jack would get a pardon, and I could plead I feared for my life. We'd get off more easily. But you? No. You'd get something much longer."

"GET OUT!" Avery roars. "GET *OUT!*"

She throws things—a vase, a picture frame. She rips a fancy lamp from the wall and chucks it at my head, but I duck just in time. Glass shatters and I run after Wren, back to Kayla's room.

"We need to go," Wren pants, helping Kayla off the bed. She leans on his arm, tears almost dried, but still looking confused.

"What's going on?"

"Give me your keys," I say. Kayla rummages in her purse and hands them to me. Wren helps Kayla downstairs, and Jack lags behind with me. Avery's screaming is waking up what's left of the party. It sounds like a banshee being squeezed out in a wringer.

"Someone's unhappy." Jack smirks.

"Wren threatened to come out with the truth about what happened to Sophia," I murmur. Jack's face falls and settles into a granite-hard determination. Wren and Kayla stumble across the lawn to her car. Just as Jack and I get out the door, rapid footsteps come down the stairs and race behind us. I turn just in time to see Avery, nose bloody from my punch, eyes wild with savage fury, her red hair like the mane of a fire goddess, and a baseball bat raised, inches from coming down on my back. I duck, the bat swinging over me, and there's a snap, the sound of something being forced, and Jack suddenly has the bat. Avery pants, shrinking away as Jack looks at the bat, observes every inch of it.

"Just like the good old days, hm?" Jack smiles predatorily at Avery. "Although the one I used was metal, wasn't it?"

Avery's fury drains so fast she looks like a punctured balloon. Terror claws at her expression as she scrabbles backward, jumps to her feet, and runs back into the house, slamming the door shut and locking it.

Jack doesn't say anything more until I've dropped off Kayla. Wren drove behind us, and got out to help Kayla to her front door. She thanked him, quietly, and he watched her go inside. Wren and I nodded at each other in a farewell, and he even nodded at Jack. When we're on the highway and I'm driving toward Jack's house, I spare a glance at him. I'd given him back his shirt, and he has his chin in his hand, fingers over his lips thoughtfully, watching the world flicker by outside his window.

He speaks first. "I broke up with Kayla."

"Shocking. I thought you two were going to last forever."

He shoots me a sardonic smirk. "Haven't you heard? Good things never last."

I switch lanes. Jack turns on the heater. It smells like skunk. He shuts it off quickly.

"What happened last night?" I ask.

"You don't remember?"

"I remember being . . . I remember being scared. Shaking."

"That's all?"

I nod. Jack goes still. His eyes are unreadable chips of ice as they always are, but for a split second I swear I see them crack on the inside with pain.

She was scared. She didn't enjoy any part of it. If she did, she would've remembered. But her fear overwrote her memories.

The wound is far deeper than I'd imagined.

I watch her face as she drives, hands white on the steering wheel. She's waiting, confused, trying to piece the blanks together in her mind. She blocked it out. Last night was too much like the time that caused the wound. I want to tell her I was trying to make her feel better, or tell her that I was trying to help (liar, you were taking advantage, just like he did).

In the sober light of morning, what I've done hits me with petrifying acidity. I forced a kiss on a drunk girl who'd been forced upon before. I'd touched a girl terrified of being touched at all. I lost control. I, Jack Hunter, the one person who keeps calm and cool and collected at all times, lost all control. And it hurt Isis so bad she blocked it from her memory.

It's better if she doesn't remember.

But the cracks fill in, icing over again, and Jack shrugs lightly.

"You were pretty drunk. Some guy with a disturbing mask jumped out at you from a corner. You were shaking fairly hard for the rest of the night."

"And why was I wearing your shirt?"

"You bumped into someone while dancing and spilled Coke on your costume. It was sticky. So I offered you my shirt, and you washed your suit off and left it to dry on the floor."

It sounds like something I'd do. I nod.

"Makes sense."

e   o   °o

She pulls up to my house, and I get out and hang in the window.

"Take care of Kayla in the next few days," I say. "She'll need you."

"Since when did you start caring about her?"

She's important to you. So I care.

I don't say that. I shrug and lie instead.

"I know what it's like. Breaking up. And GHB."

"Client of yours get too creepy?"

"Just a bit."

My eyes find her neck, and my breath hitches. There, just below her jaw, is a soft red hickey.

"Something wrong?" she asks.

If she doesn't look up and use a mirror to see under her chin, she won't notice it. I shake my head. "Nothing. Thanks for the ride."

"Thanks for helping. With Avery. And for lending me your shirt. And . . . for dating Kayla. It made her really happy."

It made you happy.

I smirk. "Anytime you want to give me another two hundred dollars to go out with one of your friends, let me know."

She snorts, and I step back and watch her pull away from the curb with something like regret festering in my chest. I tuck last night somewhere deep in my mind—lock it away for good. I'll revisit it when the longing gets too bad. But it doesn't exist, not anymore. It never happened. And that's for the best.

I'm the only one who remembers.

And that's for the best.

⊙ ○ ∘⊙

Northplains, Ohio, is a town full of secrets.

You'd think the boring Midwest wouldn't have things like savage popular girls with baseball bats and shady events that happened in the past no one wants to talk about. But it's got those by the truckload. Deception, revenge, lies. They all merge together like a vortex over the school, hanging heavy in the air on Monday.

Jack walks into the main hall, takes one look at Kayla and me on the bench, and walks right past us. Kayla, of course, bursts into tears. It took a lot of coaxing and chocolate on Sunday to convince her to come to school on Monday. I'm torn between my urge to punt him for making her cry, and knowing the breakup was the best thing for both of them. It was inevitable. A guy like Jack Hunter just doesn't date girls his own age. That's the general consensus around school. Of course Kayla only lasted two weeks! He's Jack Hunter! He runs around town with rich girls in Porsches. He got early acceptance into Harvard, a fact Mr. Evans has taken to reminding every student of when they look like they're slacking in study hall.

Jack Hunter is just meant for bigger and better things than Northplains, Ohio.

His legion of admirers makes a quick comeback. The statue in the art room has the sheet taken off its head and it's moved to the middle of the room again, the artist happily chipping away at the features. Drama Club Wailer primps and preens in front of the bathroom mirrors like a seven-year-old who's just discovered her mother's makeup. The girls have returned with an admirable vengeance.

Avery hasn't come to school in three days. No one talks about her bat-wielding fury, so I can only assume she threatened them to keep them quiet. But people say she isn't well. The official rumor is she's sick, but I know better. She's licking her wounds, trying to figure out which designer skirt will hide the tail between her legs when she finally does come back. It's only a matter of time. Sometimes I feel sorry for her. But then I remember what she did, and I just feel sorry for her body parts.

I take deep breaths to calm my rage and focus on something else. Mrs. Gregory drones on. I doodle her face on my paper and then gracefully draw a banana for a nose. I still can't remember what happened that night at the party. I was pretty drunk, so it's understandable, but I've been drunk a few times before, and though things were fuzzy, I'd always remember bits and pieces. But the other night? Nothing. It's a massive black blank smeared across my memory. I don't slip up like that—my mind is a fantastically sexy piece of equipment I keep in tip-top condition. So why can't I remember even a scrap of that night? It was probably the booze. That was more than I've drunk in a long, long time.

Kayla's taken over Avery's position as temporary queen bee. I watch her mope through the lunch line, the girls around her cooing sympathetically and insisting she'll find someone better even as they shoot sultry glances at Jack from across the cafeteria. Jack eats alone, reading a book as he munches a sandwich. I wonder what the girls would do if they knew I'd worn his shirt? Probably put an apple in my mouth and roast me to suckling browned goodness. I'm ready to die, but I'm not ready to die with a fruit in my mouth. That's a whole other ball game.

"What's a whole other ball game?" Wren asks, sliding his tray across from me and sitting.

"Ah, nothing." I wave him off. "So what's up with you, my majestic prez? Busy making peace treaties with Iran? Scouring the globe for alternative energy sources?"

"Making sure Avery comes back to slightly less power around the school. You'd be surprised how many teachers she has under her sway with blackmail. Did you know Ms. Hall is having an affair? With two different guys? And Mr. Ulfric drinks on the job in the janitor closet during recess."

"No surprise at all she's got them under her finger, then. I've seen how she works."

"Hopefully she'll have the sense not to work for a while." He sighs. "I really don't want to go to Evans about the date rape drugs she's been using."

"Or what happened that night in middle school."

Wren's eyes flash behind his glasses. "That was a bluff."

"And you huffed and you puffed, and you bluffed the house down."

Wren watches me for a moment before lowering his voice to a bare murmur. "She was our friend."

I look up from my hot dog. "Who?"

"Sophia," Wren continues. "Jack, Sophia, and me. We were best friends in elementary school. We lived next to each other. We played on the same street, in one another's yards. Every summer and winter break we were together, for days on end. It was the happiest time of my life."

He inhales and pushes his tray away.

"Avery was on the outskirts. She'd come over sometimes, since she was Sophia's best friend. She wasn't anything like who she is now. The old Avery was loud and bossy, but kind. She'd do anything to make Sophia laugh. She hated Jack—but I always knew that was because she liked him and also didn't like the way Sophia liked him. She was jealous of him getting Sophia's attention, and jealous of Sophia getting his. She was caught in the middle and it ate away at her as we got older, I think."

I try not to move, or breathe too noisily. The last thing I want to do is jolt him out of the story. Wren looks up.

"There's something I want to show you. After school. Can you drive us there?"

I nod, and he smiles.

"Good. I'll see you then. I've got a Run for Charity to organize, so, I'd better go."

"Later." I try to sound casual. I watch him leave the cafeteria, the curiosity eating me alive.

● ○ ° ○

After school, Wren instructs me on where to go. He leads me to the airport, almost all the way in Columbus. After a few more turns, we're in an airport-adjacent suburb, complete with cracked road, constant overhead noise from the planes as they go rumbling by, and faded yellow grass yards. Chipped-paint houses and trash line the streets. A pair of tennis shoes hangs mournfully from a power line above. I park and follow Wren. He leads me up the stairs of a tiny, two-story house with clean yet old-looking windows. The porch is weather-beaten and strewn with plastic kids' toys. A woman answers the door, peering through the screen.

"Wren!" Her face lights up. "Come in, come in!"

"Thanks, Mrs. Hernandez."

"Is this a friend?"

"Yeah, she's helping me at the food bank."

"Oh, how nice." Mrs. Hernandez wipes her hands on her apron and holds one out to me. "I'm Belina. It's good to meet you."

"Isis. Nice to meet you, too."

"Well, come in! Don't just stand there in the cold!"

She ushers us into the tiny house. It smells like spicy meat and fresh laundry. A porcelain image of the Virgin Mary hangs from almost every wall, and the couches and chairs and tables are shabby, but clean. Two kids race by, screaming and chasing each other with toilet brushes, using them like swords. Mrs. Hernandez snaps something in Spanish at them and they cower and immediately run into the bathroom.

"Sorry about that." Mrs. Hernandez smiles. "I've been baking tostadas all day and letting them play with whatever."

"As long as they don't wave those swords around the food," Wren jokes. She laughs and motions for us to come into the kitchen.

"Would you like some juice? I have milk, too."

"No, it's all right," he says. "We're just here for a moment. I wanted to know if you could get me your WIC paperwork. I need the PIN number to update it and I was in the neighborhood, so I figured I'd drop by."

"Of course! One second."

She shuffles upstairs. Wren turns to me and sweeps his arm around.

"It's cozy, isn't it? Four bedrooms. Three baths. Not bad for a single mom with two mouths to feed."

"It's nice, but I don't understand—"

"She works as a maid. Almost minimum wage."

"So how does she get the mon—"

"Jack."

I immediately start choking on nothing. "*What?*"

"He sends the money. Through me. To Belina, I'm a

student who works with the food bank's outreach program to supply funds to single mothers. But in truth it's only her who gets the money."

"But why—"

"I don't know what Jack does exactly to get this money," Wren interrupts coolly. "But I have an idea. If only someone could confirm it for me, I'd be very grateful."

I bite my lip. "I can't. He made me promise, Wren. He has my voice on tape—"

"I understand. That's more than enough. Thank you for confirming my suspicions."

"You can't tell him you know."

Wren chuckles. "Do I look like I have a death wish?"

"So . . ." I lower my incredulous voice. "So why Belina? What did she do?"

"It's not what she did. It's what Jack did."

It dawns on me, a slow crawl of illuminating light-thought.

"Whatever he did that time in middle school. That's linked to Belina?"

Wren nods. I'm about to ask another question when Belina trundles down the stairs. Wren makes a show of checking her papers and making small talk. So the money's not just for Sophia. He lied. But why? Because he didn't want me to know? Why the hell would Jack feel he owes Belina money? It's a nice thing to do, but it has to have a reason. I feel like I'm missing some huge part, the one clockwork gear in the middle that'll connect all the others and make them move in tandem.

"Forgive me for asking, but is there any news?" Wren softly asks Belina. "About your husband?"

Belina's dark eyes crinkle with despondence. "It's been five years now. The police don't keep me updated as much anymore."

Wren nods. "I'm sorry to hear that. I hope they find something soon."

She smiles wanly at him, then at her children in the living room. "I always pray to God for a clue, a single word from him. Some days I imagine him just walking back into the house like he never left—like he's coming home from work. But he never does."

Wren's quiet, and Belina shoots me the same thin smile.

"I'm sorry. It's rude to keep a guest in the dark. My husband went missing five years ago. But we do our best to move on, to keep living despite our pain."

I nod, my voice quiet. "That's really brave."

"No." She shakes her head. "It's just something I must do. For my children. For myself. There is no bravery, only necessity."

I understand it, but saying I understand will sound shallow, hollow, untrue. So I try to smile, try to show her I understand with my face.

Wren and I leave, Belina waving from the porch and my head filled with more questions than ever. Wren won't answer any more of them, keeping his mouth shut the entire way to his house.

I go home and scribble madly on paper like it will help me unravel the threads.

Two men hired by AveryBaseballbatSophiaWren with camera JackBelina Belina moneyHusband?JackAveryWren fear Sophia Jack Jack jack Jack Jack??? jack

Sophia
Sophiais important
Jackloves her
My stomach twists.
Jack lovesher

θ θ ° ο

There's a sad finality as Thanksgiving approaches. People start freaking about college application deadlines. Teachers nag us to finish them and turn them in. The weather gets bitter cold, the last of the trees shedding their golden fall leaves. The piles turn to mulch, and mulch turns to dirt the winter-fall rains wash out of the gutters and streets. Nothing is pretty anymore—gray skies and gray earth and gray, naked trees shivering in the breezes.

After two weeks, Kayla's conquered the act of looking at Jack without bursting into tears. Wren was there with a box of tissue on her way to mastery, though, and for that she smiles at him more and even sits with him and me at lunch. Something's brewing between them, and it makes me smile knowingly, because even if they are two hopeless nerd idiots, they are *my* hopeless nerd idiots, and I only want the best for anything of mine.

The graveyard's presence is cold and hollow, like a metal needle in my brain.

Avery's comeback was a lot more anticlimactic than we all thought it'd be. She just showed up one day for school, dressed in her same clothes and with the same savage smile on. The girls flocking around Kayla instantly swarmed back to her, Kayla not included. A surge of pride ran through me when Kayla turned her back on Avery's motion for her to come over. Kayla laced her arm in mine and we strutted away like the bad bitches we are.

Jack hasn't looked at me, much. Which isn't weird, since I know I'm a maggot on his shoe and all, but it's a little odd he doesn't like being in the same room as me, either. World history is the worst—he'll make excuses to go to the nurse's, and most days he'll just straight up play hooky and never show for class. But I see him walking around campus and going to other classes. It's only the class we share he never shows up for. I'd confront him about it, but I'm still torn about what really happened that night. His explanation made sense, but it didn't ring true. It didn't feel right.

And I'm bored. God, so bored. Now that we aren't warring, my days are filled with nothing but homework and staring at teacher foreheads, wondering where they got their worst zits when they were my age.

I sit in Evans's office, serving the last of my detention. One more day and I'm free of grading his easy-peasy papers and watching his balding head shine in the light of his self-inflicted glory.

"So, Isis." He clears his throat. "The deadline for Yale's application is next week."

"I'm not going to an Ivy, Evans. We've discussed this previously. To death."

"There's no point to life if you don't go to a good college," he insists.

"Have you watched the Food Network recently? Eating is a fantastic reason for living."

"If I may be completely honest with you, Isis, college is mostly for drinking and crying," he says. I smother a laugh, and he becomes all business again. "But where you decide to go to drink and cry sometimes gets you far. Like, for instance, Harvard. You can get a mediocre grade in a mediocre-earning field and get a degree but it will be a Harvard degree, you see? It'll speak volumes more than a Redfield degree about your level of commitment."

"And snobbery," I mutter.

"Regardless," he talks over me. "It's too late. I've already applied you for Harvard, Yale, and Stanford."

"What?" I bristle. "How—"

"Your father was very accommodating. He only wants the best for you, and provided all your personal information."

"But my required essay—"

"I pulled a few spectacularly funny yet poignant and observant essays from your English and world history classes. They fit nicely."

"My SAT scores—"

He holds up a paper. "Your father informed me you took the ACT before you left Florida, at his behest. You never got the scores because you moved, but your aunt sent them along. Take a look."

Four massive black numbers glare back at me: 32, 35, 33, and 9.

"Exemplary scores across the board! Marvelous. You must have been in a much better state of mind for that test."

"I can't—" I'm speechless. "Where do you get off deciding where I should go to college?"

"Your father also told me you're a particularly dutiful daughter, and that your mother is going through a rough patch in life. Trust me when I say I understand—"

"Do you?" I snarl. "I doubt that, baldy."

He smiles patiently. "I had a father who was ill. Cancer. I stayed behind for three years to take care of him while my friends went off to college. He kept telling me to leave, but I couldn't bring myself to. When he died, the guilt that I couldn't save him crushed me. But the way he told me he was proud of me—me, the boy who worked gas station night shifts—that made me feel even guiltier."

I go quiet, my rage simmering instead of bubbling. I had no idea Evans had a life like that.

"So what, you tell me your whole sobby life story and I feel sorry for you and decide to go to Stanford, is that it?" I ask quietly.

"No. I just wanted to tell you that I understand. I know what it's like, to be kept against your will, even if your heart wants to stay. You've written off completely the idea of going out of state. You're willing to settle for a school that wouldn't challenge you, just to take care of someone you love. Jack nearly did the same thing."

I clench my fist around the armchair. Evans smiles.

"Sometimes, we can't do the things we want to do for ourselves. Sometimes we wait for someone else to do them. You can't always wait like that. You have to seek out change on your own. But in the meantime, I had to step in."

I snort. He presses on.

"Even if you get accepted, you don't have to go. Choose whatever path you like. But I can rest easy now, knowing you can at least see the open paths before you and make an informed decision."

"So this has nothing to do with the funding you get if your students go to an Ivy?" I snap.

Evans smiles. "It's also about that. But that's only a small part."

The bell rings. I put my pen down and gather my stuff. I can feel Evans staring at me like a massive, balding elephant who smells. Like a poop-covered busybody.

I stop at the door and look over my shoulder. "Thanks. I guess."

"Consider it an apology for the pictures."

"It doesn't make up for it. You'd need like, a million cakes and a dozen clones of Johnny Depp to even begin to make up for that."

"There's a very good cloning program at Duke—"

I politely scream "*Ugh!*" and slam the door shut behind me.

chapter sixteen

KNIFE KID COMES UP to me nearly four weeks after Avery's party, right before Thanksgiving break. We're watching a movie in English, bags of chips and trays of cupcakes littering the counter from the last-day-before-break party Mr. Teller let us have. It's dark, and people are whispering and laughing and making plans for break and not paying attention to the movie at all.

Knife Kid slides into the seat beside me.

"Hello, Your Pointy Highness," I say. "What brings you to the neck of my new-girl woods?"

"You aren't new girl anymore."

"Oh? So what am I?"

"Weird girl."

I laugh. "Better than fat girl."

"They call you that, too. But weird is the most used."

I smirk. We watch the TV for a few seconds before he starts talking again. "You and Jack like each other."

I hunch my shoulders and squeeze my face together. "Are you high?"

"I saw you at the Halloween party. You danced together, and then you pulled him into that room."

I feel my mouth drop open. "I did not!"

"I saw," he insists. "I'm only bringing it up because Jack's cool. He's the only one who's never been a shithead to me in this place. And he seems kind of down. Lately. Ever since that party."

"D-Down?" I sputter. "Jack? His face muscles must have atrophied—he doesn't know how to make expressions, let alone look 'down.'"

Knife Kid shrugs. "He just seems bummed. You and him are the only two I don't fantasize about stabbing. So. I thought you should know."

"Oookay, nice talking to you. I gotta go. To India."

I make a bathroom excuse and escape, running down the hall. Jack is in PE right now; I know because Kayla's been chanting his schedule in her sleep like some weird ex-boyfriend purging ritual. I'm fueled by rage and at least seven cupcakes made by someone's talented mother. How dare Jack lie to me! I mean, I know lying was standard issue back in the day when we were still warring, and maybe it's also standard issue for everyday high school life, but c'mon! I trusted him! Bad move, but I still did it! I'm definitely not panicking about what actually went on in that room, I'm just concerned. Somewhat. And also making high-pitched *eeeeee* sounds.

I burst out the front doors. Cold air nips at me as I run
to the field, where the PE class is playing a lazy game of
dodgeball. People stand still to purposely get hit so they can
be out and sit on the lawn and text and talk. Jack is lying on
his back in the grass, looking up at the clouds. I march over
and graciously kick his ribs.

"Ow! Shit—" He hisses and sits up. His glare stops short
when he realizes it's me.

"What happened in that room?"

"Isis—"

"What happened. In that. Room!" I shout. The PE teacher
is too busy talking with the football coach to notice, but everyone else looks at me warily.

Jack runs a hand through his hair and breathes out, slowly.
Now that we're close I can see the dark circles under his
eyes. When did he get those? And why does he look skin-
nier? His cheekbones and jaw stick out unhealthily.

"It was nothing," Jack whispers. "Okay? Nothing. You just
fell asleep."

"Knife Kid said he saw me dragging you to that room. I
was drunk. I can't remember. So you better tell me the truth,
or I swear to you, it'll be a war all over again."

"What do you want me to say, Isis?" he growls. "Do you
want me to be the bad guy? Do you think I took advantage
of you?"

I slap him, but he recovers quickly. The entire class goes
silent, the dodgeball game ceasing at the sound of the slap
to watch.

"Tell me what you did—"

"I didn't do anything!" he shouts. "I didn't do anything, I swear on my life!"

His constant unfeeling, low-voiced mask is broken. Nothing about him is calm or contained. He's not the Ice Prince anymore. He's furious, his eyebrows tight and his mouth drawn in a cruel frown.

"I can't trust what you tell me anymore," I say.

"Then don't! Don't trust me. Don't trust anyone! That's the way you like it, right? That's the way you've been moving through life for the past three years, right? It's obviously working for you, so keep doing it. Have fucking fun trusting nobody for the rest of your life!" he roars.

His words sear like cold fire across my heart, leaving behind instant, dark scars. I run. I turn on my heel in one fluid motion and run. Everything is numb. I can only barely hear Jack calling after me. I'm underwater, deep, deep beneath the ocean of the past. Jack's voice turns to Nameless's.

Ugly.

Did you think that's what this was? Love?

I slam the driver's side of my car shut and start the engine. I blast past the security booth and barrel home. Stoplights are mercifully green, and the ones that aren't, I run through.

Ugly.

I don't remember parking. I don't remember getting out or running upstairs or locking my door.

I don't remember what happened that night.

That's what happens when you trust someone.

Mom is understanding. She knows this is my breakdown. The last one was just a warm-up. She understands breakdowns better than my aunt does, and much better than Dad does. She knows there are tiny breakdowns leading up to the big one. This is my Big One. I sleep for days. I don't shower. My hair is a knotted mess. Mom brings me up food sometimes, but I pick at it and leave the rest. She's so happy to help me like I've helped her. Sometimes I cry. Sometimes I don't cry and the don't-cry times are somehow worse than the crying ones. Sometimes Mom holds me, sometimes I lock her out. Kayla visits me, bringing snacks and homework and talking happily about nothing at all, and it helps. Her mindless chatter helps more than sleeping, more than crying. It reminds me I'm not the only one with problems, that Kayla's life is fraught with problems that, to her, are just as big—a missing blush color at Sephora, how she forgot there was a sale at Macy's she'd been waiting for a year on, how her little brother constantly gets into her bras and stretches them out by putting them on his head. She brings up Jack, and I snap at her to never mention him again.

"Jeez, I know you hate him, but saying his name isn't a crime, okay?"

"It might turn into one," I mutter.

"Is he . . . is he why you're so sad?"

I scoff. "As if. And I'm not sad. I have strep throat."

"You have a lovely strep voice."

I glower, and she smiles, handing me another cookie.

"Okay, I gotta go. Mom wants me to watch spitglob tonight while she goes out. Text me, okay?"

My anger fades. "Yeah. Thanks for coming over."

"It's the least I can do." She hugs me, and then wrinkles her nose. "You smell. But I love you."

"I love you, too." I grin.

I watch her go through the window, half wanting her to come back and half wanting her to never come back. After everything I've put her through, through the nasty remarks and my hidden jealousy, she's still my friend. I'm a less-than-stellar person, but she's stuck by me.

The days blur. It feels like I've been out of school for weeks, but it's only been a few days. When I'm not sleeping, I research Northplains on Google, looking for any hint of what Jack did. The newspaper archives from back then don't help. I don't even know what I'm looking for. Two men. A baseball bat. Something that scared Avery and Wren into silence. Did Jack beat them? But why would that convince him to give Belina money? Was Belina the wife of one of the men?

Belina was the wife. It all falls into place. She was the wife of one of the men Jack took a baseball bat to—

Mom screams, the sound echoing from downstairs and into my room. My blood goes cold, pumps slowly through my body.

Mom doesn't scream like that except in her nightmares.

"Get away from me!"

My feet fly down the stairs, jumping the last few and landing painfully, but pain doesn't matter right now, all that matters is getting to the door, getting to her, fighting off whoever is making her scream like that.

"*I'll call the cops!*"

"C'mon, Patricia. We both know you won't. Just be sensible about this."

Mom clutches the door for support, body twisted in terror around it. The man at the door is stocky, in khakis and a gray shirt, with a black beard and the kindest face I've ever seen—creviced with smile lines and crow's feet. But I know the truth behind it. And it sickens me. The man sees me and his face lights up in a smile.

"Isis! Good to see you—"

I pull Mom away and slam the door in his face and lock it. She trembles, terrified, and clings to me as I lead her to the couch to sit down. I pull the curtains, lock the back door and windows, and grip my cell phone tightly as I approach the door to check if he's gone. Nope. His fat, bulky ass still looms through the mottled glass of the door.

"Isis, c'mon! Patricia, tell her to open the door! I just want to talk!"

"No!" I shout. "Nobody's talking, Leo. Leave us alone!"

"You can't be serious! I drove all the way up here for a friend. I've been on the road for a whole week! I'm dusty, sweaty. Just thought I'd stop by, since I was in the neighborhood. Could use a glass of water. How about a little hospitality?"

"How about you clear off my front steps before I call the cops?"

"I've done nothing wrong, you little bitch!" Leo's voice switches from amiable to irritated. "Now open this door and let me talk to your mother!"

"This is your last warning, Leo. Leave, or I'll call the cops."

"This is an adult problem, not for snotty kids. So I'm only gonna tell you once—you open this goddamn door, or I'm breaking it."

I suddenly can't breathe.

"C'mon! Open up!"

He knocks on the door, hard, and the knocking turns to pounding. Mom screams and covers her ears. With every hard pound, she flinches and screams louder, burying herself in the couch, convulsing like each second of sound is a physical blow to her. This is not better. This is not healing. He's hurting her all over again just by being here. The slams get louder, and I grab a heavy porcelain statuette from the table with one hand and start to dial 911 with the other.

"911, what is your emergency?"

"There's— My name is Isis Blake." I hate the shake in my voice, the shake in my hands. "1099 Thorton Avenue, North-plains, Ohio. There's a man trying to break into my house."

"I understand. I need you to lock all doors and windows and get into a room."

Leo roars, using his shoulder to pound the door down, like a furious bull.

"Isis?" The emergency responder's plea is insistent. "Talk to me, Isis. Do you know this man?"

"He's my mom's ex-boyfriend. Please, you have to hurry!"

Something shatters, and I drop the phone as I watch in horror—Leo's hand punches through the glass panes on either side of the door, and he's reaching around to open the knob. Mom's scream turns primal, shrill, and she flees from the couch and runs up to her room.

The door creaks open slowly, and he stands in the doorway, dark eyes gleaming. I'm the only thing between him and her. Me, a seventeen-year-old, clutching a heavy porcelain statue behind my back and shaking like a butterfly in a hurricane.

"Step aside, kid. I'm just here for your mother, not you. I don't wanna hurt you."

I look up slowly. All the nights of Mom's crying, all of her sad smiles, all of the days she couldn't bring herself to leave her room and face me flash through my mind.

"You already have, asshole."

He narrows his eyes, taking a step toward me. It's a heavy step. My heart sinks with it. What hope do I have against a two-hundred-something-pound guy? He carves wood. He hunts deer. He's dangerous.

"Last chance. Get out of the way."

"Over my dead body." I grit my teeth.

He chuckles, sour and sinister. "You got guts. I like that."

I'm trembling. I'm trembling so hard I can feel my teeth chattering and my fingers twitching. I can't do this on my own. I can't fight this demon. I can barely fight my own.

I hear Mom's wailing from upstairs and grasp the statue more firmly.

But I have to fight. There's no one who'll come save me. No one will rescue me. No one saved me when Nameless held me down. No one rescued me in the shower afterward, not Mom, not Dad, not my aunt. I am alone. No one has ever tried to rescue me.

So I have to rescue myself.

Leo lunges for me. I duck to the side and slam the heavy statue on the back of his neck. He flinches, roaring in pain, and whirls around and grabs me. He lifts me like a paper doll, a bag stuffed with cotton, something light. I'm easy to throw. I'm flying, sailing through the air for seconds, and then sharp pain sends shock waves of agony tearing at my spine. I'm on my hands and knees, staring at the floor as it wobbles, dims, then comes back bright, then dims again.

Mom. I have to help Mom.

Leo's heavy footsteps thump toward the stairs.

I try to scream to warn her, but blackness consumes me.

⊙   ⊙   ° ⊙

Isis Blake's house is intimidating.

It shouldn't be—it's a tiny two-story that looks like it's survived at least three house fires and a tornado. The yard is unkempt and the railings and gutters are rusty and clogged with leaves. The paint peels like a bad sunburn; the windows are fogged with age and smoke exposure. The wind chime clinks pathetically against itself.

Is this really where she lives? I check the address Kayla gave me just to be sure. My GPS points straight here. It's a hole, a hovel. I expected a grander palace, with the way Isis struts about with perfect self-confidence. It's plain and run-down and exhausted-looking, the total opposite of her. It's a dump.

And yet it's still intimidating.

It's because I know she's inside. Her—the girl who wars with me, the girl who smirks at me, the girl who gave me a kiss that still lingers when I close my eyes.

The girl I injured. Twice. No, three times? How many times have I crossed the line and she just hasn't said anything?

I get out of the car and walk up to the door. The sound of someone screaming is faint, and disturbing. I look around for the source, but there's no one on the street. It must be a horror movie blasting loudly in a nearby house. I shake my head. *Stop, Jack. No distractions. You're going to apologize for that bullshit you said the other day, and you're going to do it right now.*

I'm so wrapped up in what to say when I first see her, how to play it off like I'm cool and composed, that I don't see the glass at first. But when I get to the first step on the porch, I freeze. My shoes crunch glass. The mottled windowpanes for decoration on either side of the door . . . one of them is smashed.

And the screaming is getting louder. It's definitely not a movie.

Cold dread grasps at my throat. I open the door and hiss.

"Shit! Isis!"

I collapse at her side. She's sprawled against the wall, unconscious. I push her hair from her face, check for blood anywhere. There's a dark red wet spot on the very back of her head, and a splatter of blood on the wall.

"No," I croak. "No, no, no, you can't. You can't!"

I fumble for my phone and dial 911. The operator insists there are already people on their way, and I roar.

"Make them faster! Get an ambulance!"

"Sir, we've done all that we can. Help is on the way—"

"Useless cow!" I snarl. "If she dies— So help me, if she dies—"

The screaming upstairs pitches, glass-shattering in its intensity. I swear and look around for something, anything.

There's nothing. I sprint outside and frantically unlock the trunk of my car. The baseball bat Avery waved around at the party sits there, untouched since then.

I grab it and take the stairs two at a time, my fury red-hot lava pulsing through my veins. My mind screams at me to calm down, to wait for the police, but the other part of me that's lain dormant for so long whispers encouragement. Urges me on. It's wanted this. It's missed this.

The man towers over a woman cowering on the bed—I assume she's Isis's mother. He's unbuckling his belt, holding her legs in place.

The smell of the forest comes back to me. The feel of pine needles beneath my feet. Fog encroaches, soft and white on the edges of my vision. Sophia, curled up against a tree trunk, and the shadow men advancing.

I walk behind him. Isis's mother sees me, her eyes terrified and wide as a dying fish's over the man's shoulder. He's enormous. At least twice my weight and nearly my height. His arms are thick with muscle and sinew and the scars of hard work. Evil work.

Sophia cried, her head in her hands, her wrists thin as a bird's wing.

"Help me, Jack."

I was pinned by a man, his hand holding my arms behind me. They were going to make me watch.

"Just stay still, princess. This'll all be over soon," one of the advancing shadows cackled. Some swayed drunkenly. Five of them. Five huge men, shoulders broad and grins oily in the forest moonlight.

Isis's mother looks at me and croaks, "Help me."

They started pulling Sophia's dress off. I bit the man holding me and picked up the bat he dropped. Swung. And swung. And kept swinging through the cries and the blood.

I grip the bat, spread my feet, and pull back.

The first hit gets the side of his head. The ear. His eardrum bursts instantly, blood spraying. Hot droplets land on my face. He turns to look at me, and I smile.

Another swing.

Kneecaps. They tried to grab me, but I was fast, strong, stronger than they thought. Too young to fight back, or so they thought. The first and second had weak skulls. The third pulled out a gun to shoot me and shot the fourth instead. I smiled and launched myself at the third, slamming the bat over his neck. There was a sickening crack *and he went still. The fifth barely had his pants on when I slammed the bat into his side. He staggered, reached for a gun, but I swung again.*

The man's dark eyes widen as the bat connects with his arm. Elbow. I hit three times in quick succession and there's a cracking noise. He howls, stumbling away from the bed. Isis's mother crawls under it, sobbing. The man clutches his arm, bent at the elbow in an unnatural direction.

"You fucking bastard!" he screams, and lowers his shoulder, running for me. I laugh and step aside at the last moment, and he crashes into the dresser, disoriented for a few seconds by the impact. I use those moments well.

I cracked his gun hand. He was so shocked he just looked down at it, like it was a riveting TV show instead of something that was happening to him. And I swung again. The bones cracked, his hand split open, blood and meat spraying over the pine needles. He cried. He crawled away from me and cried, begging.

"Please, man, we didn't mean— We weren't gonna—"

"L-Listen, kid, I'll just leave, okay? There's no need for—"

I swing again, into his gut. And again, between his legs. He keels over, howling, and I step on his chest and look down at him.

"There are crimes. And therefore there is a need," I say, "for punishments."

"Please—"

I smile and tap his nose with the end of the baseball bat lightly.

"No begging."

I raise the bat, level with his head, and he screams and shields his face with his good arm.

The thing in me laughs with delight.

chapter seventeen

3 YEARS, 23 WEEKS, 2 DAYS

I WAKE UP IN Satan's butthole. Everything is white—white walls, white beds, white light. Or Narnia. It could be Narnia. Did I die and go to Narnia? Because that would be *rad*. But then I see the IV attached to my arm and hear the steady *beep-beep* of my heart monitor and all hope deflates out of me quickly. Nope. Satan's butthole, aka a hospital.

I sit up from the pillows and my head tries to turn itself inside out and run off my neck. The headache splits me down the middle and sews me back up again with electric pain.

"Hairy monkeyballs!" I hiss. "Dogshit on a stick! Puke pancakes!"

A head pokes in. Wren, hazel eyes smiling, walks over to my bed.

"I knew you were awake. Who else spews such original and captivating swears?"

I feel my head. A massive, turban-like bandage has been wrapped around it. There are flowers on the small table at my side, and a smiley-face balloon cheerfully watches me from a corner, slowly rotating just to get a better view of me. From all angles.

"Where am I? Other than hell."

"Saint Jermaine's Hospital," Wren offers, pulling up a chair and sitting on it. "You've been out for a week or so."

"Mom!" I sit up. "Is Mom—"

"She's fine." Wren puts his hand on mine reassuringly. "She went to work today, but she said she'd be back at night. We've all been taking turns coming to see you. Me, Kayla, Avery—"

"Avery? Like, redhead Avery? Avery who hates me? The Avery we threatened?"

"It's weird, I know. But she brought flowers." He motions to a bunch of white camellias on the desk.

"What about Leo? The guy who broke in—"

"The police said he knocked you out, and then went upstairs. And then—"

Wren's expression cracks with uneasiness.

"Then what? What happened?"

Wren's eyes slowly move up to meet mine. "Jack. He said he came over to talk to you, and found you on the floor passed out."

"Who?"

"Who what?"

"Jack who?"

Wren smiles. "C'mon, don't play dumb. Jack. He came over, and he took care of Leo. Two broken ribs. A broken arm. A burst eardrum. Fractured skull."

I suck in a breath. Wren shakes his head and tries to smile.

"You have one, too, you know. Skull fracture. You hit your head pretty bad on the wall. For the first few days the doctors didn't know if you were going to slip into a coma or not. But you pulled through. There was some internal bleeding, and bruising. But they patched you up and you pulled through."

I look at my hands, and lift the sheet to look at my body. Almost-healed bruises cover my legs and arms.

"Leo's in custody," Wren says. "Jack's mom got him a lawyer. He's not locked up or anything, but he's on watch. The police say he's got a really good chance of getting away with no charges if you and your mom testify, but Leo's going to jail, definitely."

"I should hug this Jack guy. Show him my gratitude. Give him, like, a gift card to Starbucks at least."

Wren snorts. "Really? I thought you and Jack were at war. Do they typically give hugs during war?"

"War? No, I'm not fighting anybody. Well, I have to fight on a daily basis not to marry myself, but no. I'm not at war with anybody." I laugh. "And definitely not with this Jack guy. I'll figure out a good way to thank him. He saved my and my mom's butts after all. Is he old? Is he young? Does he go to our school? Wait . . . what's our school's name?"

I wrinkle my nose. I know I go to high school, but I can't remember the name of it. It's right on the tip of my tongue, but I don't know what it is.

Wren frowns. "East Summit High."

"Right!" I smile. "That's the one."

"They said your memory might be fuzzy," Wren murmurs. "But I didn't realize it'd be this bad. Do you remember what happened?"

"Yeah. Leo attacked my mom."

"What about before that? Do you remember the party?"

I squint, searching my memory. Instead of clear, crisp memories, all I can find is thick static.

"I—I don't know. I can't— It's weird. I feel like I do remember, but I can't— I can't find all the specifics."

"What about Jack?" Wren presses.

"What about him? He's okay in my book, if he saved my mom."

"Okay, Isis, cut it out. It was funny the first time."

"Cut what out?"

"You know Jack Hunter. Don't pretend you don't."

"Jack Hunter, huh? What a name. Sounds like the kind of name a pretentious asshole on Wall Street would have. But, uh, he saved Mom. When I couldn't. So I guess he's more of a really remarkable not-asshole."

The door opens and a doctor comes in. He smiles at me and checks the monitors.

"Good to see you awake, Isis. Are you feeling up for some cognition tests?"

"Do I get an unbearably bright light shone in my eye?"

"Yes."

"Awesome."

"Doctor," Wren says, and pulls the doctor away by the elbow. They whisper in the corner.

"Hey, I am right here! That is kind of really rude!" I shout. They ignore me and keep talking. I huff and put my arms over my chest and look out the door.

There, in the doorway, is a hot pretty boy. I say that with equal parts disgust and admiration—one, because pretty boys are usually insufferable; and two, because he's so good-looking even someone like me who dislikes pretty boys has to admit he's hot. He's tall; six two? Six three? He's lanky, not built, but the barest muscle definition stands out under his black shirt and jeans. His bone structure is something out of a Roman pantheon, but his nose is perfectly straight and his lips softer-looking. His hair is golden-brown, cut to barely grace his narrow, ice-water eyes that pierce right into me. Even if they're cold and unreachable, I can see dark shades of sorrow in them.

We stare like that at each other for a good four seconds before I yell, "Okay, I know you all want me to get better, but ordering a stripper is going too far!"

The guy, instead of getting offended, smirks. The sorrow in his eyes softens minutely, and he walks in.

Wren looks up from his place in the corner, and he rushes over to the guy. "Jack, there's something you need to know—"

Jack pushes past him and offers me a black rose.

"I figured you'd hate flowers, so I decided to get one that matched your soul," he says. I take the flower, careful not to touch any of his long fingers.

"Gee, thanks." I smile. "You must be Jack. Nice to meet

you. Also, thanks for saving my butt. And my mom's butt. From what I hear you went pretty apeshit on the guy. Claps to you."

I applaud. Jack's smirk fades slowly. The doctor hurries over to my bedside and checks the monitor, scribbling on a clipboard.

"Isis, we're going to get you into the CAT scan to see if anything's changed. You'll need another IV, so let me get that for you. Sit tight."

"Okay! Thanks, Doc." I wave at him as he scurries out. Wren is pushing Jack gradually away from my bed.

"Jack," he says with a desperate kind of urgency. "Jack, they're going to find out what's wrong, okay? They have to do more tests. He said it's probably not permanent—"

"Isis," Jack says over Wren's head. I look up.

"Yeah?"

"Stop it."

"Stop what? Being so sexy? I know, it's hard, but I just can't—"

"Stop it," he growls. "You know me."

"Uh, yes? We met like, thirty seconds ago." I chuckle. "So I guess, yeah, technically I know you."

"You're lying," he snarls.

"Lying about what?" I frown. "Look, buddy, I'm grateful for what you did, but calling a hospitalized girl a liar is going a little far, don't you think?"

Jack's eyes go wide. His fists clench. Wren pushes him back farther.

"Please, Jack, just go home. I'll call you when they do the tests, okay?" he whispers.

"You're lying! You're still mad at me so you're lying to see me squirm!" Jack shouts. Male nurses walk over to my door to see what the commotion is about.

"I'm not lying! I don't even know what you're talking about!" I yell back. My head throbs with a fresh wave of pain and I clutch it, wincing. "Can someone just get him out of here? He's hurting my head."

Jack's face goes slack, all emotion draining from it in a split second.

"Sir, if you'd come with us," one of the male nurses says.

"I'll be here with her," Wren assures him. "I'll call you if anything changes, so please, please just — "

"Isis," Jack says softly. I look over at him.

"What?"

"Do you remember me?"

"Uh, no, I was sort of knocked out when you came in and saved us. Sorry. But, you know. I'm awake now. We can get to know each other. I can buy you a puppy or something. You deserve it, for helping a total stranger."

Jack doesn't blink. He stares, the sadness back in his eyes. Sorrow clogs them, makes them dark and heavy. And then he's gone.

He doesn't come back.

○ ○ °°

The doctors do their tests. Mom sees me awake for the first time and collapses, sobbing, her arms wrapped around me for hours, apologizing. We fall asleep like that. Wren stays around me the most, and Kayla does, too. She thinks it's weird I don't remember Jack, but I keep telling her I wasn't even awake when he came in the house. She doesn't get it, though. Avery doesn't visit as much, either. She comes by maybe twice. The first time I pretend to be sleeping. She stays for only a few minutes, sitting in a chair and watching TV with me. The second time I open my eyes and start to talk, and she darts out of the room.

The doctors prescribe me medicine, and physical therapy, and tell me my memories will come back slowly, if I keep trying to remember. I do treadmill twice a day and some lady comes in and talks to me about what happened in the house, but I don't want to talk about it. Mom says I should, but I hate shrinks and she says she knows but that it will help heal me. But I'm not broken! I'm just cracked! Down the middle. On my skull. It's healing pretty well, but the doctors keep me for observation and recuperation, whatever that means.

My memories of the last few months are fractured worse than my cranium. I can remember bits and flashes—classes, parties, people waving at me or ignoring me, my lunch of tuna fish sandwiches, Mom's smile, Mom's crying. I scoop up the pieces whenever they come to me and hoard them. It's like a puzzle, and I'm desperately searching for the border pieces so I can put the rest together. I'd get depressed and down on myself, but something tells me I've done that enough this year.

One day, I take my lunch tray and eat in the second-floor lobby. There's a balcony that opens up to fresh air and a few plastic tables. The city thrums around me, the sky overcast, and the wind is chilly but refreshing. I poke at my Jell-O and chicken patty and try unsuccessfully for the millionth time this month not to die from boredom and/or terrible reconstituted astronaut-grade protein.

"Hi there," a girl's voice comes from behind me. I turn. A pretty, short girl with platinum hair smiles at me. Her skin is milk-white, and her eyes are a steely dark blue. She's thin, wearing a sweater and a flowery skirt. But there's a hospital band around her wrist. She looks so delicate, like a white dandelion or a beautiful spirit.

"Hey," I say. "Nice day."

Her button nose wrinkles as she smiles. "Yeah, but if it rains again I'm going to lose my mind."

"I hear ya." I stab my patty and motion at it. "You can sit, if you want. Watch me eat space-chicken."

She laughs, the sound melodious and sweet. She settles across from me and picks at a dead leaf on the table. I offer her my apple, and she takes it gratefully but doesn't eat it.

"I'm Isis," I say. "What's your name?"

She smiles, the weak sun catching her hair and making it shine white-gold.

"Sophia."

acknowledgments

WHOEVER YOU ARE, THANK you for reading this book. You're wonderful. Thank you for finishing, most of all. It's not easy to finish stuff these days. I should know. I barely finished this monstrosity.

But with the help of the lovely people at Entangled, this book is in your hands, whole and full of Isis and also full of poop jokes, for which I do not apologize. Thank you Stacy Abrams and Lydia Sharp for your *sharp* editing skills. Insert winky face here, followed by the 100 emoji and maybe also the eggplant emoji.

My final thank-you goes out to the people who read this book when it was just a small sprout of a thing, a self-published book on Amazon with a tiny bit of hype and a lot of hope. You were the ones who made this possible, who made my dreams come true. Thank you.

If there's one thing I've learned writing this book, it's that we're all better than we think we are. The world tries to convince us otherwise, but we are beautiful, and strong, and hilarious. We are full of good things and bad things, and together that makes us something, and something is worth much more than nothing. You are something. You are worth more than you know. The world is going to keep telling you you're worthless, but Isis and Jack will be here when it does.

We'll always be here.

don't miss the second book in the lovely vicious series

FORGET ME ALWAYS
BY SARA WOLF

All warfare is deception. Even in high school.

It's been nineteen days since Isis Blake forgot about *him*. The boy she can't quite remember. She's stuck in the hospital with a turban-size bandage on her head, more Jell-O than a human being should ever face, and a tiny bit of localized amnesia. Her only goal? To get out of this place before she becomes a complete nutjob herself.

But as Isis's memories start to return, she realizes there's something important there at the edges of her mind. Something that may mean the difference between life and death. Something about Sophia, Jack's girlfriend.

Jack Hunter—the "Ice Prince"—remembers everything. Remembers Isis's purple hair and her smart-ass mouth. Remembers that for a little while, Isis made him feel human. She made him feel. She burned a hole in the ice . . . and it's time to freeze back up. Boys like him don't deserve girls like her. Because Jack is dangerous. And that danger might be the only thing protecting her from something far more threatening.

Her past.

check out these other great reads from entangled teen . . .

LIFE UNAWARE
BY COLE GIBSEN

Regan Flay is following her control-freak mother's "plan" for high school success, until everything goes horribly wrong. Every bitchy text or email is printed out and taped to every locker in the school. Now Regan's gone from popular princess to total pariah. The only person who speaks to to her is former best-friend's hot-but-socially-miscreant brother, Nolan Letner. And the consequences of Regan's fall from grace are only just beginning. Once the chain reaction starts, no one will remain untouched . . .

WHATEVER LIFE THROWS AT YOU
BY JULIE CROSS

When seventeen-year-old track star Annie Lucas's dad starts mentoring nineteen-year-old baseball rookie phenom, Jason Brody, Annie's convinced she knows his type—arrogant, bossy, and most likely not into high school girls. But as Brody and her father grow closer, Annie starts to see through his façade to the lonely boy in over his head. When opening day comes around and her dad—and Brody's—job is on the line, she's reminded why he's off-limits. But Brody needs her, and staying away isn't an option.

HOW (NOT) TO FALL IN LOVE
BY LISA BROWN ROBERTS

Seventeen-year-old Darcy Covington never worried about money . . . until her car is repossessed. With a failing business, her Dad not only skipped town, but bailed on his family. Fortunately, Darcy's uncle owns a pawn shop, where Darcy can hide out from the world. There's also Lucas, the supremely hot fix-it guy—even if he isn't all that interested in her. But it's here amongst the colorful characters of her uncle's world that Darcy begins to see something more in herself . . . if she has the courage to follow it.

LOLA CARLYLE'S 12-STEP ROMANCE
BY DANIELLE YOUNGE-ULLMAN

While she knows a summer in rehab is a terrible idea (especially when her biggest addiction is decaf cappuccino), Lola Carlyle finds herself tempted by the promise of saving her lifelong crush and having him fall in love with her. Unfortunately, Sunrise Rehabilitation Center isn't quite what she expected. Her best friend has gone AWOL, she's actually expected to get treatment, and boys are completely off-limits . . . except for Lola's infuriating (and irritatingly hot) mentor, Adam. Like it or not, Lola will be rehabilitated, and maybe fall in love . . . if she can open her heart long enough to let it happen.